BURN COUNTRY

Also by Michael J. McCann

THE MARCH AND WALKER CRIME NOVEL SERIES

Sorrow Lake

THE DONAGHUE AND STAINER CRIME NOVEL SERIES

Blood Passage
Marcie's Murder
The Fregoli Delusion
The Rainy Day Killer

SUPERNATURAL FICTION

The Ghost Man

Burn Country

A March and Walker Crime Novel

Michael J. McCann

The Plaid Raccoon Press
2017

Burn Country is a work of fiction. Names, characters, institutions, places and events are either the product of the author's imagination or are used fictitiously. Any resemblance to actual persons, living or dead, events, or locales is entirely coincidental.

ISBN: 978-1-927884-09-6
eBook ISBN: 978-1-927884-10-2

Front cover photograph: Grandfailure/Thinkstock
Back cover photograph: DMC Design Studio/Thinkstock
Author photo: Timothy D. McCann

www.theplaidraccoonpress.com
www.mjmccann.com

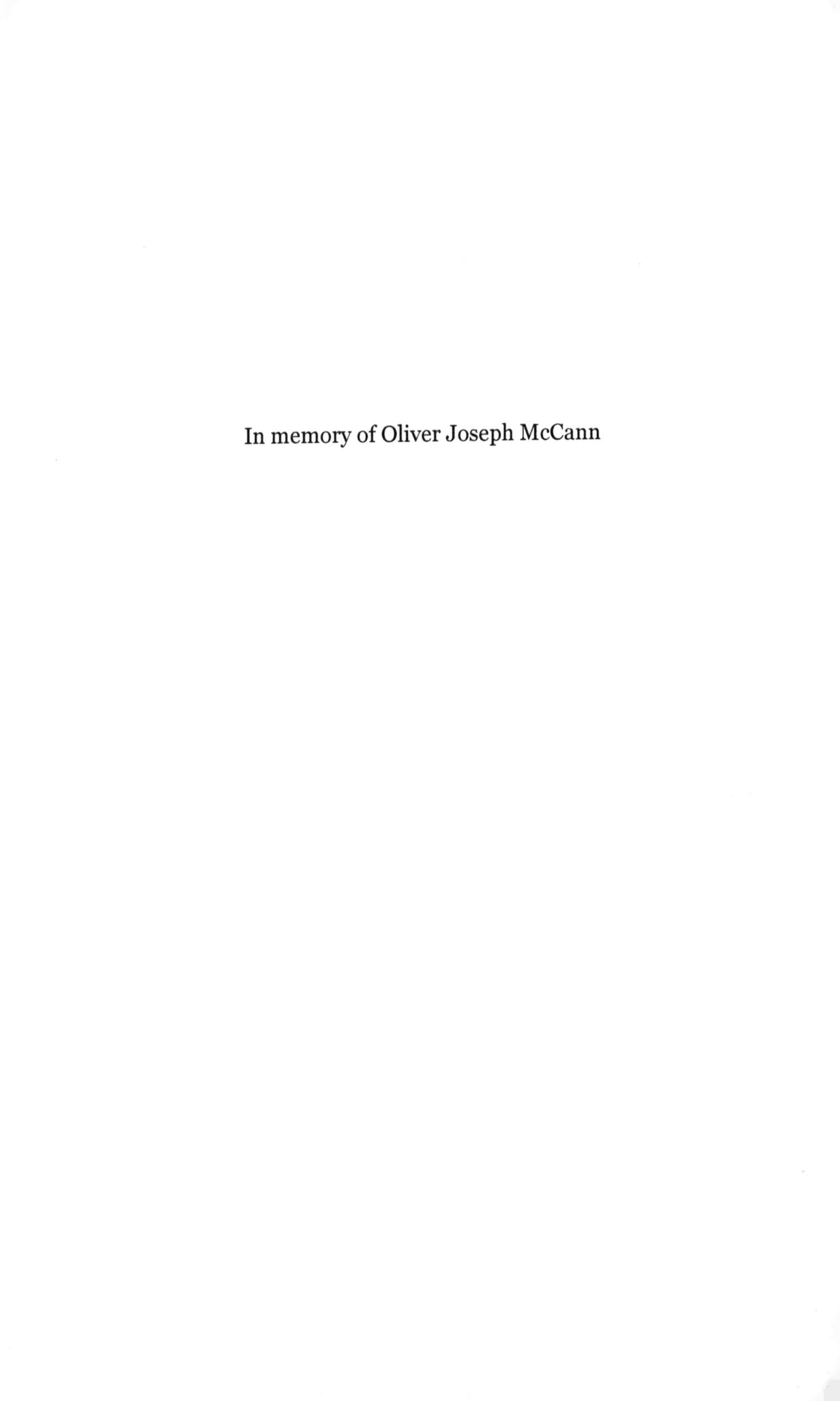

In memory of Oliver Joseph McCann

chapter ONE

As Detective Constable Tom Carty walked past the pickup trucks of the volunteer fire fighters called out to the scene from the Rideau Lakes Fire Department, he realized that the barn which had burned was not the big one behind the farm house but another, smaller one in an adjoining field. The smoke drifting in a dark cloud visible above the trees for several kilometres was actually coming from the remains of an old hay barn that had been standing, until sometime late last night, in the next field over from the house and yard.

Passing a parked Chevy Tahoe belonging to the area chief of the volunteer fire service, Carty walked up the long driveway. It was unpaved, and he picked his way along with fastidious care, avoiding puddles that had been left behind in the potholes by a recent rainfall. His breathing mask dangled by its strap from his fingers. He wore a yellow reflective vest over a navy long-sleeved t-shirt, khaki cargo pants, steel-toed safety boots, and an orange hard hat. His Ontario Provincial Police identification hung on a lanyard around his neck, and his badge was clipped to his belt.

Area Fire Chief Derek Flood saw him coming and motioned him over. They shook hands.

"It's arson again," Flood said. He pulled up the collar of his sweat-stained t-shirt to wipe at the perspiration around his mouth. His thermal turnout jacket, unbearably hot on this humid August morning, hung on a nearby fencepost, along with his helmet, fire protection hood, and respirator. His gloves were tucked under the suspenders holding up his turnout pants. He took a long pull at a bottle of water.

"Number five," Carty said, looking at the mud and hay clotted under Flood's boots. He and Flood were about the same age, early forties, and Carty considered him a friend. They participated in the same charity golf and softball tournaments, co-captained friendly tug-of-war competitions on Canada Day between law enforcement and fire and rescue, and manned the grills together to serve up hotdogs and hamburgers at various summer festivals and fundraisers in the township.

The firefighter spat out water and wiped his mouth. "I could smell accelerant this time. I've already called the OFM." The Office of the Fire Marshal had sent an investigator to look into four previous fires that had been set in Rideau Lakes Township since mid-May. As the detective constable dedicated to this area from the Leeds County Crime Unit of the OPP, Carty had investigated them as well.

"Another thing," Flood went on, "something burned in it this time. Maybe an animal caught under the loft when it collapsed. You probably smelled it back on the road."

"I smelled it." Carty looked around the yard. The back door of the nineteenth-century stone house, which led out onto a deck, was wide open. Across the lawn there was a small, new-looking building, a granny cottage or studio of some kind, with large windows and a skylight. Beyond the studio an open shed made of grey barn board housed an antique Massey tractor and a riding lawn mower, but there were empty spaces where you'd expect to find a car or truck belonging to the people who lived here. Behind the shed, on the other side of a fence and a gate, Carty saw an empty chicken coop, a garden of some sort that was sadly overgrown with weeds, and the big barn he'd first thought was the one that had burned.

"Neighbours down the road called it in," Flood said. "Nobody's home. Back door of the house was open like that when we got here. No animals in the barn, by the way." The push-to-talk mobile phone in his pocket popped and scratched out his name. He threw aside his empty water bottle and fished out the phone. "I'm in the yard."

"On my way, Derek," someone said. "Sit tight."

They watched an all-terrain vehicle bounce across the field from the burned-out barn. Carty recognized the ATV as part of the equipment inventory of the fire station located in the nearby village of Elgin, along with the pumper and tanker still parked in front of the blackened structure in the next field. Slowing to pass through a gate, the four-wheeler skirted a fenced-in corral and zipped through the barnyard. It slowed again to navigate another gate, then rocketed across the inner yard to where they waited. The young man driving the ATV killed the engine and stood up, stripping off his helmet and respirator. Carty recognized him as a farmer named Egan who lived just outside Jones Falls, about fifteen kilometres away.

"It's out, right?" Flood shoved the phone back into his pocket. "It was out when I left. Don't tell me it's not out."

"It's out, Derek." Egan shrugged out of his thermal turnout jacket and threw it across the seat of the ATV. "That's not the problem."

"Okay, so what's the problem?"

"That damned stench we could smell? That we thought

was an animal?" Egan ran his hand through his thick black hair and spat on the ground. "It was a body, Derek. Somebody died in that goddamned fire."

chapter TWO

"Okay, how about this one?" Kevin Walker gathered up the playing cards from the coffee table and began to shuffle them as Caitlyn, sitting cross-legged on the floor across from him, watched closely. Kevin leaned back against the footrest of his La-Z-Boy recliner as though to hide his movements from her.

Unimpressed, she rolled her eyes.

Five-year-old Brendan, sitting on the recliner, pushed his bare foot gently against Kevin's back as he watched cartoons on the television in the corner of their basement play room. One of Brendan's socks was draped over Kevin's shoulder and the other was somewhere behind the couch. Brendan preferred to be barefoot, although Janie invariably yelled at him when she caught him without his socks and slippers on. It was an ongoing battle that would not be settled any time soon.

Kevin fanned out the cards and extended them to Caitlyn. "Pick a card. Any card."

"This is lame, Kevin."

"No, it's not. It's magic. Come on, pick a card."

Caitlyn dutifully pulled a card out of the middle of the pack.

"Don't show it to me. Just look at it and memorize it."

As she frowned at the card with the fake intensity only an eight-year-old can muster, Kevin squared up the cards and put the deck down on the table. "Okay now, my lovely lady, show the card to the other spectators, if you will, please."

"You'll see it."

"No, I won't. I'll close my eyes."

"You can see it through the cracks in your lids."

"The cracks in my lids? No, I can't. Okay, here." He picked up a magazine from the table and held it in front of his face. "Can you see my eyes now?"

"No."

"So I can't see you, either. Hold the card up in front of your face and show it to Brendan."

He listened to cartoon sound effects. No one spoke. A commercial began on the television.

"Did you show it to him?"

"He's not looking."

"Brendan, look at the card your sister's showing you."

"Okay," Caitlyn said, "he looked at it."

Kevin tossed the magazine aside and picked up the deck of cards, holding them out to her with a wide, phoney smile. "And now, my young princess, I will show you an astounding feat of magic. Place the card you have chosen back into the deck without revealing it to me."

Caitlyn reached forward and hesitated, not sure what to do.

"Just push it anywhere into the middle of the deck," Kevin said. "Face down, so I can't see it. That's it."

When she'd put her card back, he moved the deck behind his back. "Your card is very warm. Very warm! I can feel it, right through all the other cards."

"No you can't."

"Yes I can, because it's a magic card. In fact," Kevin brought the deck back out and passed his hand over it several times, "it's so magical it has revealed itself to us in an incredible way!" Using his thumb, he began to push the cards, still face down, from his right hand into his left, one at a time. "Where's that magic card? Where is it? Where is it?" He suddenly came to the five of diamonds sitting face up in the deck. "There it is! It's magic!"

"You cheated."

"No I didn't. How did I know it was that card? You didn't show it to me."

"You saw it when I showed it to Brendan."

"No, I didn't. Plus, you put it face down into the deck, and now it's face up, revealing itself to us. Admit it, Cait. It's magic!"

Kevin's cellphone, sitting on the coffee table, began to vibrate.

Giving her the cards, he picked up the phone and glanced at the time—9:29 AM—and the caller identification—*S. Patterson.*

"Walker."

"Let's roll, Kevin. Another barn fire, and a possible homicide this time." Detective Sergeant Scott Patterson, Kevin's supervisor, recited an address just north of the village of Elgin in Rideau Lakes Township. "Get your ass in gear."

"It may take a few minutes," Kevin said. "I'm watching the kids for Janie while she's at work. It *is* my day off, remember?"

"Not any more. Get moving." The line went dead.

"Don't leave," Caitlyn said. "I won't make fun of your tricks any more."

Kevin gave her forearm a gentle squeeze. "It's not that, sweetie. It's just work, that's all."

"Mommy's doing Nanna's hair this morning. She's going to be *pissed* at you."

"Pissed!" Brendan parroted behind Kevin, his eyes still on the TV.

"Language, please." Sighing, Kevin called Janie and braced for the worst.

Half an hour later, when Janie's mother let herself in the side door and came up the stairs into the kitchen,

Kevin gave her a hug and a peck on the cheek. “Your hair looks lovely, Barb.”

“Butt kisser.” She patted his arm. “Go ahead. We’ll be fine.” She smiled at Caitlyn. “Won’t we?”

Watching Kevin secure his holstered firearm to his belt, Caitlyn rocked up onto her tiptoes. “Kevin was showing me magic!”

“Magic! Is that so?” Barb looked up at Kevin who, at six-foot-five inches and an athletic 235 pounds, towered over her. “What’s all this about?”

Kevin shrugged into his suit jacket and ran a hand over his short brown hair, checking himself in the mirror at the top of the stairs. “From a book. I’m teaching myself.”

“From the library!” Caitlyn chirped. “Kevin got me my own library card, Nanna!” The Elizabethtown-Kitley Township Public Library’s Spring Valley branch was located next door to the OPP detachment office where Kevin worked, and he’d started taking Caitlyn there on his days off, hoping she would develop an interest in reading.

He knelt down and gave her a hug. “Be good for Nanna, Cait-bug.”

“I will. Catch the bad guy!”

“Always.”

As Kevin backed his Ford Fusion motor pool vehicle out onto the street and hurried away, he glanced at the dashboard clock. It was already 10:06 AM. Elgin was about a twenty-minute drive away, which meant he’d be arriving at the scene almost an hour after having received the call out.

Patterson would not be pleased.

Sparrow Lake, the village west of Brockville where Kevin lived, had a population of about six hundred people. Most of them seemed to be out all at once on this humid Monday morning. He slowly worked his way along Main Street and up to the village limits where he stepped on it, anxious to make up time. He headed north to County Road

42, turned left, and then had to slow down to navigate his way through Athens, which was just as busy as Sparrow Lake. Once he was able to jump back up to highway speed, he followed 42 west to Delta, where he was forced to slow down once again, after which he ran another five kilometres at something above the legal highway limit to Philipsville, where he endured yet another slowdown. Eventually he reached County Road 8, where he turned left and floored it in a straight run southwest as fast as he could push it.

Kevin was used to the challenges of local geography that went along with policing in a rural jurisdiction covering just over two thousand square kilometres with only thirty-five thousand inhabitants scattered along county roads and back lanes that hooked and bent around countless lakes, swamps, and rivers. He was used to it, but he didn't like it. How the crow flew and how the car travelled were two very different things, and he was constantly pushing the envelope not to arrive late these days, it seemed.

He reached an open stretch where there were no trees. Through the windshield on the passenger side he could see a large, trailing cloud of smoke that had risen into the air from a spot somewhere below the horizon to the southwest. He gritted his teeth and gripped the steering wheel even more tightly.

Thank God for Barb. Janie's regular day care person was on vacation this week, and while Barb had agreed to take the kids, this morning she'd been Janie's first appointment at the hair salon, which was why Kevin had booked the day off, in order to baby-sit. Janie had been stressed. She did her mother's hair free of charge, and this morning it had been a full permanent treatment and God knew what else, but on top of her mother, Janie's appointment calendar was booked solid for the day, thanks to a reception of some kind in the village later this week. She was wired for sound. Dropping the kids off at the hair salon had not been an option. Kevin valued his health too much to have tried pulling that stunt.

Life with Janie was a bit of a challenge these days.

As he approached Elgin from the north on County Road 8, the speed limit dropped to forty kilometres an hour. Passing a sign welcoming him to the village, he braked again and drew up behind a short line of traffic crawling past a set of wooden barriers blocking access to Charland Road. Predictably, everyone wanted to look down the road before passing the intersection. At the barrier, he lowered his window and held out his badge and identification to the uniformed officer, who waved him through.

"It's about two and a half kilometres down," the constable said, his uniform shirt dark with perspiration.

"Thanks." Kevin eased through the opening and drove on. Charland Road was narrow, with no shoulders to speak of on either side. He passed a series of ranch-style semi-detached houses on one side and corn fields on the other until he came to a T-intersection. Another set of barriers had been set up here, and Kevin again lowered his window and held out his identification and badge for inspection by the uniformed officer on duty. This time the officer wrote his name and badge number down in a log book and stuck the clipboard through the window for Kevin to sign. This was the outer perimeter that had been established to contain the crime scene, and Kevin winced as he rolled through, knowing that his time of arrival had been duly noted for the record.

As he drove on, he could see that the smoke had dissipated considerably below the tree line. He passed more corn, a house, a barn, and then pulled over behind a long line of vehicles parked along the side of the road. He got out and hurried toward the crime scene tape at the end of the driveway of the large hobby farm just ahead.

Farther down, a fire truck and a pumper edged out onto the road, their job obviously done. A few steps from the driveway, he paused next to an unmarked grey Crown

Victoria and glanced inside. On the passenger seat he saw a black leather handbag that was a cross between a computer bag and a soft-sided briefcase. Recognizing it, he groaned.

If *she* was already here, then he was indeed very, very late.

chapter THREE

Detective Inspector Ellie March had awakened this morning to the sound of a loon calling out across Sparrow Lake. As its cry echoed and faded, she lay for a long time with her head on the pillow, listening to the silence, thinking about nothing in particular.

Later, when she took her first cup of coffee out onto the back deck, the surface of the water was still and quiet. The air was heavy and humid. Her muscles tingled pleasantly from her morning exercises, and the hot coffee tasted good. She spotted a distant bird, likely the loon she'd heard, moving slowly across the water close to the opposite shore. As she watched, it disappeared. She waited. Eventually it surfaced again, metres away. It shook itself languidly, then continued to drift.

She took the coffee down onto the dock, smelling the water in the breeze coming off the lake. She walked out to the end and looked down. The water was about a metre deep. The bottom was a patchwork of rocks, mud, and weeds, not good for wading or swimming but fine for boating. Her next-door neighbour, Ridgeway Ballantyne, had a paddle boat that she'd borrowed once, a week ago, for a leisurely tour along the shoreline. It was moored to Ridge's dock now. Looking over, she promised herself she'd take it out again soon in an attempt to escape the humidity.

Movement below her caught her eye. Beneath the

surface of the water, a school of small fish eased into the dark patch caused by her shadow. They inevitably appeared whenever she came out onto the dock. According to Ridge, they were juvenile smallmouth bass that lived in the tall weeds along the shore. Eventually they would reach adulthood and move out into deeper water. For now, they hung out under her dock looking for crayfish, insects, and minnows. There were about a dozen of them at the moment, ranging in size from approximately fifteen centimetres down to six or eight centimetres in length.

As she raised the coffee cup to her lips, several of the smaller and more timid ones flicked out of sight, spooked by her movement. Undaunted, one of the larger ones moved out of her shadow and ascended toward the surface, anticipating a treat. Previously she'd shared bits of her food with them, crumbs of toast or pieces of a hotdog bun, but this morning she only had the coffee. It amazed her that they seemed to see her from down there and were able to track her movements so carefully. She'd almost come to think of them as pets.

Her morning exercises included a tai chi routine in which she visualized a school of koi she'd seen at an aquarium when she was a child. The movement of the fish helped her focus on the moment and relax. Lately she'd begun seeing the bass instead of the golden fish. She took it as a sign that she was settling into her new home.

She sat down cross-legged on the dock, right at the very edge, so that she could watch them idle back and forth below her. She shifted her weight and took her cellphone out of the pocket of her track pants, setting it down on the dock by her knee. Wrapping both hands around the coffee cup, she raised her eyes to the distant shoreline. The warm breeze coming off the lake sandpapered her cheeks. The weathered boards of the dock warmed her flesh through the track pants. It felt good. She loved warmth and hated the cold.

A cicada began to buzz somewhere behind her, up in one of the trees.

Today would be spent finalizing reports on a homicide case in Lanark County in which a middle-aged woman had shot her husband in bed while their eight-year-old daughter was away on a sleepover with friends. It was a very sad and disturbing case. The man worked only part time, and there'd been very little money coming in. The house, located on a back concession road, was unfinished and in disarray. The husband had a history of drug problems and spousal abuse. The woman called 911 herself and calmly waited for police to arrive. She made a full confession, and forensic investigation left no doubt as to what had happened. Interviews with neighbours, relatives, and friends confirmed the mental cruelty and physical abuse that had been going on for several years in the home.

It was a fairly straightforward case for Ellie and the investigating detectives working out of the Lanark County detachment, as far as it went. What made it difficult, and disturbing, was what the woman had done in the twenty minutes between killing her husband and calling 911. After firing a single shot through his left temple, she left the gun at the end of the bed and went into the kitchen for a chef's knife. Slowly, carefully, and with obvious deliberation, she used the knife to mutilate his body from head to toe. When she was done, she walked out of the bedroom, threw the knife into the waste paper basket in the bathroom, and washed her hands. Then she called 911.

Several respondents to the scene threw up. The identification sergeant made three attempts before he could stay in the room long enough to photograph the body. Even Ellie admitted to herself, afterward, that it was the most horrific scene she'd ever attended.

Thinking about the tasks that were left to her before wrapping up the case—the calls to be made, e-mails to be sent, and documents to be uploaded into the system—

helped objectify it all to a certain extent. Thinking about administrative details helped convert the shock and revulsion into calm efficiency.

She focused on the feeling of the warm air on her skin and the smell of the water. It still required conscious effort to keep her emotions safely compartmentalized. These things, she knew from long experience, took time to work through.

She raised the cup to her lips and found it empty. She'd finished the coffee without realizing it.

She looked down into the water, but the fish had grown bored with her and disappeared. She saw only herself, her shoulder-length brown hair beginning to show threads of grey, her cheekbones high and freckled, her eyebrows unplucked, her eyes narrow and sober.

Plain and awkward Ellie March, whose head was filled with horrible things.

On the deck next to her knee, her cellphone began to vibrate.

chapter FOUR

Thirty minutes later she was staring across a field at the burned-out wreck of a hay barn as Detective Constable Carty brought her up to speed. Behind them, Detective Sergeant Scott Patterson, his complexion matching his clipped red hair, quietly tore into Detective Constable Kevin Walker for his late arrival.

"As I was saying," Carty said, glancing at his notebook, "it's known as Spencer Farm. Twenty acres, twelve in hay and the rest in bush. It belongs to a local heritage society in trust, but was owned by the late Senator Constance Spencer until her death two years ago. The property used to be much larger, apparently, and was held by the Spencer family for multiple generations. It's being leased to Senator Spencer's husband for a dollar a year. He's some kind of painter or artist or something. That's his studio in the back yard."

"Any sign of Mr. Spencer?"

Carty shook his head. "Spencer was her family name, not his. His name's Lang or Lane, something like that. I'm still trying to track him down. He didn't spend a lot of time here, from the sound of it."

"He wasn't in the house?"

"No. We cleared it and there's no one home. Doesn't look like anyone's been living there recently. No dirty laundry in the hamper or garbage in the waste paper baskets, that sort of thing. There were signs it was ransacked by an unknown subject, so we're waiting on the warrant before we search it. There were footprints entering and leaving, and some kind of small wheel tracks, like a hand cart or dolly."

"Is Mr. Lang or Lane our victim?"

"Possibly," Carty shrugged. "We'll know soon enough."

"What about the studio?"

"Signs of a violent disturbance, visible through the windows. Overturned table, what looks like blood spattered on the floor, and holes in the gyprock suggesting someone used a hammer or crowbar to look for something in the walls. Again, we're waiting on the warrant before we go in."

Ellie watched the fire department pumper edge down the road between the parked vehicles on its way back to the fire station. She'd been told that the first responders had arrived eleven minutes after receiving the 911 call, which she thought was very good for a rural volunteer service. "Okay, so tell me about the fire."

"The OFM investigator's en route," Carty said. "Gordon Findlay. Good guy; he investigated the others as well."

"There's no doubt it's another arson?"

"It's arson, but different from the others. He used an accelerant this time, and there's no immediate sign of a road flare, which was used as the igniter in the other cases. Maybe a match or a cigarette. We'll have to wait to be sure."

"And there's a fatality."

"Yes. Before now, there wasn't even livestock lost."

"Tell me about the body."

"The coroner's still here," Carty replied carefully, "with Martin. I haven't gotten an update yet, so you should probably get it directly from them."

"Mmm." Ellie glanced behind her at Kevin, who was following Patterson across the yard for a look at the studio. She looked back at the burned-out barn and nodded. "All right. Let's go take a look."

They rode in Flood's Tahoe, the fire chief behind the wheel, Ellie in the front passenger seat, and Carty in the rear. Flood drove through the barnyard and around the corral, then across the hay field, following a well-worn set of wheel tracks to the barn.

"Tom tells me you've moved out here to the boonies from the big city," Flood said, glancing over at her.

"Down from Orillia," Ellie corrected, "but I'm originally from Toronto, yes."

"How do you like all this country living?"

"I like it just fine." She looked at his straight brown hair, which stuck up all over the place, the stubble on his jaw, and the boyish dimple in his cheek. "What about you, Derek? Are you from around here?"

Flood nodded. "Grew up on a farm just outside Portland. Fifth generation, so you could say I'm a local."

"Never been through Portland that I know of."

"You must have blinked and missed it." Flood parked a short distance away from the scene. They got out. He opened the back hatch of the Tahoe and handed Ellie an orange hard hat before putting on his own. She saw him looking at her footwear, low-cut black leather safety shoes she'd dug out of her bedroom closet before leaving the cottage.

"Steel toes," she said.

"Okay." Flood held out a respirator.

Ellie shook her head. The air still stank of smoke, soggy scorched wood, and the tang of burned flesh, but it was breathable. She hated wearing things that restricted her peripheral vision and made it sound as though she were speaking from the back of a cave. Carty, she saw, had left his on the back seat of the Tahoe.

"Good morning, Ellie." OPP Identification Sergeant Dave Martin stepped over to them. Short, precise, and irreverent, Martin was in charge of the East Region's

Forensic Identification Unit. He didn't offer to shake hands with Ellie, but nodded and gave her a fleeting smile.

"Hi, Dave. What have we got?"

"Another arson. The structure's not stable, so you should stay outside. The roof's caved in down at the far end, where the tin's been gone for a long time. This end's still up, but the beams and posts look pretty iffy."

"We've got a crew coming in to brace it up before the search," Flood said.

"It helped that there was rain on the weekend," Martin added. "The hay was damp and it didn't burn as well as our guy hoped it would."

Ellie looked at the smudges of mud and ash on the knees and cuffs of his white coveralls. "What about the body?"

Martin peeled back his hood and accepted a bottle of water from Flood. "Thanks. Derek here confirms that the body was right in the area of origin, just inside the door, but it seems the guy got a lot of accelerant on a post right next to it and that brought down the loft on top of the body, like this." He held his open left hand on an angle above his bottle of water. "Ended up protecting the body. And while it was coming down, it dumped a whole crapload of damp hay on the corpse which smothered the flames."

"Oh?"

Martin grimaced. "Well, it didn't happen immediately. The face and the rest of the upper body are burned away." He looked at Carty, who stared back at him. He glanced at Flood, who looked down at his boots. "Bad news is, the body was moved. By one of the firefighters. He grabbed the legs and started to pull it out from under the debris. When the right arm snagged and came off—"

"We're very sorry about this," Flood said, turning to Ellie.

"The coroner's already expressed her displeasure," Martin went on. "As far as I'm concerned, it was fine because we discovered that when the killer dumped the body, the left hand ended up under the vic's butt, and because most of the combustion was on the top and right side, and because it stopped when the hay came down on it, the left hand was protected enough that I was able to take prints. We're running them now."

"I see." Ellie watched a small woman in blue coveralls walk out of the barn. She removed her white hard hat and respirator and shook out shoulder-length auburn hair. She handed the hat and respirator to a paramedic behind her, saw Ellie, and came over.

"You must be March," she said. "I'm Dr. Fiona Kearns. You need to stay out of there; it's not safe. *And*, our victim's not a very pretty sight. We don't want you losing your breakfast all over our crime scene."

Ellie frowned. Kearns was the new coroner for Lanark-Leeds, replacing the very disagreeable Dr. Yuri Dalca, who'd retired from practice a month ago and moved to Arizona. A general physician in Perth, Kearns was known for her extensive background in emergency medicine and a recently-published book based on her experiences, which was apparently already a bestseller. The word was that she would be the next regional supervising coroner on her way to becoming chief coroner for Ontario, unless she received a higher calling in the interim. Politics was rumoured to be in the mix.

"Call me Ellie." She held out her hand, but Kearns had already turned away to take a tablet from the paramedic.

Ellie waited as she swiped through photos on the tablet, but apparently Kearns had nothing more to say to her. Glancing at Martin, Ellie motioned with her head and walked toward the barn.

"Don't say I didn't warn you," Kearns called out over her shoulder, still busy with the tablet.

The barn was about twenty metres by ten. At one time it had had double doors on the front, facing the road, but they'd long since disappeared to wherever barn doors go when they're taken off and not put back on again. Ellie followed Martin to the right of a curving trail of small green cones indicating the safe path around evidence flagged by yellow numbered markers.

"We've got about a metre's worth of tire tracks from the vehicle that brought the body in from the road," he said, pointing. "The fire trucks and guys in boots chewed up the rest." He stopped in front of the barn entrance and pointed again. "You can see where some kind of ramp was lowered from the back of the vehicle, and here," he pointed once more, "where the vic was wheeled down onto the ground and into the barn."

He stepped just inside the doorway, glancing up cautiously. Ellie stood beside him. Flood brushed against her left shoulder as he moved slightly ahead of her, obstructing her view.

"Over there," Martin said, lifting his hand to his face as the stench of the burned body asserted itself, "is what's left of an office chair. I'm guessing he was tied or duct-taped to the chair, perhaps in the studio, put into the vehicle, brought over here, cut loose and dumped from the chair, then set on fire."

Ellie tried to step around Flood, but he shifted and shook his head. "Better not. As incident commander for this fire I'm responsible for your safety. Now that the coroner's done her thing, I don't want anyone else coming in until the investigator gets here and we can get everything braced up or torn down or whatever the hell we have to do. Okay?"

Ellie nodded. She could feel the residual heat from the extinguished fire as it radiated from the ground and the remains of the structure. The body lay about three metres away from her. The stink of it filled her lungs, causing her stomach to involuntarily tighten. It was a blackened, charred ruin. "Any indication yet as to cause of death?"

"That would be my question," Kearns called out from

behind them, "and I'd be happy to answer it back here, if you don't mind."

Ellie turned and slowly retraced her steps along the trail of green cones. "Can you say yet if the fire killed him?"

Kearns flashed her white, straight teeth. "You're assuming that the victim was male."

Ellie waited.

"As a matter of fact, he was. Furthermore, I'm quite certain that death was caused by blunt force trauma." She held up her tablet and turned it around, showing Ellie a close-up photograph of the corpse's head. "At the right upper portion of the skull there's considerable damage from what looks like a blow from a hard, slender object of some kind. I'd say he was struck while tied to the chair in the studio and bled out while the attacker was in the house doing whatever it was he was doing. Chances are pretty good that when he came back, the assailant found the victim dead and decided to dispose of the body here and set it on fire to cover his tracks. Which, as we all know, is usually a waste of time." Kearns swiped to a close-up photograph of the victim's left hand, swollen and red but relatively intact. "This kind of fire seldom burns hot enough to completely destroy all the evidence. There's always something we can use to make an identification, as we've seen already this morning."

"Serge has a full set of photos as well," Martin said, referring to Identification Constable Serge Landry, who was working the scene under Martin's supervision. "He's back in the yard, shooting the exterior of the studio right now."

Ellie nodded.

"You'd just better hope," Kearns said, turning on Flood, "that no evidence was lost when your probie disturbed our body. As it is, it's going to be prominently mentioned in my report."

She turned away abruptly and strode off to the

ambulance, handing the tablet back to the paramedic, who'd apparently been recruited as her gofer.

Martin sighed. "What is it with coroners around here?"

"Make sure nothing gets missed," Ellie said, looking back at the barn.

"Of course, Ellie. That's what I do."

She headed back to the Tahoe with Carty. "Have you talked to the person who moved the body?"

"Briefly," he replied. "Bishop's with him now. The kid's a little upset."

Flood opened the passenger door of the Tahoe for her. "You have to understand something. We're not a professional firefighting service. I have ten volunteers, but I never know at any given time how many are going to be able to respond when we get a call out, or which ones I'll get. Five made it out today, which is average for a Monday morning. Egan and Mannion are farmers, the guy who drives the pumper manages the big hotel at Jones Falls, and Byrnes works in his father's store in Elgin. They had to leave work to get here."

Ellie got into the Tahoe. She left the door open and turned to face him.

"Our volunteers pass the CPAT tests down at St. Catharines," he continued, referring to the standardized Candidate Physical Ability Test administered by the provincial firefighters screening service, "which we pay for. Then they take our training here at home. After working all week in their regular lives they give us their weekends, and we put them through the programs identified by the OFM for level one and level two firefighters. Byrnes had to get to eighty hours of training before we'd let him respond to a call with us. He's up to about ninety hours now, and he'll finish probation in a few months."

"Probation's a year, isn't it, Derek?" Carty asked.

"That's right." Flood looked at Ellie. "He's a good kid,

and he does a good job for me. He just, well, panicked when he saw the legs sticking out. For a moment he thought he was in a rescue situation instead of a recovery one."

Ellie said nothing, looking over Flood's shoulder at Martin, who was hurrying toward them with his cellphone to his ear. When the identification sergeant reached them he ended the call and put his hands on his hips.

"We have an ID on the victim," he announced. "The shit's about to hit the fan."

Ellie frowned. "Why?"

"He was a VIP from Ottawa, Ellie. Independent Senator Darius Lane."

chapter FIVE

They gathered in front of the shed as Ellie and Dave Martin brought them up to speed. Kevin leaned back against the nose of the Massey tractor, notebook and pen out, and glanced at John Bishop, who stood next to him. The stocky detective's short-sleeved white shirt was dark with perspiration, and his upper lip was beaded with moisture. Kevin watched him use his tie, an ugly, puce-coloured thing with some kind of faded floral pattern, to mop at his forehead and mouth. He caught Kevin's look and rolled his eyes.

"Now for the political bullshit. Got your shovel ready?"

Kevin smiled faintly. The news that their victim was a member of the federal Senate had been met first with disbelief by the team, then amusement. But when Bishop suggested that their victim might have been killed by someone hoping to abolish the upper chamber one bloodsucker at a time, Patterson tore into him with even more acid than he'd shown Kevin over his late arrival.

The tension level went up immediately.

They were getting as much background information as they could, Carty explained, but things were still sketchy. Lane was apparently a well-known artist who'd been appointed to the Senate last year by the prime minister to fill the vacancy left by the victim's late wife. Carty hadn't heard of Lane before, but Kevin was familiar with his work, having seen an exhibit featuring his paintings in the National Art Gallery in Ottawa a couple of years ago. Post-modern romanticism, if he remembered correctly. However, he figured it was wise to keep his mouth shut as Carty droned on about Lane's condominium in Ottawa, his lack of a driver's licence, and other bits and pieces they'd been able to pull together so far.

Dogs in the doghouse should stay quiet in the doghouse until the master calms down.

"Given the victim's prominence," Ellie was saying, "we're going to have to investigate on multiple tracks. The motive may be connected to his paintings, which are apparently fairly valuable, or it may be related somehow to his government responsibilities. Having said that, we can't rule out the serial arson angle just yet."

She looked at Patterson. "I'd like to have Tom work as the primary investigator. He's familiar with the arson cases, and it's his back yard."

Patterson looked at Carty, who nodded without changing expression.

Ellie folded her arms. "Mona Sisson did a good job as file co-ordinator on the Hansen case. Is she available again?"

"Yes," Patterson said. "And Wiltse's already working on our paper. We should have it all by mid-afternoon." Detective Constable Ben Wiltse was the warrants co-ordinator for the crime unit, and it was his responsibility to prepare and submit search authorizations on behalf of the team while Sisson, as file co-ordinator, would scrutinize and file all reports and other documents generated by the investigating officers.

"Then pull everyone in who's not already here. I'll get Rachel Townsend on board right away. There's going to be a media firestorm when the victim's ID hits the news, and I expect it'll be handled from the commissioner's office this time, but we'll need Rachel to co-ordinate statements for us at this level and keep the reporters off our backs." She looked at Carty. "We need to know right away if there's any next of kin, we need to know what was taken from the house, and we need to know how Lane got down here from Ottawa in the first place, since he didn't have a driver's licence."

Carty nodded. "Will do." He pointed at Bishop. "I want you and Kevin to start working the arson angle right away. Grab the files on the others from my office and go through them for anything that might connect to this case."

"We hear and obey," Bishop smirked.

Ignoring his tone, Carty said to Patterson, "Let's move Leung from the area canvass and have him look into the victim's connections to the art business. Community response can handle the door-to-door." Working at the regional level out of Smiths Falls, the community response team included nine experienced detective constables who could be tapped as resources in major cases like this one. "If the arson angle's a dead end, I'd be willing to bet this has something to do with the theft of some valuable paintings from this house, maybe by someone not from around here. I'll get Leung started on it right away."

"Good idea," Ellie said.

Bishop turned to Kevin and pooched out his lips. *Good idea*, he mouthed.

"Smarten up," Patterson growled, catching the exchange.

"Hey," Bishop shrugged, "I'm always happy to work the dead ends, boss."

"Let's get started," Ellie intervened. "We'll meet at four to see where we're at." She pulled out her cellphone and walked away.

"Was it something I said?" Bishop asked, watching her punch in a number and lift the phone to her ear.

"She's calling upstairs," Carty said, his tone flat. "They'll have to inform the commissioner." He pulled out a set of keys and tossed them to Kevin. "Everything's in the filing cabinet in my office. Get moving, okay?"

Bishop smacked Kevin on the shoulder. "I rode down here with Leung, so you're driving. Let's blow this dump before he asks us to clean the frigging toilets next."

Sighing, Kevin headed back down the driveway. Great. Bishop in a sour mood. Not exactly his favourite thing in the world to have to deal with. But after having already taken flak from Janie and Patterson this morning, maybe he'd have better luck with Bishop, with whom he usually got along just fine.

After such a bad start to the day, how much worse could it get?

chapter SIX

Fifteen minutes later Ellie and Patterson met Inspector Todd Fisher at the command post that had been set up near the inner perimeter at the end of the driveway. The Leeds County detachment commander had been on his way to the scene when Ellie called, and as he followed them up to the house he wrinkled his nose at the smell that still hung heavy in the air.

"God, I hate doing fires. What's happening with the area canvass?"

"Underway," Patterson replied, explaining that detectives had already covered the few residences in the immediate area and had moved on to the village itself, hoping that someone in Elgin, perhaps at the general store or hardware store, could tell them something about the victim and his activities when he was down here in Rideau Lakes rather than up in Ottawa.

"Anything in the ditches?"

Patterson shook his head. "The usual trash. Nothing thrilling, so far."

A short, fussy man with wavy grey hair and thick black eyebrows, Fisher briefly toured the farm, looking in the back door of the stone house and peering through the window of the studio, before reluctantly accepting a ride across the field to the burned-out barn. Kearns was supervising the removal of the body from the scene and couldn't spare him time to chit chat, so he had his look, got back into Flood's Tahoe, and endured the less-than-smooth trip back to the dooryard, where Ellie was waiting for him.

"Leanne's expecting us." She led the way back up the driveway to the road. "We'll take my car."

Since Fisher had caught a ride from his office to the scene in a cruiser, the arrangement was self-evident as far as he was concerned, so he clasped his hands behind his back and said nothing.

When they reached Ellie's Crown Vic, she threw her handbag onto the back seat as Fisher opened the door, pulling out his cellphone. She drove down to the end of Charland Road and swung around the dogleg that connected to Highway 15, which would take them north to Smiths Falls. Fisher called Chief Superintendent Leanne Blair, the East Region commander. Leanne was Fisher's immediate superior. He assured her that the scene was fully secured and work was well underway under Detective Sergeant Patterson's more-than-able supervision. He listened for a long moment to whatever Leanne was saying, assured her they would be there in time, and put away the phone.

"Conference call with Moodie in an hour."

Ellie nodded. It would take them about half an hour to reach the regional headquarters building on the outskirts of Smiths Falls, and they'd have another thirty minutes or so to sit with Leanne and get their ducks in a row before speaking to Commissioner Moodie. Her thoughts raced ahead. Given the extremely high profile of the case, Moodie would likely want a media strategy handled out of General Headquarters in Orillia, which meant that Rachel Townsend, the media relations officer Ellie preferred to work with, would be required to follow marching orders issued by GHQ. The political side of the case would also see them dealing with the federal government, which meant the RCMP—

"You don't seem overly excited about all this," Fisher said, breaking into her train of thought.

"I don't follow you."

"Well," he turned sideways in his seat to look at her, "I would have thought this would be your big break. A senator? Ellie March, already a rising star, and now this?"

Ellie glanced over at him but didn't respond. Homicides were many things to many people, but to her they were never a "big break."

"From what Leanne says," Fisher went on, "you'll have Tony's job just as soon as your rabbi can find a quiet place to put him out to pasture."

She glanced at him again. Was he trying to provoke her? The suggestion that she would participate, even passively, in a move to push aside her own supervisor, Tony Agosta, in order to further her career aspirations was ludicrous.

"Look, Todd," she said, "I just got appointed. The last thing I'm interested in is someone else's job."

She'd recently completed a rather long and stressful competitive process to reach the rank of detective inspector after having been seconded into the job on an acting basis for nearly two years. Her substantive position in the Criminal Investigation Branch had been at the rank of detective staff sergeant, and she'd made a name for herself as an effective interrogator before moving on to a temporary assignment as a CIB major case manager at the acting rank of detective inspector. Now that she'd finally earned her commission, the job was hers on a permanent basis. Ellie was determined that her career focus for the foreseeable future would rest entirely on major case management in general and homicide investigation in particular. Internal politics didn't interest her in the slightest.

"Everyone knows your rabbi's next in line to be commissioner," Fisher said. "Word is, he won't wait to pull you up with him."

Ellie sighed. Fisher was referring to Deputy

Commissioner Cecil Dart, provincial commander of Investigations and Organized Crime at GHQ. Dart's son Craig, a detective constable in the Leeds County Crime Unit last winter, had fallen through the ice of Sparrow Lake while being pursued by an armed suspect. Ellie had risked her own life to pull him to safety. She'd also heard the rumours that Dart the elder hoped to make commissioner soon and use it as a springboard into politics, following the footsteps of a former commissioner whose political career had seen him briefly occupy a cabinet position in the federal government before he and his party were soundly thrashed in the last general election. She'd also heard the talk, from Leanne in particular, that Dart remained grateful for what Ellie had done for his son.

"He's not my rabbi," she said flatly, "and nobody's pulling me up anywhere."

Fisher murmured, " 'The lady doth protest too much, methinks.' "

Ellie didn't reply. She knew it sounded lame, even to her own ears. Dart was welcome to feel gratitude if he wished, and there was nothing she could do about it. The bottom line was that she never expected help in her career, she never asked for it, and she never wanted it. She didn't have the personality for networking and cultivating relationships. Her focus was on her work, and the rest be damned.

After a moment, she spared another glance at Fisher. He was looking down at his hands, his mouth slightly open. Unaware that she was looking at him, he bit his lower lip, shook his head, and sighed.

She didn't like Fisher and knew he didn't like her either. It wasn't misogyny on his part, despite the stories she'd heard about his sexism before her assignment to the Hansen case last winter. She'd had enough dealings with him now to realize he respected Leanne Blair, for example, and had no problem reporting to a woman. According to Scott Patterson, he did nothing to discourage female uniformed members from coming into his detachment. It was just that he had a sour disposition and was a very unhappy human being. And he definitely didn't like Ellie March.

She slowed for a stop sign. Peripherally, she saw him stir, looking around, as though uncertain of where he was.

"Not too much farther," she said.

He nodded, covering his eyes with his hand.

chapter SEVEN

The OPP East Regional Headquarters building in Smiths Falls was a two-storey, 50,000-square-foot facility divided into two halves—one housing the Forensic Identification Services unit that provided evidence processing within the region, and the other accommodating administrative staff and regional senior management. Completed in 2012, construction of the new building had been funded by the Ontario government as part of a total investment of $93 million in OPP facilities across the province.

Upstairs on the second floor on the admin side, the office of Chief Superintendent Leanne Blair, the regional commander, was appropriately comfortable—large, well-lighted, and furnished with attractive-looking furniture. An oil painting of a brick house by Kingston artist James Keirstead, a former OPP constable, adorned one wall, while another was covered with the usual plaques, certificates, and photographs one would expect to find on the power wall of an experienced law enforcement professional.

The atmosphere in the office at the moment, however, was anything but comfortable. Leanne had drawn her chair over from behind her desk to a round table in the corner. Ellie sat on her right, her back against the wall. Todd Fisher sat across from her, frowning at his knuckles. Regional media relations officer Constable Rachel Townsend, feeling very junior at the moment, made up the foursome. In the centre of the table was the source of their discomfort, a conference call telephone device connecting them to the OPP commissioner in his office in Orillia.

"Thank you, Ellie," Commissioner Ted Moodie said as she completed her briefing. "It sounds like you're telling me this fire's not connected to the others."

"We haven't ruled it out, sir, but given the significant differences in modus operandi we're looking in other directions as well. Because we found preliminary indications that the house had been searched and items removed, as I mentioned, we're investigating the distinct possibility that paintings or other valuables belonging to the victim may have been stolen and that the homicide occurred during the robbery. Once we've got the warrant in our hands and we've processed the house, the studio, and the rest of the property, we'll be in a better position to explore that line of investigation more thoroughly."

"I see." Moodie hesitated. "Cecil, you have a question?"

"Yes, sir." The voice of Deputy Commissioner Cecil Dart came through the speaker. "What about a political motive?"

Ellie glanced at Leanne, who raised her eyebrows. "Darius Lane was appointed to the Senate nine months ago," Ellie replied. "He was on the standing committee on social affairs, science and technology. He helped prepare a report on social inclusion in Canada, but I'm not sure what he's been working on since. We'll be looking into it. He apparently had a condominium residence in Ottawa not far from Parliament Hill, so we'll need to look at that as well."

"We'll need to have the RCMP *and* Ottawa Police on board and squared away before that happens," Dart observed.

Ellie compressed her lips, saying nothing.

"I'll be contacting my RCMP counterpart," Moodie

said, "to let them know we'll expect their assistance on the government angle." He sighed. "As soon as we're done here, though, I'll be briefing the premier. She'll call the prime minister. The minister of public safety and the Senate speaker will be brought into the loop, not to mention the director of CSIS, the Ottawa chief of police, and who knows who else I'm forgetting at the moment. The death of a senator creates instant waves, as I'm sure you understand. The ride is going to be anything but smooth."

Both rooms went quiet for a moment as they all thought about what lay ahead.

"With that in mind," Moodie continued, "John will control all information released to the media."

"Any and all statements will be issued solely from my office," John Goss said, entering the conversation for the first time. As director of Corporate Communications and Strategy Management, he was Moodie's right hand in Orillia in terms of media relations. "Is that understood, Constable Townsend? You'll be provided with text statements that can be handed out to local media, and you can read those statements to the press, but there'll be no deviation from them, no Q-and-A, and no ad libbing or off-the-cuff comments."

"Yes, sir," Rachel said. She glanced at Leanne, who nodded her reassurance.

"Ellie," Moodie said, "I need you out front on this investigation. There'll be a lot of moving parts, and I need you to keep a tight grip on everything."

"Yes, sir. Understood."

Moodie sighed again. "All right, look. As much as we all like plausible deniability in high risk cases, I want Ellie to report directly to me on this one. Is that understood?"

"Are you sure that's necessary?" Dart asked.

"Yes, it is. And whatever Ellie needs, I expect all of you to make sure she gets it right away. Leanne, will that be a problem?"

"No, sir." Leanne glanced at Ellie. As regional commander, Leanne reported to the deputy commissioner of Field Operations, a different stovepipe in the organization than that occupied by Ellie and Dart. Technically, she was responsible for the homicide investigation while Ellie was, in essence, a highly-qualified resource on loan from GHQ to manage the case on her behalf. It was Leanne's responsibility to provide the people, vehicles, equipment, and investigative and forensic expertise to work the case, drawing on her crime units, community response teams, emergency response teams, forensic identification unit, and any other resources at her disposal. She glanced at Fisher. As commander of the detachment in which the homicide had occurred, he was her managerial boots on the ground. If Ellie asked for something or someone and didn't get it, it was on Fisher's forehead that the little red laser dot would settle.

As usual, he wore the expression of a man who'd just downed a bottle of vinegar.

"Then I think we understand the situation," Moodie said. "Ellie, this is where you'll call to reach me directly." He recited his cellphone number.

Ellie wrote it down in her notebook. She would program it into her cellphone as a speed-dial selection when they were finished.

"Let's get to work, then."

When Leanne reached forward and stabbed the button to end the call, everyone around the table sat back and exhaled.

Ellie made a final note, set down her pen, and looked up.

"Well, March," Fisher said, "this is a pretty shit storm we've fallen into. I hope you're up for it."

"I guess I'd better be," she replied.

chapter EIGHT

Compared to the regional headquarters building, the facility housing the Rideau Lakes OPP satellite detachment just west of Smiths Falls was a bit of a step down in terms of luxury accommodations. Shoehorned into the former South Elmsley municipal building on Highway 15 between a meeting hall for seniors and a five-bay township garage, the office was home base for eight patrol constables, a court officer, a sergeant, a secretary, and Carty, the lone detective constable dedicated to Rideau Lakes Township.

Kevin parked in front of the flagpole next to the front door and got out. He glanced at Bishop, who slammed the passenger door and spat on the pavement. The detective was still out of sorts, and Kevin knew from experience it would be a good idea to take the lead here in order to avoid pissing people off unnecessarily.

Inside, Kevin walked up to the security glass and smiled at the secretary, a middle-aged woman he hadn't met before. She didn't return the smile. He held up his badge and Carty's keys.

"I'm Detective Constable Walker from the crime unit. This is Detective Constable Bishop. Tom Carty sent us over to look at a couple of his files." He jingled the keys.

She glanced at his badge, buzzed them in, and turned her back. Whatever was on her computer monitor was evidently more interesting than he was.

Kevin led the way down a narrow hallway. He paused at an open door and looked in at Sergeant Kent Evans, whom he knew slightly.

"Sergeant Evans, how's it going?"

"Walker, Bishop. What brings you boys up here?" Short and thin, Evans reminded Kevin of an old-fashioned bank clerk with his trimmed moustache, receding hairline, and rolled-up shirt sleeves.

"Tom sent us on a mission." He tossed the keys lightly in the air and caught them. "We have to look through some of his files."

Evans closed the report he'd been reading and put it into his desk drawer. "The fire, huh?"

"Yeah."

"Tom's been talking about how bad he wanted to catch this guy before he hurt someone."

Behind Kevin, Bishop peeled off his suit jacket. "Yeah, well, I guess it's too late for that now."

"You're right about that. Anything I can do to help?"

Kevin motioned with his head down the hallway. "Tom's office is just down here?"

"Down at the end."

"Thanks. We'll let you know if we need anything."

"All right, boys. Good hunting."

Kevin used one of the keys on Carty's ring to open the office door. He looked in at a tiny space not much larger than a maintenance closet, with room for a desk, a chair, a gunmetal grey four-drawer filing cabinet, a visitor's chair, a coat rack, and not much else.

"Christ, I'm not doing this in here," Bishop groused.

"Yeah," Kevin agreed, edging in. "It's so small, even the mice are round-shouldered."

"What? There's mice in here, for chrissakes?"

"Never mind." Kevin flipped through the keys on the ring and unlocked the filing cabinet. He pulled open the top drawer and skimmed through the files until he found what he was looking for. There were four accordion files labelled with numbers from their records management system and "Arson—Crane," "Arson—Mason," "Arson—Roberts," and "Arson—Wierdsma" typed below the numbers. He pulled them out and shut the drawer. He spotted a pack of yellow adhesive Post-it notes on Carty's desk and dropped it into his jacket pocket. "Let's find someplace to work."

Bishop led the way back up the hall. He rapped a meaty palm on Evans's doorframe and stuck in his head. "Got anywhere we can look at this stuff?"

"Meeting room's full of boxes right now," Evans said, standing up. "Old files being sent out to archives. But the kitchenette has a table." He squeezed past Bishop and led the way up the hall to a small room at the far end. The table was covered with the usual junk a working crew is usually too rushed or too lazy to throw out or put away—a jar of coffee whitener and packets of sugar, empty yogurt containers, fast food packaging, half-empty Styrofoam cups, magazines and newspapers, dead flashlight batteries. Even cleared, it would be too small for what they wanted.

Bishop snorted. "Not cleaning that up, man. Besides, we gotta spread out." He pointed at the accordion files under Kevin's arm.

Evans shrugged. "I think Pat's in next door. Maybe you could use a table in there."

"Is there AC?"

"It's probably on." Evans slid past Bishop into the hall. "There's an art class in there tonight."

Kevin led the way back through the reception area and out the front door. Two parking spaces down from his Fusion there was another entrance which led into the meeting hall side of the building. Evans tried the door, found it open, and went in.

Bishop looked at Kevin and rolled his eyes. "Too bad it's not euchre night. I could use some extra cash."

They walked through an inner door into a reception

hall that was about the size of a grade school gymnasium. Tables had been pushed back against the walls, and stackable chairs were set up in a semi-circle in the middle of the floor, presumably for the upcoming art class. The air was cool, indicating that the air conditioning was indeed turned on and working to keep the humidity at bay. A short, white-haired woman was running a vacuum cleaner around the floor. She saw them out of the corner of her eye and shut it off.

"Help you? Oh, it's you, Kent." She came over, peeling off blue latex gloves as she examined them over thick black-framed glasses. "What can I do for you?"

"Got a couple of detectives here need some room to spread out with a few files." Evans indicated Kevin and Bishop with his thumb. "Thought maybe they could borrow a table of yours for what, an hour or two?" He looked at Kevin.

"Sounds about right," Kevin agreed.

Pat shrugged. "Help yourselves. As long as you don't mind me vacuuming while you're trying to work."

"Not at all." Kevin looked over at the tables along the wall on the left. "Maybe over there?"

She waved. "Make yourself at home."

Bishop pointed at a galley-style opening across the way. "Is that the kitchen?"

"Yep."

"Got any coffee in there?"

Pat put her fists on her hips. "I can make some. Dollar a cup."

"Sold." Bishop glanced at his watch. It was nearly one o'clock. "What about lunch?"

Pat stuck out her bottom lip, thinking. "There might be a couple containers of chili in the fridge left over from Saturday night. I could nuke them for you. Two-fifty each."

"Bring it on."

"How about you, dear?" Pat asked Kevin.

"Sounds good."

"Will you boys need to make copies?" Evans asked as they watched Pat march off toward the kitchen.

"Maybe," Kevin said.

"Gonna say, our photocopier's busted right at the moment. The guy's supposed to come out tomorrow to fix it. We've been using the club's."

"How much does the old shark charge you for that?" Bishop asked.

"Ten cents a copy."

"Guess we'll just have to make a lot of notes."

"Okay, then." Evans clapped him on the shoulder. "Have fun."

Bishop trooped over to the far wall and dragged out a table. It was the kind found in most meeting halls like this one—thin, varnished eight-by-four plywood on tubular metal legs. It made a racket as he pulled it across the floor. Kevin put down the accordion files and helped Bishop with another one for himself.

"Just in case you're wondering," Bishop said as he went back for two stacking chairs, "I never, and I mean never, sit with my back to a room. Just saying." He grabbed the top two files and shoved the others toward Kevin. "Let's get this circus on the road." He sat down and snapped off the elastic cord on the flap of one of the files.

Kevin picked up the remaining two folders. He had ended up with the Mason and Crane files, which meant that Bishop had taken Roberts and Wierdsma. Sitting down, he opened the Mason file and did a quick inventory. Carty had neatly filed an array of documents in the folder's slots according to its type or origin. He pulled out an incident overview document and gave it a glance.

"This is the first one, isn't it?" he said. "May 16? Mason?"

"Could be," Bishop replied. "I'm looking at Roberts,

July 18."

Kevin grabbed the other folder and took a look. "This is Crane, June 4."

Bishop dug into the second folder in his pile. "Wierdsma. June 24."

"Okay, so he had them filed in alphabetical order, but as it turns out, I've got the first two cases and you've got the last two."

Bishop used his arm to push aside the Roberts file he'd started with. "Let's do this in chronological order."

"Sounds good." Kevin made room in front of him and started to unpack the Mason folder.

"Does Carty get under your skin like he does mine?" Bishop asked. "Or am I the only one who's allergic to fucking assholes?"

"He's not that bad."

"Mr. Primary Investigator, thank you very much." Bishop snorted. "Not that I'm pissed because I've got more service time than him, which doesn't seem to count for anything around here. It's his whole attitude, like he's better than the rest of us because he was a fucking MP in the army. Excuse fucking me."

"He's all right," Kevin repeated.

"I had no problem when you were primary on the Hansen case, Kev, even though you only had a couple years. You did a real good job, plus you knew the locals in the township. Made sense. But I wouldn't mind having a crack at primary too, for chrissakes. Given my seniority, and all. Just a *fucking* thought."

"It's Carty's township," Kevin said, not wanting to talk about his own experience a year ago as primary investigator in the Hansen homicide investigation. Although he'd been excited at the opportunity to lead the team under Ellie's direction, and they'd successfully closed the case, it had not turned out well for him on a personal level. The killer had proven to be his former mentor with the now-defunct

Sparrow Lake Police Service, where Kevin had started out as a police officer and detective, and the man had played him for a fool the entire time. Kevin had considered requesting a transfer to another detachment afterward, but the idea had prompted an incendiary response from Janie when he'd run it by her, and he'd decided to stick it out where he was rather than provoke a war at home.

"Plus," Kevin added, "he's been working the arsons already."

"Yeah, well, look who's working them now." Bishop picked up a stack of photographs and dropped them down again.

"Shut up, I'm trying to read."

"Okay, okay. Here." Bishop leaned over and spun a letter-sized printout across the table. Kevin picked it up. "It's a map of the township with the four fires marked on it. He's got a comparative analysis, too."

Kevin flipped through his documents and found copies of the same map and analysis. "Yeah, got it. I guess he put a copy in each file."

"Such an orderly mind," Bishop said. "I feel so inferior."

Kevin studied the map. Rideau Lakes Township covered a land area of just under 730 square kilometres in an approximate diamond shape in the northwest corner of the county. It was south of Perth, southwest of Smiths Falls, west of Brockville, and northeast of Kingston. Home to a little more than 10,000 people, it contained about 4,000 private dwellings, a large percentage of which were waterfront properties on the 840 kilometres of shoreline along its lakes and rivers. The four dwellings in question, Kevin saw as he looked at Carty's map, were all located in Bastard Ward or very close to it, in the eastern corner of the diamond. Carty had drawn lines joining each of the four locations to the others. Interestingly, the lines intersected at the top of lot 18 in Concession VI, between the hamlet of Harlem and the village of Philipsville, near County Road 8. Kevin had passed within a kilometre of the spot on his reckless drive down to the scene this morning. Perhaps Carty had thought the intersection point was significant.

"He says here," Kevin murmured, re-reading Carty's comparative analysis, "that periodicity on the fires was working out to be about twenty-one days. So, three weeks between each one. Which means he would have been due for his next one last week."

Bishop shrugged. "Maybe he went on vacation. Up north to play tourist at a forest fire or some damned thing. I don't know. Who cares?"

After Pat had delivered their chili and coffee, accepted their payment and tips, and returned to her vacuuming, Kevin spent the next half hour reading through the file on the Mason fire, the first known case in the series.

Located on Forfar Road south of Portland, the property was owned by Donald Mason, a forty-eight-year-old truck driver who was on the road that night. His eighteen-year-old daughter Brenda and her boyfriend were alone in the house all evening. At approximately 10:15 PM they were watching television in the living room when Brenda heard a noise outside the window and saw some kind of movement in the darkness through a gap in the curtains. When the boyfriend went outside to investigate, he saw someone run around the corner of the house. He went back inside for a flashlight, but by the time he returned outside there was no one in sight. He discovered a small wooden step stool on the lawn under the window. A moment later he saw flames coming from a small, old barn in the back field. As he ran inside to call 911, he thought he heard a vehicle drive away, but didn't remember seeing headlights on the road.

In an interview after returning home, Donald Mason told Carty the wooden step stool belonged to him. He kept it in a shed that doubled as a garage and workshop. After an inspection of the shed, Mason reported to Carty that a canvas messenger bag filled with road flares was missing.

Flipping to the report from Gordon Findlay, the investigator from the Fire Marshal's Office, Kevin saw that the arsonist had apparently used one of Mason's flares to start the fire in the barn. Findlay's report stated that road safety flares contained strontium nitrate, which caused them to ignite and burn with a red flame. They had a fuel combination of sulphur, wax, and sawdust. They produced temperatures of more than 2000 degrees Celsius and could be ignited simply by pushing a button on the end of the flare. In the rubble of the barn Findlay had discovered a residue containing strontium oxides, sulphides, and sulphates indicative of a flare. On top of that, he'd also found the igniter button, which often did not burn in cases like this. An inspection of the button, Findlay wrote, indicated it had belonged to an Orion Emergency Road Flare, a common make. Mason had bought a bulk quantity of that same kind of flare online last fall. He always travelled with a handful of them in an emergency road kit in his truck. The rest of his supply was stored in the messenger bag stolen from the shed.

A canvass of the neighbours produced nothing useful. No one had seen or heard anything suspicious in the hours leading up to the fire, and no one remembered an unfamiliar vehicle on the road. If the arsonist had scouted the Mason property in advance, he'd managed to do so while remaining invisible. The Masons didn't own a dog or livestock, so there was no barking or any other commotion to alert the neighbours.

No useable footprints or other physical evidence was recovered from the scene. Latent fingerprints lifted from the step stool matched only Donald Mason and the boyfriend, who'd unthinkingly picked it up and thrown it across the lawn.

Following up on the voyeurism angle, Carty had checked the provincial sex offender registry for possible suspects. There were only two offenders registered in the surrounding area, one living in Westport village and the other in Smiths Falls. Neither had a prior conviction for voyeurism or trespassing at night, and both had iron-clad alibis for the night of May 16. A check of CPIC, the Canadian Police Information Centre database, turned up no one else with an arrest or conviction for Peeping Tom offences in the area.

A second search of the database for arson cases turned up only two in the area, both in Brockville. One involved insurance fraud and the other was a case of vandalism in which a middle-aged man set fire to his neighbour's car in a dispute involving the man's wife. Carty talked to the Brockville Police Service and interviewed both men without result.

Kevin spent the next half hour on the Crane file. Just over two weeks after the Mason fire, on Tuesday, June 4, just before dusk, twenty-eight-year-old Matthew Crane was returning home from work at a house construction site in the village of Athens, where he was sub-contracting as a drywall installer. While driving westbound on County Road 42, he passed a slow-moving pickup truck. He apparently cut back into the lane too close to suit the other driver, who blew his horn and flashed his high-beam lights. For the next seven kilometres Crane saw the pickup in his rear-view mirror, which apparently had speeded up to follow him, and when he turned left onto Harts Gravel Road, the pickup was still there. Turning onto Coons Road, where he lived, Crane saw the pickup sticking with him, and when he turned into the driveway of the house he was renting, the pickup slowed down. Crane got out of his car in time to see it accelerate away again. He could offer no description of the truck other than it was light-coloured, grey or light blue or silver or dirty white, medium size, maybe a Ford or Toyota. He couldn't give a licence plate number. He was fairly certain, though, that it was an Ontario plate.

That night Crane awoke to a neighbour pounding on his door just after midnight to tell him the barn behind his house was on fire.

Because Crane was just renting, Carty took a statement from the landlord, David Knowlton, who lived in Athens. According to Knowlton, Crane had lived in the house for the past two and a half years without incident. He paid his rent on time and was a model tenant. Once it was clear there was no damage to his house and attached garage, and that the fire had not spread from the barn to the surrounding property before being put out, Knowlton expressed little concern for the loss of the barn itself. It was unused, and he'd been thinking about tearing it down and selling the barn boards, which he understood were worth a few bucks from interior decorators looking to repurpose them in home renovation projects.

John Jordan, the neighbour, told Carty he was reading in his living room when he heard a vehicle on the road between his house and Crane's. Because it was only a few minutes short of midnight, when traffic on the road was rare, he'd parted the curtains in time to see a pair of headlights race by in the direction of the Harts Gravel Road intersection. He couldn't identify the make or model of the vehicle, but thought it was a pickup truck. When asked if he knew anyone who drove a pickup, Matt Crane had recalled the road rage incident. With no other information on the truck, though, there was little Carty could do to follow up.

The Fire Marshal's report read almost identically to the one he'd submitted on the Mason case. Findlay had discovered similar evidence pointing to another of Mason's road flares as the igniter of the fire, leading to a conclusion that arson was again the cause. A search for physical evidence once more yielded nothing of significance.

With no apparent element of voyeurism this time but a solid basis to believe the two fires were connected, Carty interviewed Bill Quigley, the area fire chief of the Delta station that had responded to the blaze, asking specific questions about past and present volunteer firefighters who might have a reason to set fires. Carty had been thinking, no doubt, of a former volunteer who'd been found responsible for a rash of barn fires in Lanark County over a decade ago. The only person Quigley could think of who'd ever displayed any erratic behaviour at all was a man named Patrick Lennon. Carty then contacted Derek Flood, who'd responded to the Crane fire, with the same question. Flood had no other names for him, but remembered Quigley bringing up Lennon's name more than once in meetings.

Carty interviewed Lennon at the home of his brother, who ran a small farm on Otter Lake Road. Recently divorced, Lennon was currently living in his brother's basement and working for him on a part-time basis. A former military veteran, he suffered from post-traumatic stress disorder and had volunteered for the fire department as part of his rehabilitation program. He'd quit after six months. His brother vouched for Lennon and said he was certain he was downstairs in his room all evening on June 4. Lennon drove a medium-green Toyota Tacoma pickup truck, but his brother swore Lennon hadn't been off the farm for the past three days. Lennon himself repeated the same claims, insisting he'd never heard of Donald Mason or Matt Crane before and had no reason to bear them any ill will. He said he quit volunteer firefighting because he'd discovered he had a pathological fear of fire as a result of his military experiences. Without evidence to the contrary, Carty had no choice but to turn his attention elsewhere.

"You boys want any more coffee?" Pat asked, breaking Kevin's concentration.

"Uh, no thanks." He watched her gather up his empty cup and chili container, napkins, and plastic utensils onto a plastic serving tray. "It was good." The truth was, he'd been so absorbed in what he was reading he hadn't paid any attention to what he'd been eating or drinking.

"How about you?" she asked Bishop, adding his garbage to her tray.

"No, I'm good." The stocky detective frowned. "Do you really charge Evans ten cents a page to use your photocopier?"

Pat looked at him over the rims of her glasses. "What do you think?"

Bishop watched her walk away, then shook his head at Kevin. "I think she'd charge admission to her own funeral, the bloodsucker."

"Are you done with those?" Kevin asked, pointing at Bishop's files.

"Yeah, I was just re-reading stuff. Let's swap."

Kevin spent less time reading the other two case files, knowing that Bishop had reviewed them in depth. The third barn fire had occurred the night of June 24 at the farm of Peter Wierdsma on Visser Road, just below Otter Lake off County Road 5, about fifteen kilometres south of Smiths Falls. Wierdsma ran a large dairy operation that included one hundred and twenty-five head of cattle and a small cheese factory, but the barn that had burned down was an older one in which Wierdsma kept a pony belonging to his daughter. The pony was found running loose in the next field from the fire, suggesting that the arsonist had chased it from the barn before doing his thing.

Among the interview reports filed by Carty was one detailing his second visit to Patrick Lennon. Once again his brother, Mark Lennon, alibied him. Carty noted that Patrick "became agitated during the interview and had to be physically restrained by his brother." There was nothing in the file that Kevin could see which pointed to Lennon as a promising suspect.

The fourth fire had been set just under a month ago, on July 18, at the farm of Dr. Gordon Roberts on Daytown Road, north of Delta. A quiet, retired orthopaedic surgeon, Dr. Roberts raised Olympic-class competitive horses on a hundred-acre farm. His sixteen-year-old granddaughter was an amateur equestrian who rode in national competitions. Roberts had just finished building a new horse barn at a cost of a hundred thousand dollars, but the animals had not yet been moved in. A collection of antique horse buggies had been stored in the barn, and the arsonist had removed straw-filled seats, stacked them in a pile, and set fire to them with another flare. In this instance the igniter button was not recovered, but the tell-tale residue of a road flare was found at the point of origin.

Interestingly, Carty had made note of a conversation he'd had a few days after the Roberts fire with Constable Mary Ann Arthur and Constable Wayne Thompson of the Smiths Falls Police Service. While Carty was attending a charity event in town sponsored by local law enforcement officers and first responders, Arthur and Thompson approached him with questions about the barn fires, which were now getting extensive coverage in local and regional media sources. During their conversation, Arthur recalled having responded to a nuisance fire in the washroom of the local Burger King in March. The restaurant manager reported that one of her cashiers had had an altercation with a customer over the amount of change she'd given him. After a loud argument the customer stormed into the washroom, emerged a few minutes later, and left the building. Almost immediately afterward a fire was discovered in the waste paper basket in the washroom. The manager put it out with a fire extinguisher.

While questioning witnesses in the restaurant, Arthur took a statement from a man who'd seen the argument and watched the customer leave the restaurant and drive away. He gave Arthur a licence plate number which matched a Ford Ranger truck registered to a man named Larry Pool on County Road 8, north of Philipsville. Larry Pool turned out to be disabled, but his twenty-two-year-old son Jeremy admitted to having been in the Burger King and arguing with the cashier. He denied setting the fire, however, and in the absence of any evidence to the contrary he was not charged.

Carty interviewed Jeremy Pool at home. His father alibied him for the Roberts fire, swearing he was watching television with him that night, and insisted the same was true for the other fires, as well. Carty noted in the report, though, that Larry Pool appeared intoxicated at the time of the interview and that the young man was evasive and generally unco-operative.

"I don't get it," Bishop said suddenly, tossing paper aside. "What's the connection? Peeping Tom, road rage, an old pony, and a bunch of buggies. It all seems completely random."

Kevin sat back, trying to remember what he'd read about serial arsonists. While there were a number of known motives for arson in general, including profit and vandalism, serial arsonists tended to be motivated by revenge, excitement, or social or political extremism. Kevin frowned. According to the *Crime Classification Manual*, if he remembered correctly, crime concealment was another motive for arson. Concealment of murder, for example. But did that particular scenario fit the profile of a serial arsonist? He'd have to look it up again to be sure, but he didn't think so. It made him feel even more discouraged. They were retracing Carty's steps through a series of fires that were looking more and more unrelated to the Darius Lane case.

"Besides," Bishop went on, interrupting his train of thought, "there're hundreds of fire bugs around here anyway, so take your pick."

Kevin frowned. "What do you mean?"

"This is burn country, man. Starts every spring. They get out along the side of the road and set fire to the ditches in front of their properties to burn off the weeds and whatever. In the summer they're clearing fields and making gigantic bonfires out of tree branches and stumps. They all got burn bins in their yards for their garbage and crap, and no permits for them. Personally, I think half the population of this province just loves watching shit burn. Like I say, take your pick."

Kevin sighed, packing documents back into the accordion file. "Carty didn't get very far. The closest he came to suspects were the Pool kid and Lennon, the soldier with PTSD."

"We should check him out," Bishop said. "Maybe he's got some kind of political agenda against the government. Maybe he wanted to make some kind of anti-war statement by killing a senator."

Kevin said nothing, re-reading the Pool interview report. There was something sticking in his mind, something...

He tossed aside the report and grabbed the map on which Carty had drawn all the lines connecting the first four fires. He looked again at the intersection point, just above County Road 8.

"Check this out, JB." He stood up and slapped the map down on the table in front of the stocky detective, jabbing his index finger at the spot where all the lines intersected. "This is less than a kilometre from where Jeremy Pool lives."

Bishop looked at the map for a moment, then grinned up at Kevin. "You're not just another pretty face, kid. Let's go have a talk with the little prick."

chapter NINE

When Ellie bought the cottage on Sparrow Lake where she now made her home, she had enough left over in her savings to pay for a few upgrades and improvements. She brought a contractor up from Kingston to build an addition onto the northeast corner where the tiny laundry had been located. Once it was finished, she moved the pocket-sized washer and dryer combination into the new room along with a pantry stocked with several months' supply of canned food, cases of bottled spring water, and bottled preserves purchased from a woman at the Brockville farmers' market. Other shelves held emergency supplies and a fully-stocked military-grade first aid kit that cost her $149.99 online and contained everything from bandages and tape to sutures, surgical blades, and clamps. She put a fold-up cot in there as well, in the unlikely event that someone would visit her and need to stay overnight.

The original laundry room became a walk-in closet for her linen, bedding, off-season clothing, and footwear. She left the master bedroom untouched, but attacked the guest bedroom with a vengeance. She paid the contractor to haul away the old furnishings and replaced it with office furniture from federal government surplus. The items were all mismatched—the filing cabinet was plum-coloured, the desk was mahogany, the credenza was oak, and the corner table was light birch. She didn't care, since the furniture was solid, large enough to suit her purposes, and relatively inexpensive, being second-hand.

There was just enough room left over in her new office for her gun safe, which had made the trip down from Orillia along with her clothing, files, a few personal possessions, and precious little else. Inside the safe went her SIG Sauer P229, a 9 mm Glock 17, a Remington 870 pump-action shotgun, and a Colt C8 carbine, along with ammunition for each weapon. The two long guns and the SIG were departmental-issue weapons. The safe was secured with a biometric fingerprint recognition lock keyed only to her.

She put a medium-sized whiteboard on the wall and set up her communications system on the corner table. It included a satellite telephone she could use either at home or on the road when a cellphone connection was unavailable, and a desktop radio set connecting her to the Government of Ontario Fleetnet radio network used by the OPP and the provincial ministries of Health, Natural Resources, Transportation, and Corrections. The radio enabled her, should the need arise, to get in touch with OPP provincial communications centres, individual detachments, EMS and fire services, area hospitals, highway maintenance operations, and various OPP talkgroups such as tactics and intelligence. Civilians routinely used scanners to monitor these channels as a form of entertainment, but for Ellie the radio provided a backup system in case her cellphone and satellite internet connection both went down at the same time.

When it came to preparedness, Ellie firmly believed that redundancy was a good thing. She wasn't a wild-eyed survivalist wanting to live free or die, but she definitely intended to be able to do her job without interruption no matter what might happen. Having been raised in a small apartment above a shoe store in the middle of downtown Toronto, and having lived her entire adult life up to now in high-rise apartment buildings, she wasn't exactly sure what to expect out here in cottage country. She thought it wise to be ready for anything.

While the cottage was now set up as her base of operations, she continued to spend much of her time in field detachment offices while managing cases in the region. She led team meetings, observed interviews and interrogations, and spent as much time as she could with the investigating detectives and regional intelligence co-ordinators as they pieced together evidence and followed up on leads. As a major case manager she was expected to remain at a high level, overseeing, advising, and clearing roadblocks, but as an experienced detective and highly-regarded interrogator she often found herself rolling up her sleeves and getting into the thick of things. It was, for better or for worse, her way.

Once the commissioner had been briefed on the Lane investigation, Ellie's intention was to drive down to the detachment in Elizabethtown-Kitley, a few kilometres north of Brockville. This office was the administrative host facility for the Leeds County detachment and the base of operations for the crime unit, and Ellie had once again been given temporary office space in the building for the duration.

She was driving south on County Road 29 and had just passed the turnoff to Toledo when her cellphone buzzed. She hit the hands-free. "March."

"Ellie, it's Scott. Just wanted to give you a heads-up on a development here at the scene."

She frowned at the tone of Patterson's voice. Something was obviously upsetting him, and he was making an effort to control his temper. "What's going on?"

"We have some guests here at Spencer Farm. An INSET guy named Soroby and his sidekicks. Says he's here to conduct the RCMP's national security threat assessment."

"Jesus Christ." Ellie glanced in her rear-view mirror, saw that no one was behind her, and stepped on the brakes. “Wait one.” She slowed the car and edged out onto the shoulder at a spot where the ditch on her right was very shallow, almost non-existent. She threw the gearshift into Park, pulled the phone from the hands-free set-up, and got out.

She moved around the back of the Crown Vic onto the shoulder. “Run me through it.”

“Our friend is Sergeant Edgar Soroby, INSET Quick Response Team, Ottawa. RCMP, of course. He showed up with two other guys, a crime scene investigator, and an attitude a fucking mile wide. Says his orders are to process the scene for evidence of a possible threat to national security. When I told him to fuck off, he got on the phone and talked to some Mountie named Merrick, who wanted to talk to me. So I says, ‘Gimme the fucking phone’ and I talked to this guy. He says, ‘Call Detective Inspector March and tell her I’d like to speak to her forthwith.’ So I’m calling to pass along the message.”

“ ‘Forthwith.’ ” Ellie felt her annoyance level climbing the ladder as she paced back and forth behind the Crown Vic. “Really.”

Integrated National Security Enforcement Teams, referred to as INSETs, were created by the RCMP after 9/11 to function at an operational level, tracking and interdicting known or suspected terrorists working on Canadian soil. The teams included personnel seconded from other law enforcement agencies, primarily the Canada Border Services Agency and local police forces, including the Ottawa Police Service and the OPP.

“Is our guy with them?” she asked, referring to the OPP member of the INSET team.

“No. Just Soroby, two other Mounties, and their forensics dude.” Patterson sighed. “Look, Ellie, Wiltse tells me we’re still an hour or two from having the paper to start working inside. I can’t have these fucking idiots traipsing all over the place, screwing up chain of custody and fuck knows what else."

Ellie's phone beeped, telling her she had another incoming call. "Scott, I'll get back to you." Without waiting for his response, she hung up and switched over to the incoming call. "March."

"Ellie, it's Leanne. I've just received a request from the RCMP for co-operation in their investigation of Senator Lane's death."

Ellie's jaw tightened. "You mean, they'd like to co-operate in *our* investigation of the Darius Lane homicide. Listen, Leanne, they've already got INSET at Spencer Farm trying to force their way in, and Patterson tells me some prick named Merrick wants me to call him *forthwith* so that he can straighten me out—"

"Actually," Leanne interrupted, "I have Assistant Commissioner Merrick here with me in the office right now."

Ellie tightened her grip on the cellphone. "Great. Let me talk to this idiot."

"I'll put you on speaker." The audio dropped in tone and took on a hollow timbre. "I'm here with Assistant Commissioner Dan Merrick, Ellie."

"Hello, Detective Inspector March," a tenor voice called out, "Danny Merrick here. I'm sorry to make your acquaintance this way, but we all need to move quickly on this thing."

"Listen," Ellie began, "I don't know what you think you're—"

"Sorry to interrupt you," Merrick cut in, "but it's not a matter of what I think, Ellie, it's who the victim was. May I call you Ellie? Please call me Danny."

"I need you to explain to me right now why the RCMP is causing a disruption at our crime scene when we've got better things to do than waste our time with a bunch of inter-agency bullshit."

"It's the farthest thing imaginable from bullshit,"

Merrick calmly replied. "Please let me explain."

"All right! Okay. Explain."

"Senator Lane was sitting on a committee that had access to extremely sensitive information," Merrick said, "and it's my job over the next twenty-four to forty-eight hours to oversee a national security threat assessment to determine whether or not this country has just experienced a serious intelligence breach or perhaps the first move in something on a larger scale."

"Wait a minute," Ellie frowned. "Are you implying this was a terrorist attack of some kind? You think Lane was killed by foreign interests? Is that what you're saying?"

"I'm neither saying nor implying it, Ellie. What I *am* saying is that as of right now and until my job is done, that's the number one hypothesis that has to be proven or disproved. This is coming from the top down. It's not something I've dreamed up to keep me busy on a quiet Monday afternoon, believe me. Although the OPP still has jurisdiction, yes, and it's your case, no question about that, circumstances have put me in the rather delicate position of having to insist on, rather than ask for, your co-operation."

Ellie gritted her teeth, aggravated by his calm, placating tone. Her prior experiences with the RCMP had been mixed, and she'd often found them to be arrogant and condescending. God's gift to Canadian policing. This guy, however, was going out of his way to be deferential. As though he were teaching a seminar on situation defusion to a classroom of junior bureaucrats.

"All right," she said, "here's how this'll go. We'll share our findings on the physical evidence with you as soon as we get it. And we'll give your people appropriate access to the crime scene as soon as we've finished processing it. That way we still do our job and you get whatever information you need to do your threat assessment."

"That's great, Ellie, I really appreciate it, but I'm afraid

I'll need a somewhat different arrangement than that. Sergeant Soroby has escorted two of our best investigators to the crime scene along with a crime scene specialist who works exclusively on national security cases. These three individuals have extensive experience in looking for things your people haven't been trained to recognize. International terrorism is a whole different arena, Ellie, and we're the ones who are qualified to play in it. Surely you understand this, given the current war against ISIS and recent history here in Ottawa with the attack on the national war memorial and the Parliament buildings. Our domestic vigilance has quietly ramped up since then, and we need to get out in front of this particular incident right now before it gets away from us."

"Leanne, are you buying this?"

When the regional commander hesitated, Merrick said, "Look, Ellie, this comes right from the PMO. Do you understand what I'm saying? Our threat assessment has been given top priority by the prime minister himself."

"Unbelievable," Ellie whispered through clenched teeth. She stopped pacing and leaned against the trunk of the Crown Vic. She lowered the phone from her ear for a moment and breathed deeply.

Across the road, a woman wearing jeans and a tank top was on her hands and knees on the front lawn of a white bungalow. She stared over at Ellie as she pulled weeds out of a circular garden in the middle of the lawn and tossed them into a wheel barrow. Ellie turned away. She hadn't even been aware of having stopped in front of a house on the highway, so focused had she been on Patterson's call.

"All right," she said, raising the phone again, "will it make the prime minister happy if your specialist accompanies my people as they process the scene? I'm not talking about Soroby and the two other guys; they can go get a damned coffee and cool their heels somewhere else. Meanwhile, we do our job, we preserve the integrity of the scene and chain of custody of all physical evidence, and your forensics specialist can observe and advise without getting in the goddamned way. Does that sound doable, Assistant Commissioner Merrick?"

"It does. Yes. Look, I have a suggestion. If you could meet me in Ottawa tomorrow morning face to face, say at ten o'clock, we could talk this over and I'll brief you as far as I can on how the situation's unfolding from our end. How does that sound?"

"Where?"

"Come to our headquarters on Leikin Drive. Do you know where that is?"

"Yes."

"Excellent. Thanks, Ellie. I'll see you then."

You sure as hell will, Ellie thought, ending the call and shoving the cellphone into her pocket.

Across the road, the woman gave her one last look over her shoulder as she pushed the wheel barrow full of weeds around the side of the house.

chapter TEN

On the way down from Carty's office to the Pool residence on County Road 8, Kevin stopped at a convenience store so that Bishop could use the washroom. While he was waiting, he picked up a dollar coin from the bottom of the cup holder in the centre console and rolled it across the tops of his fingers. Then he practised the classic palm movement, holding the edge of the coin between his fingers, sliding it into his palm, and keeping it there with the muscles contracted enough to grip the coin without spreading his fingers. It was a basic concealment technique, and he checked the back of his hand each time he tried it to make sure it looked relaxed and natural.

He practised with both hands, then tried the movement known as the French Drop. He held the coin up in his left hand, gripping its edges with the tips of his fingers. He then covered it with his right hand and pretended to transfer the coin to that hand while actually dropping it down into the palm of his left hand. He pulled his clenched right fist away while closing his left hand around the coin, held both fists out, facing down, and then turned his right fist up while pointing at it with his left index finger. He rubbed his fingers together and opened the hand. Empty. The coin appeared to have vanished. It was a classic bit of misdirection, using his pointing finger and his eyes to direct attention away from the hand still holding the coin.

Like the classic palm movement, it was an important element in any sleight-of-hand routine.

He was practising with the coin in his other hand when Bishop opened the passenger door and got in.

"What the hell are you doing?" He slammed the door and peeled the wrapper from a Fudgsicle.

"Practising." Kevin started the trick again from the beginning. He held up his empty hand, grinned, then reached for the back of Bishop's head as though to pluck the coin from behind Bishop's ear.

"Mmmph," Bishop complained through a mouthful of cold slush. "Fu' off wi' tha' shi', will ya?"

Laughing, Kevin dropped the coin back into the cup holder and started the engine. "You're no fun at all, you know that?"

Bishop swallowed and slurped at the Fudgsicle, which was already starting to melt from the heat of the day. "What the hell are you doing? Magic tricks?"

"I'm teaching myself." Kevin pulled out onto the highway and accelerated, chasing the shadow of the Fusion up the hot, black pavement.

"What the hell for? Are you gonna start a second career as a clown at kids' birthday parties? Christ, Kev."

"It's just for fun." Kevin checked his mirrors, then set the cruise control when their speed had reached 85 kilometres an hour. "Plus, it's interesting. I'm learning a lot about misdirection. Forcing attention to one spot while doing something at another spot, where they're not looking."

"I know what misdirection is, Kev. I'm not a fucking moron." Bishop slurped thoughtfully. "So again. What the hell's the point?"

Kevin glanced at the dashboard clock and saw that it was almost three o'clock. They were about fifteen minutes away from the Pool address, give or take. "I don't know. I've never been very good at lying. I wanted to see what it feels like to fool people. Deceive them. Make them believe something that's not true."

"Fucking deep." Bishop polished off the rest of the Fudgsicle and dropped the stick on the floor next to the crumpled wrapper.

Kevin said nothing, disliking garbage in the vehicle but not wanting to offend Bishop by asking him to pick it up again and put it in the little waste paper basket behind his seat.

"Seriously, Kev, how about pulling a rabbit out of your hat and finding the shithead who's setting these fires? That'd be an impressive trick."

"What's your feeling on the Pool kid?"

Bishop shrugged, wiping his mouth on the back of his hand, then rubbing the hand on his thigh. He'd spent more time than Kevin on the Roberts file, which included Carty's interview report on Jeremy Pool. "I don't know. Carty obviously thought he might be good for it, given the little episode at Barf King, but he couldn't shake anything loose. We'll see."

The house was set back from the road, half-hidden by cedar trees that at one time might have been an attempt to construct a hedge before being allowed to grow wild. The driveway was a set of wheel tracks cratered with large potholes. Kevin eased forward carefully, not wanting to damage the undercarriage of the Fusion.

They pulled up into a yard that was cluttered with junk and refuse. Kevin stopped behind a light blue Ford Ranger pickup truck with an aluminum cap on the back and a thorough coating of road dust along the sides. The rear licence plate was completely covered, but Kevin could see the contours well enough to tell that the plate matched the one in Carty's interview report.

He shut off the engine and looked around. A rusted Honda Civic sat on cement blocks in tall grass, its wheels gone. His eyes moved to an old box freezer, dented and rusting, abandoned against the wall of a woodshed, an oil drum used for burning garbage, a motorcycle with no engine, and a rusted-out household fuel oil tank on its side, weeds growing up through jagged holes.

"Dog." Bishop pointed.

It had been making a racket since they'd pulled in. Kevin looked at the German Shepherd and collie mix that had run out to the full length of its chain to bark at them from the driver's side of the pickup truck. It was a very large dog. The fur stood up on its neck and back, and it showed long yellow teeth as Kevin made eye contact with it. The chain was wrapped several times around the trunk of a large Manitoba maple tree behind the house. Each time the dog lunged forward, the chain snapped tight, then it dropped as the dog bounced back. Snap, drop. Snap, drop. Hoping it was secure, Kevin opened his door and got out.

The house itself was a two-storey frame structure with a long, pitched roof at the rear extending over a back shed. At one time the walls had been painted white but now they were badly faded and peeling. Someone had made an aborted effort to repaint the house some kind of cream colour a year or two ago, but had quit after going halfway up. There was a front door facing the road, but weeds and litter made it obvious that it was never used. A few steps from the front end of the pickup truck was a side entrance.

Kevin followed Bishop around the passenger side of the Ranger toward the side door. As soon as they were clear of the pickup truck, the dog rounded the front end and made another mad lunge, snapping the chain taut before recoiling onto its hind legs.

Bishop cursed, his hand moving inside his jacket to touch his gun. Kevin walked around him and pounded on the aluminum screen door with his fist. Through the open inner door he could see intermittent flashing light, and between the barks of the dog he could hear the sound effects of a video game. He pounded again and shouted,

"Hey, anyone home? Police!"

No response.

Bishop pushed in and pounded on the door. "OPP, answer the door right now!"

The video game abruptly stopped, and between the barks Kevin heard shuffling feet. A thin young man with messy black hair, a thin moustache, and a prominent Adam's apple stared at them through the screen of the aluminum door. "What?"

Kevin held up his badge. "OPP, are you Jeremy Pool?"

He nodded, staring at Kevin.

"I'm Detective Constable Walker, and this is Detective Constable Bishop. We need to ask you a few questions. May we come in?"

He shrugged and walked away.

Bishop's hand shot out and pulled open the screen door. Kevin stepped into darkness, his eyes not ready for the relative gloom inside the house after the bright sunlight outside. He moved forward tentatively, Bishop crowding in behind him. As his pupils dilated, Kevin made out a kitchen area on his left and a doorway on the right. Jeremy Pool turned right, and Kevin followed him into a cluttered living room. Jeremy sat down on the floor in front of a widescreen television. He picked up an Xbox controller and resumed playing his video game. It was a military action first-person shooter similar to *Call of Duty*.

Kevin looked around the room and saw a middle-aged man sprawled in a recliner chair. He wore jeans, a stained green t-shirt, and plaid carpet slippers. He appeared to be asleep. The air in the room was heavy with the odours of stale perspiration, marijuana, and alcohol.

Bishop moved forward and yanked the cable of the controller out of the game console. "Shut this shit off and pay attention, kid. We're going to ask you questions and you're going to answer them. Time to focus."

Jeremy looked at him for a moment, then said in a

quiet, flat voice, "Can't turn it off without the controller, man. Plug it back in."

"You plug it in." Bishop tossed the end of the cable at him.

Jeremy caught it deftly, stood up, and plugged it back into the console. As Bishop moved over to a side cabinet covered with ornaments, debris, and half-empty liquor bottles, Jeremy saved his game and shut off the console and television set.

"Who's this?" Kevin asked, looking at the man in the recliner.

"Larry. My father." Jeremy stood in the middle of the floor, his arms crossed, his left foot slightly forward. He wore jeans and a plain navy t-shirt. His narrow feet were bare and dirty.

"Is he all right?"

"He's okay. He'll sleep it off, then start in again when he wakes up tonight."

Bishop held up a pink ceramic pig with beady black eyes and a big grin. "Anybody else live here?"

Jeremy shook his head. "That belonged to his mother. My grandmother."

"How about this?" Bishop put down the pig and held up a plastic bag half-filled with marijuana buds. "This your grandmother's, too?"

Jeremy nodded at Larry. "His. Medicinal. For the pain."

Bishop snorted. "Yeah, right. Never heard that one before."

Jeremy shrugged. "It's true." He unfolded his arms and pointed at the recliner. "His doctor's certificate and registration form are in the side pocket of his chair."

Kevin saw folded papers sticking out of the side pocket of the recliner. He pulled them out and looked them over, then folded them up and put them back again. "We're not here about weed, Jeremy. Where were you last night, from six o'clock on?"

"Here. Why?"

Bishop tossed the bag of weed aside and walked over to the recliner. He tapped the sole of Larry's slipper with the toe of his shoe. "Can anybody verify that? Maybe this guy?"

"He'll probably remember. We watched a couple of movies, then I put him to bed."

"What time was that?" Kevin asked.

"I don't know. I guess around one or one thirty."

"What movies did you watch?"

Jeremy pointed at a stack of DVDs on a stool beside the television set. The DVD on top was a copy of *Memento*, starring Guy Pearce.

"That's an unusual one," Kevin said. "What did you think of it?"

"Good. Weird, the way he wrote stuff all over his body to remember it."

"Got a girlfriend, Jeremy?" Bishop asked.

"No."

"Do you like girls?"

Jeremy shrugged. "Sure."

"Ever look at girls through their windows at night? For kicks?"

"No."

"Do you like animals?"

"Sure."

"Ever have a pony?"

"A pony? No."

"But you wanted one, right? Maybe when you were a little kid? Ride around on your own little pony?"

Jeremy shook his head.

"Is that your pickup truck outside?"

Jeremy folded his arms again and crossed his legs, left foot in front of the right. He was such a skinny kid that it almost looked as though he was trying to braid himself. He motioned with his chin at the recliner. "His."

"Do you drive it?"

Jeremy nodded.

"This guy better not be getting behind the wheel," Bishop said. "How about showing us your driver's licence and the registration and insurance for the truck?"

"What for?"

"Because I want to see them, smartass. That's what for."

Jeremy shrugged and slowly unwrapped himself, reaching into the pocket of his jeans. He pulled out his wallet, fished around in the bill fold, and handed Bishop his licence.

As Bishop looked it over, Kevin watched Jeremy. It was very plain he'd dealt with the police before. Most kids his age would be upset, nervous, scared of being caught or accused of something they hadn't done, but Jeremy demonstrated the calmness and affected disinterest of someone with experience in being interviewed by the police. Kevin wondered if he'd spent time on the street or had a juvenile record that Carty hadn't been able to access in his systems searches.

Bishop handed Kevin the licence. It bore the correct name and address, and the photo looked fairly recent. The date of issue was two years ago, and the date of birth indicated that Jeremy was twenty-two years old.

Bishop said, "Now, how about the paper for the truck?"

"They're outside," Jeremy replied. "In the glove compartment."

Kevin tipped the plasticized licence so that it caught the light. He could see smudged fingerprints and a light patina of dirt, indicating that it was handled on a regular basis. "Who buys the alcohol?" he asked, giving it back to Jeremy.

"I don't." Jeremy tucked his licence back into his

wallet.

"You mean to tell me he does?"

Jeremy shook his head. "A friend of his. Lives down the road. I keep telling him not to, but he just laughs at me. Sneaks it in when I'm not here. He's a worse drunk than Larry is. Look, why are you asking me all these questions? Why do you want to know where I was last night?"

"What's the matter, kid," Bishop said, "don't you check out the news when you're online?"

"We don't have the Internet. Can't afford it."

"TV, then. Your cellphone."

"We can't afford that stuff. Look, tell me why you're asking these questions, or I think you should leave."

"Don't tell us what we should do," Bishop said, stepping close to him. "We know you like setting fires. We know what you did at the Barf King."

"I didn't do that. Someone else did."

"Yeah, right. Some other pyro nut job."

"It wasn't me."

"Not what the manager said, kid. According to her, you got into an argument with an employee, went into the can and then left, thirty seconds after which the washroom was filled with smoke. You got a thing about setting fires, Jeremy?"

"No. And I didn't do that. Like I told them, there was another guy went in right after me. He must have done it."

"C'mon, don't try to con me, kid. You set that fire and you set all the other fires that have been happening around here lately, didn't you? We've got you figured out, so you might as well just get it over with and tell us about it. We're real good listeners."

"I didn't set those other fires, either. I told the other guy that."

Kevin had been running his eyes around the room, looking at the walls. There were corner shelves with knick knacks, a cheap battery-operated clock that had stopped at seven minutes after ten, a faded colour picture of Jesus that looked as though it had been purchased in a discount store in the 1970s, framed photographs of elderly people who were likely long since dead, and nothing else of interest.

"Do you like art, Jeremy?" he asked.

"Art? Not really."

"Interested in paintings? You know, pictures by Van Gogh or Picasso, that kind of thing?"

Jeremy said nothing, looking puzzled.

"Ever hear of a Canadian painter called Darius Lane?"

Jeremy shook his head.

"Get down to Elgin much?"

Jeremy shrugged. "No. Never. Why would I? Nothing there."

"Where do you work, kid?" Bishop cut in. "You've got a job, don't you?"

"Not right now."

"What about before?"

"I worked last winter in Smiths Falls. At the lumber yard."

"Get fired, or quit?"

"Laid off. Me and another guy. Not that I cared. Bunch of good old boys. Hillbillies."

"Living off your old man's disability, are you?"

"I'm on unemployment right now, okay?" Jeremy flung his hands out. "Do you know how hard it is to find a job around here? I'm trying! Leave me *alone*!"

Bishop stepped back. "Okay, kid. Settle down. Mind if we look around a little? See if you've got any artwork lying around that doesn't belong to you?"

"Yes, I *mind*. I think you should leave!"

Kevin glanced down at Larry Pool. He was still unconscious. A dark stain had spread across his lap.

He caught Bishop's eye and motioned with his head toward the door.

Bishop said, "Let's go outside and look at that truck, kid. You first. Let's move."

"I just want you to *go*, and leave me *alone*."

"Come outside with us," Kevin said. "Show us the paperwork for your dad's truck, then we'll get out of here and let you get back to your game."

"Fine." Clenching his fists, Jeremy marched past them. He went out into the hall and crashed through the aluminum screen door, letting it bang shut behind him.

Bishop rolled his eyes. "Welcome to the loony bin."

Outside, they squinted at the bright sunlight. Kevin fumbled for the sunglasses in his jacket pocket and put them on as Bishop cursed, sidestepping to avoid the lunging dog, which he'd momentarily forgotten.

"Quiet, Jack!" Jeremy ordered, opening the passenger door of the Ranger. "Go and lie down!"

The dog barked once more at Bishop, then turned and trotted back to its dog house under the tree.

Jeremy sat down on the passenger seat of the truck, one foot on the ground. He opened the glove compartment and pulled out a plastic folder. "Registration and insurance," he said, handing the documents to Bishop.

Bishop glanced at them and handed them back as Kevin looked into the interior of the truck. It was filled with garbage—fast food wrappers, junk mail, a half-eaten apple, pistachio shells, and other waste. Behind the driver's seat he could see a balled-up blue windbreaker, and behind the passenger seat a pair of rubber boots. Tattered work gloves stuck out of one boot, and a rolled-up red baseball cap was shoved down into the other.

"Do you like to drive?" Bishop asked.

Jeremy shrugged.

"Ever get mad at other drivers? You know, for doing stupid shit like cutting in front of you?"

"No."

"Know anybody who lives on Coons Road, Jeremy?"

"I don't know where that is."

"Did you follow a guy after he cut you off two months ago, then come back and burn down a barn behind his house? Was that you, Jeremy?"

"No. Now leave me alone."

Kevin circled around the back end of the truck. The cheap aluminum cap had a white top, and the frame was unpainted. Through the sliding windows on the side he could see more garbage, along with a red plastic gasoline can, a chain saw, assorted tools, a few chunks of firewood, and an axe.

No canvas bag containing road flares. Nothing to suggest that Jeremy drove around setting barns on fire.

"Cut firewood, do you?" Kevin asked.

"Yeah. We heat the house with it in winter."

Kevin looked into his eyes. They were still, grey eyes that held the emptiness of rural poverty. Other than the Xbox, which had not been a recent model, and the DVDs, which looked as though they'd been bought second hand, Kevin had seen no sign of the other electronic toys most young males Jeremy's age owned. He'd said he didn't have a cellphone or Internet access, and Kevin believed him. A quick scan of the roof of the house showed no satellite dishes, either for television or Internet. The truck was fourteen years old and in rough shape, the house was in serious disrepair, and their clothing was far from new.

"Got any road flares, Jeremy?" he asked.

"No. Leave me alone."

Bishop shook his head and got into the car.

Kevin held out one of his business cards. "If you hear anything about the barn fires around here, give me a call."

Jeremy took the card. Without looking at it, he said, "Sure."

Kevin took one last look around the yard, then got behind the wheel and drove away.

chapter ELEVEN

"I can't believe they can just swoop down and butt in on our case like this," said Detective Constable Mona Sisson. "Can they do that?"

"Yes," Carty replied, tight-lipped.

"They're being allowed access," Patterson said, glancing at Ellie, "because it's considered a potential national security threat. So they're not butting in, they're 'observing and advising.' "

"I'd tell them to observe this," Sisson said, holding up her middle finger.

"We'll set up a video conference for you," Bishop quipped, "and you can let them know exactly how you feel."

"Do it," Sisson said, turning her upheld finger in his direction. "See if I give a shit."

"You guys should relax," said Identification Sergeant Dave Martin. "Chadwick's a good guy. He helped. I'm not pissed, so why should you be?"

"He's a friend of yours," Carty said. They were talking about the RCMP forensics specialist brought to the scene by the INSERT sergeant.

Martin nodded. "We've known each other for a while. He was fine. Really. Don't try to make a problem where there isn't one."

Down at the end of the table Kevin sat quietly, his eyes

on his notebook. His expression was thoughtful as he turned a page, reading something he'd written earlier.

The only other participant in this evening's case meeting who'd had virtually nothing to say so far was Detective Constable Dennis Leung, the newest member of the crime unit. He sat on Ellie's right, listening to the others with a neutral expression on his face. Leung had transferred into the detachment this spring from Toronto, where he'd been assigned to the Alcohol and Gaming Commission of Ontario. He was here to replace Craig Dart, Cecil Dart's troubled son, who'd transferred up to Sudbury.

Ellie had heard that there'd been some kind of problem which led to Leung being moved out of the AGCO, but she didn't know the specifics. She hadn't actually met the man until Patterson introduced him to her in the hallway just before the meeting. On the surface he seemed quiet, polite, and professional. Time would tell whether or not he was a good detective.

"Let's go over what we've managed to piece together so far," Ellie said. She looked at Dave Martin. "Care to fill us in on your progress to date?"

"My team's still processing the house," he replied, hands folded in front of him, "but we've done the studio building and the big barn and shed. I can save you the trouble of worrying about the last two. No one's been in the barn since before last winter, guaranteed, other than rats and birds and feral cats. The antique tractor and riding lawn mower in the shed haven't moved in a long time, and we didn't get a single useful latent or trace from there."

"So what about the studio, then?" Ellie turned a page in her notebook and clicked her ballpoint pen.

"Definitely our primary for the homicide. There's a small office desk but no chair, so we can work on the assumption the office chair found in the torched barn came from there. The desk had been searched. Papers, stationery, office supplies tossed all over the place. Holes were punched in the walls, looks like by a wrecking bar of some kind, and the floor was damaged by the same tool, presumably when our offender checked for loose boards or a trap door or whatever. None of which existed."

"Looking for something that wasn't there," Ellie said.

"A reasonable assumption. We've got the victim's prints and two other sets." Martin glanced at Carty.

"Sheila McGuigan," Carty supplied, "a sixty-one-year-old part-time housekeeper who comes in once a week, using her own key, to clean the house and studio. She's also a part-time personal support worker employed at a nearby long term care facility, which was how they popped her prints. She says she was last in the studio two days ago to clean."

"We've already found her prints in the main house as well," Martin put in.

Carty looked up from his notes. "The other prints belong to a man named George Gleck, forty-five, lives in Elgin, works as a courier with access to Ottawa International Airport, which explains why he's on file. He works on the side around the village as a maintenance man doing odd jobs, including plumbing, electrical work, and carpentry. Four days ago he repaired the ceiling fan in the studio. It had stopped working. The housekeeper confirms she let him in and was present the entire time he was there. Apparently they're friends."

"Interesting." Ellie raised her chin at Martin. "What else?"

"Plenty of physical evidence in the studio. Blood, sputum, urine, feces. We'll find out soon enough if any of it *isn't* from the victim. A few hairs and other trace elements. Mrs. McGuigan apparently says she was in there two days ago to clean"–he glanced at Carty, who nodded–"and so it's quite probable everything we have was left last night."

"Assuming she's a decent housekeeper," Kevin said.

"We checked," Carty said. "She is."

"Okay," Ellie said. "That's good."

"We've made some progress on the fire," Martin went on. "I had a chance to talk to Gordon Findlay before coming over here." The investigator from the Office of the Fire Marshall had arrived at Spencer Farm shortly after noon and had begun his investigation, assisted by area fire chief Derek Flood. "It's definitely arson, and it's definitely different. The site search is still ongoing, but Findlay had already taken samples and assured me the accelerant was acetone. Which, as you probably know, is used as a solvent to thin lacquer and varnish, to remove nail polish, stuff like that." He looked up at Ellie. "It's also used in art restoration and conservation to clean soot and grime from oil paintings or to remove old varnish if you're going to re-varnish a canvas."

"You can also find it in pretty much any garage or workshop," Carty said. "I've got some at home. I use it to clean oil residue off of engine parts."

"And it's in most drug labs," Bishop added, tipping his chair back. "Can you spell 'precursor,' kids?"

Ellie shifted. "Anyone find an empty container nearby? Maybe in the ditch?"

"Nope," Patterson said immediately. "Nothing like that in the area search."

Martin coughed. "Sorry. Still some soot in my throat, I guess. Anyway, according to Findlay we're definitely looking at an amateur. Too much accelerant, and it was spread all over the damned place. Frankly, an experienced arsonist would have left Lane taped in the chair, piled dry hay on top of him, applied adequate accelerant to burn the body, made another pile to burn the barn around him, and called it a day. This guy was back and forth and in and out, like he was making it up as he went along."

"If that's the case," Kevin said, "maybe the acetone was an accelerant of opportunity. Maybe it was in the vehicle with him at the time and he just grabbed it."

Bishop snorted. “I like that. ‘Accelerant of opportunity.’ ”

“It’s too early for that kind of speculation,” Carty frowned. He looked at Martin. “Did you learn anything about the vehicle used to transport the victim from the studio to the barn?”

“We’ll run the tire treads in the database later tonight,” Martin said, “but the wheelbase measurements suggest a van or mid-size pickup truck.”

“Ford Ranger size?” Kevin asked, thinking of Jeremy Pool.

Martin shook his head. “One hundred and fifteen inches. The Ranger’s smaller. One-eleven something. One-eleven point six. No, this is more like a cargo van. You know, like the Sprinter that we use. That sort of vehicle.”

Ellie watched Kevin and Bishop exchange knowing looks, then said, “Just to finish with the fire, there was no trace of a flare this time?”

Martin shook his head. “Findlay’s thinking that maybe a cigarette was used.”

“Other physical evidence?”

“We took casts and photos of the small wheel tracks at the back of the house. What we’re looking at there is a hand truck, the kind that converts to a four-wheeled cart. You can buy them at Canadian Tire.”

“So something was taken from the house through the back door using the hand cart,” Kevin said. “Loaded into the same truck, presumably, that was used to take the body over to the little barn.”

“Supporting a theory of robbery and homicide,” Carty said. “Something large and heavy, like a crate full of paintings, was removed from the house. The killer caught the victim in his studio, secured him to the chair with duct tape, interrogated him as to the whereabouts of these paintings, put holes in the gyprock to see if they were hidden in the walls, found out they were in the house, went in and got them, used the hand truck to carry them outside to the cargo van, went back into the studio and killed Lane, loaded him into the truck still taped in the chair, drove over to the old barn via the road, wheeled him into the barn, splashed acetone everywhere, set it on fire, and left with the stolen goods."

"Sounds reasonable," Patterson said, looking at Martin. "Doesn't it?"

He shrugged. "I don't see any holes in it yet. But the night's still young."

"Maybe," Kevin said, "the senator was interrogated in his studio by someone looking for sensitive information or some kind of documents connected to his government committee work. After being tortured he finally told them they were in a safe in the house, the killer or killers removed the safe, killed Lane, then burned his body in the barn as a way to buy time and throw us off the scent with a false connection to the string of arsons in the area."

"I don't buy the national security angle," Carty said, his voice flat. "Let the Mounties waste their time on that."

"Either way," Kevin replied calmly, "there's still one important question we haven't answered."

"Which is?"

"How did Lane get down to Elgin from Ottawa? He doesn't drive, so how'd he get there?"

"What about the bus?" Leung asked, speaking up for the first time.

Carty shook his head. "It only comes down as far as Crosby, once a day, Monday to Friday. A shuttle for people working in Ottawa. And he'd still be a lot more than walking distance from the farm."

"Taxi?" Leung asked. "Limousine service?"

"You make a good point, Dennis," Carty allowed. "We need to follow up on it. Start checking it out right away."

"The other possibility," Kevin persisted, "is that he was picked up by his killer or killers in Ottawa, maybe at his condo, and brought down here specifically to turn over whatever it was the killer or killers wanted to take from him."

Carty frowned. "You keep saying 'killers.' You think there was more than one?"

"We don't know yet one way or another, do we?"

"Kevin's absolutely correct," Martin chipped in. "Without reviewing all the physical evidence, I can't rule out the possibility that there was more than one person involved."

"Maybe he was whacked by a team of ninja terrorists wearing black ski masks and funky tights," Bishop offered.

"Not funny," Patterson snapped.

"Dennis," Ellie said, "tell us about the victim. What have you been able to put together so far?"

Leung adjusted his glasses, looking down at his tablet. "I've provided Mona with a biographical sketch," he said carefully, "so it's available to everyone. He's a very interesting person. *Was*. I can walk you through it now if you like, Detective Inspector March."

"Call me Ellie. Please, go ahead, Dennis."

Leung raised his eyebrows, scanning the tablet's screen. He wore a charcoal suit, a pearl-grey shirt, and a pink tie. Ellie saw a simple gold wedding band on the ring finger of his left hand. On his right hand, in contrast, was a large, flashy ring inset with a bezel-cut ruby and small diamonds.

"Darius Lane was born in Port Hope, Ontario," he began, "on January 8, 1939. His father was a barber and his mother a housewife. There are no known surviving family members, by the way. After high school he attended the Ontario College of Art in Toronto, from 1957 to 1961, working part-time in a tavern on the Strip—Yonge Street, that is—to help pay his way. The first showing of his work was at the well-known Isaacs Gallery in 1961, an exhibit featuring Dennis Burton and several other local artists. It was a disaster for Lane, because all the attention went to Burton and his dreadful dadaism, garter belts, and depictions of female genitalia. Commentators wrote that Lane's romantic modernism was 'ridiculously dull and uninteresting,' quote-unquote." He glanced uncertainly at Ellie.

"Go on," she said.

"Okay. For the next ten years he struggled to find wall space for his work, and drifted from job to job, staying in the downtown Toronto area. Alcoholism became a problem, and he spent quite a few nights in the drunk tank. He went homeless between jobs and was picked up several times for vagrancy. Finally, in 1971, at the age of thirty-two, he took a bus to Bowmanville and worked for a year on a horse farm until he was let go for causing a small fire in one of the barns. He was a heavy smoker and was careless with a cigarette. He was drunk at the time. Damage was slight and no one was injured."

"Seemed to have had a thing for barns and fire," Bishop said.

"I guess you could say that. Anyway, he drifted to Kingston and found jobs washing dishes in restaurants downtown. He lived upstairs in an old apartment house near the Queen's campus and was trying to paint again. His next-door neighbour saw him working on a canvas in the back yard one day and went over for a look. The neighbour, Dr. Charles Stewart, was a professor of art history and conservation at Queen's. He liked what he saw. He took Lane under his wing, got him a job framing pictures at a downtown gallery, and for the next three years helped him fight the alcoholism and put his life back together." He glanced at Ellie again. "Some of this information comes from archived newspaper interviews and magazine articles."

"All right," Ellie said. "Continue."

"Fast forward to 1979, when Stewart became interim director of the Agnes Etherington Art Centre on campus and helped Lane get a few of his pieces into some shows. He sold a couple of paintings and apparently re-invented himself artistically. Then, in 1981, it happened."

"What happened?" Mona Sisson asked, pretending to be hanging on every word.

"Um, he sold his most famous painting, called *The Fire in a Boy's Heart,* to Pierre Elliott Trudeau."

"Wow," Mona said, surprised despite herself. "Trudeau?"

Leung nodded. "He was visiting Kingston and made an unplanned stop at the gallery. This was shortly after the patriation of the Constitution. He looked around, saw Lane's painting, and bought it on a whim. It ended up hanging in a bedroom at Harrington Lake, the prime minister's country retreat, although I believe it's now at Rideau Cottage, which the current prime minister is using as his residence right now. Anyway, the sale put Darius Lane on the map for the first time."

"I can imagine."

"After that he moved to Ottawa and worked out of an apartment on MacLaren Street. He was elected to the Royal Academy of Arts, was represented by galleries in Toronto and Ottawa, sold quite a few pieces, and started drinking heavily again. He ended up getting thrown out of his apartment, sank all his money into a house in Rockcliffe, lost that through non-payment of taxes, and wound up back on the street until he met Senator Constance Spencer. She apparently picked him up, dusted him off, got him back to work one more time, and eventually they married. Nine years later she passed away from cancer, and he ended up succeeding her in the Senate."

"So what was he worth?" Ellie asked.

"I should be able to answer that question tomorrow," Bill Merkley said, speaking up for the first time. As the regional intelligence co-ordinator assigned to the case, his responsibilities included executing warrants and production orders for financial records, and analyzing and reporting on them for the team. Banks were generally given a thirty-day time frame in which to respond to a production order, but in extremely important situations an RIC might be able to obtain information over the phone from a bank contact in advance of the formal response to the order. "My guy was out of the office today. I'll talk to him in the morning."

"Okay," Ellie said.

"I haven't been sitting around doing nothing, though." Merkley thumbed his straight brown hair out of his eyes. "When Senator Spencer passed away, her will was submitted to the courts for probate. The forms used for the filing are publicly accessible. They don't give me all the numbers, but I was able to see that her net worth was about three million dollars."

"So who got what?" Bishop asked.

"The executor was someone named James Brett. Turns out he's a cousin of hers who lives in Rideau Lakes. Nice guy. We talked for almost half an hour." Merkley fingered his moustache as he glanced through his notes. "According to Mr. Brett, she had almost two million in various equities that were liquidated. Her real estate included the farm, the condo in Ottawa, and another condo in the Bahamas. She left the farm to a local heritage society with the proviso that Lane be allowed to live there until his death. She left the condo in Ottawa to him, and the condo in the Bahamas was sold. The proceeds, along with a million bucks, went into a trust that was set up to disburse funds to several charities, including the Ottawa Mission, the Ottawa Food Bank, and a couple others in Leeds County. Another million went to Lane, and the rest was divided among various relatives and friends."

He smiled at Ellie. "I can't say for sure right now how

much money Lane had himself, but my sense is that it wasn't much. I'm told that the Ottawa firm Cole, Haley and Barnes handled all his finances. They paid his bills, invested his capital for him, made sure he had enough cash in his wallet, and kept him out of trouble. Remember, this guy had a history of homelessness. He wasn't exactly a model of financial responsibility."

"As for his paintings," Leung chipped in, "I called a friend who told me Lane's work is almost exclusively either in private collections or hanging in galleries. He wasn't known to keep them himself. When he finished a canvas, he lost interest in it. The paintings were shipped to whatever gallery was handling his stuff. From 1984 to 1997 that was the Gibson Gallery in Ottawa, the Scott Gallery briefly, the Watson Gallery in Toronto in 2002, and something called The March Hare Gallery in Ottawa from 2002 to present day."

Ellie frowned. "Are you saying it's unlikely there were paintings in the house?"

"We're really not sure at this point," Merkley replied. "Dennis and I have been putting this stuff together as best we can, but there are still a lot of holes."

"I understand." Ellie looked around the table. "Anyone have anything else to share right now?"

"Only that the victim was worked over pretty good before his death," Martin said. "Dr. Kearns likes to talk to her tablet while she's working."

"I think it's called dictation," Mona said.

"Quite so, my dear. God knows she won't talk to me unless she absolutely has to. I'm only a sergeant." He winked at Patterson, who rolled his eyes. "Anyway, both the victim's elbows and his left kneecap were shattered ante-mortem with the same blunt instrument that delivered the killing blow to his head. My betting money's on the wrecking bar that was also used on the wall. His right kneecap, by the way, was still intact."

"That would be when he started talking, no doubt," Kevin said.

"A smart guess."

Kevin glanced at Bishop and said to Carty, "We'll continue to follow up on the other arsons."

"Fine," Carty replied, not interested.

"Stay with it," Ellie told Kevin. "I want to be able to rule them out or in as soon as possible."

"You got it," Kevin said.

Frowning at Carty, whose eyes were down as he wrote in his notebook, Ellie gathered up her things and walked out.

chapter TWELVE

Kevin leaned against the back fender of Bishop's unmarked black Crown Vic and watched the leaves of an aspen tree quiver in the breeze as Janie ripped into him on the phone for the second time that day.

"Why?" she snapped. "What the hell is it now?"

"Bishop and I have to interview a guy," he said. "I'll be home later."

"You do what you want, Kevin. We're going to bed early. I'm exhausted. I've been on my feet all day, Brendan's been driving me nuts since I got home, and I've got a terrible headache. Don't wake us up when you come in or you'll regret it."

"I won't, Janie. I'm sorry."

He was apologizing to a dead line.

He got into the passenger side of the Crown Vic. Bishop was also on his cellphone, his face a careful blank as he listened. "Yes, dear," he said after a moment. "I'm not sure, maybe eight or nine."

He paused, then said, "There are leftovers in the fridge. Just microwave some of that. I can pick up something for myself, don't worry."

He waited. "No, dear. Of course not. I'm with Kevin. We have to go see somebody."

"For the case we're working on."

"Yes, Walker."

"He's sitting right next to me, Jen."

"I know. I understand. I'm sorry, Jen. Of course. Me too. Bye."

Bishop slipped the cellphone into his jacket and backed out of the parking spot. When they were out on the highway he floored the accelerator, his jaw clenched.

Kevin kept his mouth shut. He'd heard the water cooler talk about Bishop's wife, Jennifer. She suffered from anxiety and severe depression, and she constantly called him at work. She'd experienced several miscarriages and, after they'd given up trying to have children, she'd gone into a severe downward spiral. She was apparently on medication, and Bishop drove her to Kingston once a month for therapy. According to Mona Sisson, a tireless gossip, Bishop had played around on the side after the last miscarriage. Jennifer caught him at it and attempted suicide. Bishop was now bending over backward to try to put things right. She called him four or five times a day. He explained what he was doing, who he was with, and talked her through whatever was upsetting her. Mona's opinion was that Jennifer was obsessed with the thought that Bishop would cheat on her again, that he was getting ready to leave her. Bishop was pretty much at the top of Mona's list of people she didn't like. Which was saying something, since it was a pretty long list.

Kevin had met Jennifer only once, as she avoided the social functions that usually brought cops and their spouses together. She was a quiet, withdrawn woman with a pretty face and a slender, fragile-looking build. Kevin had no idea if any of what Mona said was true, and he refused to pry. It was none of his business. As far as it went, though, he felt sorry for Jennifer, and because he liked Bishop, he felt sorry for him as well.

"I think we're wasting our time." Bishop said suddenly, rolling his shoulders to relieve the tension in his muscles. "I don't think this Lennon doofus is our guy."

"Why not?"

"Just a feeling. I'm more interested in the Pool kid." He frowned. "His old man looks like a real loser."

"It's multiple sclerosis. That's what it said in the paperwork for the medical marijuana."

"Oh, shit."

"Yeah." Kevin looked out the window. He'd read a few articles on the condition, which involved damage to the nerves in the brain and spinal cord. Patients with MS experienced pain and numbness, muscle spasms, loss of co-ordination, and cognitive and emotional problems. Alcoholism, depression, and suicide were often by-products of the disease.

Kevin said, "Some studies suggest that CBD, cannabidiol, can reduce pain associated with MS, but if I remember correctly, it's an aerosol mist product, not the bud for smoking, that patients use."

"Well, he's not going to help the kid's alibi if he's bombed out of his fucking gourd all the time."

"Agreed."

Hutchings Road was yet another narrow, shoulderless strip of pavement lined with trees, fences, and farmers' fields. The Lennon place was a twenty-acre property that backed onto Newboro Lake. The house, a tidy white frame structure, was close to the road. As Bishop pulled into the driveway, Kevin saw a barn and outbuildings, grazing cattle, and fields dotted with large rolls of hay.

Bishop parked behind a dusty red pickup truck and shut off the engine. "I got this," he said, opening his door and rolling out.

"Okay." Kevin followed him around the side of the house. Parked in front of the red truck was a dark green Toyota Tacoma pickup truck. Even with its coat of road dust, Kevin thought it was still a stretch to match it to the light-coloured pickup described by Matt Crane as having followed him home on June 4 after the road rage incident, although Crane had said it might have been a Toyota.

The humid air was oppressive after the air conditioning of the Crown Vic. Flies buzzed around firewood stacked against the wall. An underfed, feral-looking cat stuck its head out, stared at them, and disappeared around the corner.

Kevin saw a trail of smoke coming from the far side of the house and suddenly smelled the aroma of grilling meat. He glanced at his watch and saw that it was almost seven o'clock.

Bishop pounded on the aluminum screen door with the edge of his fist. "Hey! Anybody home?"

"Just a minute," a woman's voice called from somewhere inside.

Kevin watched Bishop use his shirt sleeve to wipe his damp forehead. They listened to the sound of feet approaching. A redhead in her mid-forties opened the door. "Yes? What is it?"

"OPP, ma'am," Bishop said, holding up his badge. "Does Patrick Lennon live here?"

The woman frowned at the badge and called over her shoulder, "Mark? Can you come here for a minute?"

As the woman shut the screen door, Bishop said, "Mind if we come in, ma'am?"

She ignored him, holding the door shut from the inside. After a moment she was joined by a tall, muscular man who came outside, closing the door behind him.

"I'm Mark Lennon. What do you want?"

Bishop flashed his badge again. "OPP, Mr. Lennon. Detective Constable Bishop. This is Detective Constable Walker. Is Patrick Lennon at home right now?"

"He hasn't been off the farm for three days," Lennon said, folding his arms and looking down at Bishop. "Maybe you cops could piss off and leave him alone this time. He hasn't done anything wrong."

Kevin stepped forward. Lennon wore a tight grey

t-shirt and jeans. He was fit, well-muscled, and obviously trying to physically intimidate Bishop, who was several inches shorter, much thicker around the waist, and short-winded from the heat. Kevin, however, was an inch taller than Lennon, carried about fifteen pounds more muscle, and hadn't been physically intimidated by anyone since adolescence.

"We need to talk to him," Kevin said, well inside Lennon's personal space. "Is he here or not?"

Lennon locked eyes with him. Kevin returned the stare, his face expressionless, his breathing easy. It wouldn't take long, and it didn't.

Lennon stepped back. "He's with his bees."

Bishop snorted. "His what now?"

"His bees." Lennon pointed.

Kevin looked across the field, noticing for the first time a collection of white boxes near enough to the tree line to catch the early evening shade. It was an apiary, the home of a colony of honey bees. A white-clad figure moved slowly between the boxes. He wore bulky headgear and carried a pot of some sort in his hand.

"Great," Bishop said. "Bees. Call him over here."

Lennon took out a cellphone and called a number. "Pat? It's me. Can you come back to the house? It's the cops again."

Kevin watched the distant figure set down the pot and wave his arm around in obvious anger.

"Yeah, I know. I hear you. I was about to call you for supper anyway. Steaks are ready. Yeah, I know, but if you talk to them, they'll go. All right." Lennon ended the call. "He's coming."

As Kevin watched, the distant figure of Patrick Lennon whirled and fired his cellphone into the trees. Marching over to an all-terrain vehicle parked a discreet distance from the apiary, he started the engine and circled around, heading toward them.

"He's not happy," Mark said.

"Obviously." Bishop shook his head. "Looks like he's gonna need a new phone."

"I'll go out and find it later. Hopefully it won't be broken. You guys need to lighten up on him, okay? He's not a pyromaniac. Just the opposite. He has nightmares about explosions and fire. He's a veteran, for God's sake. Cut him some slack."

"Does he have nightmares about burning down people's barns?" Bishop asked.

Kevin watched Mark's lower lip suck in, and knew what he wanted to say. Wisely, Mark swallowed the words and walked toward the approaching ATV. Kevin followed, with Bishop close behind.

Patrick Lennon stopped the ATV a few yards short of the driveway and got off. The veiled hood of his white bee suit was unzipped and pushed back, revealing a shaved head, a tight jaw, and angry eyes. He was shorter than his brother and about six years younger. His leather beekeeping gloves were shoved into a patch pocket on his thigh, and his hands were clenched into capable-looking fists as he strode toward them.

"Just answer their questions and they'll go," Mark said.

Bishop shouldered past him, once again holding up his badge. "Patrick Lennon? Detective Constable Bishop, Detective Constable Walker, OPP. We've got a few questions for you."

Patrick Lennon slapped the badge out of Bishop's hand and kept going. "Get off this property and leave me the hell alone."

"Whoa!" Bishop shouted, spinning around. "Hey, buddy! Time to take a ride!"

Kevin stepped into Patrick's way and held up a hand. "Easy, now. Hang on a sec." Patrick tried to move around him. Kevin blocked his path again. "Just give us a minute, then we'll go."

Patrick stopped. "I heard about the fire, it was on the news. I didn't set it. That's it, pal. Take it or leave it."

Kevin looked over Patrick's shoulder at Bishop, who had retrieved his badge and was coming up behind Lennon with fire in his eyes. He turned to Mark and said, "Let's go somewhere we can sit down and talk."

Anxious now to defuse the situation and keep his brother out of trouble, Mark put his hand on Patrick's arm and said, "Come on, let's go around to the gazebo. I'll get you a Coke."

Patrick shook off his brother's hand, but nodded and walked toward the house. His brother followed. Kevin intercepted Bishop, who angrily shook his head and went to move around him. Kevin put a big hand on Bishop's forearm and stopped him.

"Simmer down. Let it go. I'll take it."

"Fuckin'—" Bishop snarled, then spat on the ground and nodded, knowing he needed to step back and cool off.

Kevin caught up to Mark Lennon. "You're certain he didn't go anywhere last night?"

"Positive. We ... had a bit of a fight. He found a bottle of brandy I'd hidden away last Christmas. He's not supposed to drink because of his medication and because, well, it brings out the anger. He got drunk. I smelled it on him when he came upstairs to get something to eat. His apartment's in the basement. We had it out, then he went downstairs again and that was it. He didn't come back up until this morning."

"Is there another exit from the basement?"

"No."

Bishop caught up to them. "Got any road flares?"

Mark looked at him. "I'll tell you what I told the other guy, both times he came out here. I keep a few in an emergency kit in my truck. I'll show them to you."

He walked up to his truck, opened the passenger door,

and reached behind the seat for a black zippered bag. He opened it and handed Bishop a flare. It was a different brand than the Orion flares the arsonist had stolen from Donald Mason and had used to start the other barn fires.

"What about him?" Bishop asked, handing back the flare.

"He doesn't have an emergency kit in the truck. He doesn't drive very much. I take him to his appointments and stuff, or Mollie does. He doesn't have any flares. He didn't start those other fires, and he didn't start that one last night."

They followed Mark around the house into the back yard. Mollie Lennon looked up at them from the barbecue, where she had lifted up the steaks and was scraping off the grill. She glared but said nothing.

Across the lawn, between a crab apple tree and a tall maple, the Lennons had set up a ten-by-ten screen house. Patrick stood inside, stripping off his bee suit. He draped it across the back of a lawn chair and sat down.

"I'll get his Coke," Mark said. "You two want anything?"

"Sure, I'll take a Coke," Bishop said.

Kevin saw that Mark's eyes were pleading with them not to cause trouble. "Yeah, thanks," he said.

Inside the screen house, they sat down in chairs on either side of Patrick.

"How long have you been keeping bees?" Kevin asked.

"This is my third year."

"I'd be nervous of getting stung."

"I was at first. It happens a few times, then you figure it out. And they get used to you." He ran a hand over his bald head and wiped the perspiration on his t-shirt, which was already soaked.

"Where did you serve in Afghanistan?"

"Kandahar, mostly."

"I understand you were wounded."

"That's right."

"When was that?"

Patrick didn't respond.

Mark walked into the screen house with a small tray. He handed a can of Coke to each of them and sat down next to Kevin. "Everything all right?"

"Fine." Patrick popped the tab on his can and took a long drink. He leaned back, touched the cold can to his forehead, then unexpectedly smiled at his brother. "Next time do a better job hiding that stuff, will you? I still feel like dog shit."

"There's nothing else left in the house, Pat."

"That's what you said before." Patrick looked at Kevin. "I'm not supposed to have booze. That's what I was doing last night, to answer your question. Getting blitzed downstairs in my room."

"Did you go out for anything?"

"No, I *passed* out. End of story." He took another long drink, glanced at his brother, and held up his left hand. The last two fingers were missing. "This is what you wanted to know about. February 14, 2010. Valentine's Day. Second day of Operation Moshtarak. It was a pacification offensive to drive the Taliban out of the town of Marja. I raised my hand to signal to one of my buddies, and felt a tug. I looked at my hand, and two fingers were gone. Just like that. Gone. Like a total idiot I decided that was a good time to charge the enemy. I covered about ten yards and caught the edge of an IED blast that took out one of our vehicles. Concussion, and shrapnel here." He tapped his left shoulder, under the t-shirt.

"After he was hospitalized," Mark said, "he had a bad bout of infection. We almost lost him then. I'm just glad to have him home now."

"Sounds tough," Kevin said.

"PTSD's the real bitch," Patrick said to his Coke can. "I'd already been over there too long and was feeling pretty messed up. Then this. All I could think about afterward was how I'd never play the piano again. I couldn't get it out of my head."

Bishop made a noise.

Mark shot him an angry look and then said to Kevin, "Pat played in a country music band. He was really good. Music was everything to him, back then. I still think you should play, Pat. You could still play."

Patrick shrugged, staring at the can. It was obviously an old subject that had been debated into the ground.

"Why did you volunteer for the fire department?" Kevin asked.

"Part of my rehab. Supposed to help me build a rewarding civilian career, as they like to say, by transferring all my great military skills to something useful at home. Didn't work. Dumb-ass fucking idea."

"Why? Why didn't it work?"

Patrick gave him a long look.

"Stress," Mark said. "Everyone thought he was ready for it. They thought the action would do him good, but it was a huge mistake. In the middle of a training exercise he just ran out. Took him six months to get back to where he was before he started."

"Turns out I'm a pyrophobic," Patrick said. "Afraid of fire. Where the fuck did that come from, right? Can't even stand to watch someone light a cigarette. Can't sit in front of a fireplace. And I sure as fuck can't set fire to barns and hang around getting my rocks off watching them burn to the ground. Are we done now?" He put down his can of Coke and rubbed his face with his hands.

"Look," Mark said, standing up, "he gets therapy and counselling, meets with his VAC case manager on a regular basis, does everything they ask him to do. Can you please leave him alone?"

"Patrick," Kevin said, "where were you on the night of July 18?"

"Here."

"Do you know Dr. Gordon Roberts?"

Patrick shook his head.

"Is he a shrink?" Mark asked.

"Patrick, where were you on the night of June 24?"

Patrick sighed raggedly. "Here."

"Do you know a man named Peter Wierdsma?"

"No."

"What about Matthew Crane or Donald Mason? Do you know either of them?"

Patrick shook his head again.

Bishop took a last swig of Coke, put down the can, and said to Kevin, "Let's go."

Kevin held out a business card to Mark Lennon. "Call me at that number any time."

Mark stared at the card. "Why the hell would I want to do that?"

"Just take it. In case you need to talk to me. About anything."

Mark kept his hands at his sides. Kevin put the card down on the table and walked out of the screen house.

Back inside the Crown Vic, Bishop started the engine and shook his head. "Told you that doofus was a waste of time." He spun his tires in the gravel driveway and swung out onto the road.

"Sometimes," Kevin said, "you come off as such an asshole."

"I'm paid to be an asshole, Kev. That's how we get this fucking job done."

Kevin could think of nothing to say to that.

"Same goes for you, by the way," Bishop added. "You need to start remembering that. You can't do this job trying to be everybody's fucking pal."

Kevin stared out the window, wondering if Bishop was right.

chapter THIRTEEN

After arriving home at the cottage and warming up some leftovers for a quick meal, Ellie was tidying up the kitchen when she received a call from Tom Carty.

"I just got off the phone with Burton," Carty said without preamble, referring to Dr. Carey Burton, the director of the forensic pathology unit at the Kingston General Hospital. "I called to confirm the details on the Lane autopsy. He tells me the body's been transferred to Ottawa. Did you know about this?"

Ellie walked over to the sliding glass doors leading out onto the deck and put her forehead against the glass, closing her eyes. She listened to the steady hum of the air conditioning unit in her bedroom window for a moment before asking, "When did this happen?"

"Late this afternoon, apparently. Kearns ordered it. Did she call you?"

Ellie opened her eyes and shook her head. "No, she didn't. I'll get back to you."

She looked up Fiona Kearns's number and dialled it. It rang through to voice mail. She left a message for Kearns to call her back right away. It took fifteen minutes for the coroner to return the call.

"This is not a good time, March. I'm just about to walk into a fundraiser with my agent and publisher. What did you want?"

"Dr. Kearns, did you sign off on a transfer of the Lane remains to Ottawa?"

"Of course. They had an opening for the post tomorrow morning. Is that all you called for?"

"It didn't occur to you to inform us this was happening?"

"Danny Merrick led me to believe he would speak to you about it. At any rate, you've obviously been informed of it now, haven't you?"

Ellie took a breath. "What the hell has Danny Merrick got to do with it?"

"Look, March, I don't have time for this. The body's at Ottawa Hospital. The pathologist is Dr. Glen Davies, a good friend of mine. I believe the time slot begins at ten a.m. Take it up with Danny Merrick. Now if you'll excuse me—"

The line went dead.

Ellie quickly looked up the number Merrick had given her and dialled it. When he answered, she snapped, "Did you tell Dr. Kearns to transfer the Lane remains from Kingston to Ottawa?"

"Hello, Ellie. Ah, I didn't tell her to, no, because that's her call, not mine. But I did suggest it to her, yes. Didn't she call you about it this afternoon?"

"She most certainly did not."

"I'm very sorry. You're only hearing about it now?"

"Yes, damn it."

"I'm very sorry about this. Dr. Burton wasn't able to do the post until tomorrow afternoon, so I asked Dr. Kearns if she thought we might be able to get it done in the morning in Ottawa. She made a call and got us a ten o'clock opening up here. I thought she said she'd inform you right away."

Right, Ellie thought. This was the kind of interference that gave the RCMP the reputation they so richly deserved. "According to her, you were going to call me. Next time you have a bright idea for my investigation, Assistant

Commissioner, let me know about it first before you suggest anything, all right?"

She ended the call and shoved the cellphone into the leather holder clipped to her belt. She put her feet into moccasins, found her cigarettes on top of the fridge, grabbed a bottle of beer, and went out onto the back deck. She allowed herself one cigarette a day, at the end of the day, with a drink to help her relax before going to bed. It was a little early, but she lit the cigarette anyway and inhaled deeply.

Dusk had fallen about half an hour ago. She took a long pull on the beer and stared at the moonlight spilling across the uneven surface of the lake. Once her anger had subsided, she called Patterson and relayed the change of plans for the autopsy. He agreed to spread the word to Dave Martin and Tom Carty.

She ended the call and concentrated on her cigarette. After a few long moments, she became aware of music coming from next door. She looked over and saw people on the back deck, which was brightly lighted by several large spotlights. It was her neighbour, Ridgeway Ballantyne, and two others, a man and a woman. They were playing musical instruments, and Ridge was singing.

The place next door was a huge, two-storey log structure similar to a hunting lodge. It had three large bedrooms and a loft upstairs, and a recording studio on the main floor in which Ridge, a professional musician, did contract work for advertising companies and media outlets. Now seventy, he'd managed to save most of his money after a meteoric career in the 1960s and 1970s as a founding member of the Scottish psychedelic folk band The Amazing String Players, and a chunk of it had gone into the property on Sparrow Lake.

They finished playing, and their laughter drifted over to her. Ridge bent down to pick up a cigarette from an ash tray on the deck. He caught sight of her silhouette, outlined in the motion-sensitive porch light behind her head, and waved. She waved back. He beckoned her over.

After coming home, she'd changed into jeans and a navy t-shirt with the OPP logo embroidered on the left chest. Her hair was uncombed and her face, without makeup, was damp with perspiration. She felt grouchy and out of sorts.

What the hell.

Beer bottle in hand, cigarette in the corner of her mouth, she pushed away from the railing and slowly walked over. As she climbed the stairs leading up onto his deck, she heard him say, "I'd rather not bother with the piano. Let's just stick to the stringed instruments this time, shall we?" His husky, slightly gravelly voice still retained much of the accent that marked him as a native of Glasgow.

As she stepped up onto the deck, he stood and grinned at her. "Welcome, Ellie March. Welcome! Now we're all set with an audience. How are you doing this fine summer evening?"

"Not bad."

He studied her face for a moment and lost the grin. "Oh, yes. That's right. I heard about what happened to the senator. That would be you on the case, of course." He grabbed a nearby Adirondack chair and pulled it over. "Never mind. Sit for a few and listen. Something else to think about."

"Thanks. I hope I'm not intruding." She bent down and stubbed out the last of her cigarette in his ash tray.

"Not at all. This is Stephen Simms," he indicated the man standing behind a tall bass violin, "and his wife, Margie Bolton. This is Ellie March."

Simms tucked his bow under his left arm and offered his hand. "Nice to meet you, Ellie. Ridge has mentioned you before."

Ellie shook his hand. "Good to meet you." He was in his early fifties, plump and balding, with crow's-feet at the corners of his eyes and dimples that sank into his cheeks as he smiled at her.

"You're the one with the police, aren't you?" Margie asked, looking at the logo on Ellie's t-shirt. Her violin in one hand and her bow in the other, she didn't offer to shake hands. She was about the same age as her husband and a few inches taller. Her strawberry blond hair fell in waves to her shoulders. She wore a tight t-shirt, and her jeans rode low on her hips. Her feet were bare.

"That's me, all right." Ellie sat down in the Adirondack chair.

"Would you like another beer, Ellie?" Ridge asked. "Or something a wee stiffer, perhaps?"

"Thanks," Ellie said, wagging the bottle in her hand, "when I'm done this. I take it you three are The Happy Teazel?"

Ridge laughed. "We are, indeed. We've got a gig coming up two weekends from now in Merrickville."

"I hope I'm not interrupting your rehearsal."

"We're just putting together a set list," Stephen explained. "The songs we'll play. It's not exactly a rehearsal, yet. Still plenty of time for that."

"Bloody humidity," Ridge muttered, re-tuning his guitar.

"You live in Athens, don't you?" Ellie asked.

Stephen nodded, lowering his head to listen as he applied a gentle pressure to a tuning peg and plucked the corresponding string.

Ridge played a few arpeggios and then slid into a slow melody in a minor key.

"Ah," Stephen said, raising his bow. He began a soft bass accompaniment. A few bars later, Margie took the melody on her violin as Ridge chorded along.

Ellie drank the last of her beer and held the empty bottle in her lap, staring out across the water as Ridge began to sing:

The moon shone bright
Like a light from the shore
I was left in the darkness
Begging for more
She held out her heart
and pulled it away
I was left in the darkness
with nothing to say.

His voice sounded like a cross between Van Morrison and Levon Helm. Despite his age and the natural roughness, he sang with strength and on pitch. The song reminded her of an old album by Fairport Convention, a folk rock group a friend of hers had listened to years ago:

Don't pull away, don't pull away
Please give your heart, turn night to day
Lost in the dark, a ship going down
If you leave me here, I'll surely drown.

The cellphone on Ellie's hip began to vibrate. She pulled it out and looked at the call display. It was Merrick. She eased up out of the chair and caught Ridge's eye. He winked at her and nodded.

She walked over to the railing to take the call. "March."

"I've confirmed the post-mortem begins at ten, Ellie," Merrick said, "but you and I are scheduled to meet at the same time, remember?"

"That can wait."

"May I make a suggestion?"

Ellie hesitated for a beat, then said, "What?"

"Your people can attend the autopsy while you and I keep our meeting. I think it's very important we have our face-to-face right away. You'll understand once you get here."

Ellie thought quickly, then nodded. "All right. Let's do that."

"Okay. You'll be here at Leikin at ten tomorrow morning, will you?"

"Yes."

"All right. Good night, Ellie."

Ellie ended the call, aware that he'd said *here at Leikin*, as though he were still at work in his office at RCMP headquarters on Leikin Drive. Unpaid overtime for an assistant commissioner?

She made a quick call to Scott Patterson. "I'm meeting with Assistant Commissioner Merrick tomorrow morning at ten, so I'll skip the autopsy. Did you talk to Martin and Carty?"

"Yeah, they'll both be there."

"Good. Look, we need a clear understanding of the ante-mortem injuries to the elbows and kneecap, and if we're looking for a pry bar or a tire iron as the weapon. Is it round, or does it have corners. Right?"

"Got it."

"I'll talk to you later." She ended the call and turned around, aware that the music had stopped. Ridge was writing something on a piece of cardboard while Stephen leaned down to listen as he fussed again with another tuning peg. Margie was staring at her.

"You must lead a very exciting life."

Ellie put away the cellphone. "I guess you could say that."

"Have you ever shot anyone?"

It was a question civilians sometimes asked without thinking, and Ellie answered automatically. "No, thankfully. It's not something you ever want to have happen."

"It must be awful, seeing someone who's been murdered."

"Yes, it is. But you get used to it."

Margie shuddered. "I don't see how you possibly could."

Ridge put the cap on his Sharpie and stood up. "Let's get you that stiff drink now, lass."

"I'm very sorry to have interrupted," Ellie said.

"Not at all. Wine, or whisky?"

Ellie sighed. "Whisky, please. Neat."

"Coming right up. Stephen, Margie, anything?"

"Water, please," Stephen replied.

Margie nodded. "The same, thanks."

As Ridge left the deck and went inside, Ellie turned to the other two. "I *am* very sorry. It's annoying when people's cellphones go off when you're trying to play."

"I suppose you have to keep it on all the time," Margie said.

"Unfortunately, yes."

Stephen smiled. "Don't worry about it. Margie and I have played in some pretty woolly places in our time, believe me, so a cellphone vibrating is nothing." He looked at his wife. "Remember that night at the King Eddie, the summer we were married?"

"Oh, God. Yes."

"We were with a Celtic band back then," Stephen said to Ellie, "and one Friday night we were playing at the King Edward Hotel in Kingston, down near the waterfront. It was wall-to-wall military students, and in the middle of a set they started a fight. Tables overturned, bottles flying, it was a regular donneybrook. We just kept playing while they tore up the place."

"So we're used to distractions," Margie said. "Don't give it a second thought."

"That's kind of you." Ellie glanced back toward the door through which Ridge had disappeared. *I hope he brings the bottle out with him*, she thought. Her one-drink limit was going to go out the window tonight, for sure.

chapter FOURTEEN

It was well after nine o'clock in the evening when Kevin finally got home. The house was quiet; the kids were asleep, and Janie had gone to bed. In stocking feet he crept into the kitchen and opened the fridge. Front and centre was a large bowl covered with tin foil. A piece of paper was taped to the foil, and written on the paper in red crayon was "Kevin." He'd half-expected it to say "Eat this and shut up," so it was a relief instead to see just his name, carefully printed by Caitlyn.

He took the bowl over to the counter and peeled off the foil. It was macaroni and cheese with sliced-up hot dogs, Caitlyn's favourite. He was pleased she'd saved some for him. He put it into the microwave to warm up, hoping the noise wouldn't disturb Janie. Then he grabbed a can of beer from the fridge and went into the living room. He sat down in his battered La-Z-Boy recliner, turned on the television, and muted the volume. He flipped around the channels, passing a news broadcast showing footage of Spencer Farm shot earlier in the day, and settled on a baseball game.

Something felt lumpy and hard against the small of his back. Leaning forward, he pulled out one of Brendan's socks. He draped it over the arm of the recliner, smiling. He was very fond of Janie's children, and they seemed to have taken to him. Brendan had been only six months old when Kevin and Janie began living together, and in essence he'd been the only father the boy had known. Plus, he and Caitlyn got along famously. Perhaps when he and Janie got married—

He stopped himself right there. He'd been waiting for a good time to propose, but she'd been in such a horrible state of mind the last while that he'd kept his mouth shut. He'd tried a couple of times to ask what was bothering her, but she'd shut him down. He knew from experience to bide his time with her and ride it out.

Sighing, he turned his attention to the bowl in his hand. He'd forgotten to put salt and pepper on the mac and cheese, but he was too tired to go back into the kitchen to get them.

The bowl was half empty when he heard Janie's footsteps behind him in the kitchen. She got a glass from the cupboard, poured herself something from the fridge, and scuffed into the living room to look at him.

"You're home."

"Hi, babe. Sorry I woke you." She looked small and tired. A larger version of Caitlyn after a long and exhausting day. Her shoulder-length black hair was tousled, and her eyes were red-rimmed.

"I was awake," she said to the television.

"Are you feeling okay?"

She looked at the milk in her glass and drank a mouthful. "Mmm hmm."

"Sorry I got back late. We had to interview some guy, then Bishop dicked off and I had to—"

"It's all right." She sat down on the arm of the couch across from him. "How was it?"

Rough, he wanted to say. Patterson reamed me out, Carty gave me the high hat all day, and Bishop was his usual charming self. Not to mention being handed a bunch of stale cases that anyone could see were unrelated to the main event. It was only his second murder investigation, and after having been the primary on the first one, he felt as though he were watching from the sidelines this time around.

"Okay," he said instead.

"They said on the news the guy was burned up."

"After he was killed."

"Gross." She finished her milk and stared at the glass.

"You look tired, babe. You should go back to bed."

When she didn't reply, he continued to eat.

After a few moments she stood up. "Don't stay up too late," she said, putting a hand on his shoulder as she scuffed back into the kitchen.

"I won't." He finished the mac and cheese and washed it down with beer.

At least she didn't seem to be mad at him any more.

chapter FIFTEEN

Located in the southwest suburban neighbourhood of Barrhaven, RCMP national headquarters on Leikin Drive in Ottawa was a seven-building complex sitting on fifty-four acres. Officially referred to as the M.J. Nadon Government of Canada Building, it was named after the sixteenth commissioner of the RCMP. Ellie had visited their previous headquarters facility on the Vanier Parkway several times during her career, and from what she could see as she slowed to turn into the front entrance, this new location was a serious upgrade from the old one.

She pulled up to the security booth, lowered her window, and handed the wallet containing her OPP identification and badge to the commissionaire. “I have a meeting with Assistant Commissioner Merrick at ten.”

The commissionaire looked from the identification to Ellie and back again, wrote something down, and handed the wallet back to her. Leaning out of the booth, he pointed over the roof of her car. “Park in the visitors’ lot on the right, Detective Inspector March. Someone will meet you there.”

Ellie waited for the barrier to lift, then drove forward. She turned right, found the visitors’ parking lot and, after a bit of searching, pulled into an empty space. As she shut off the engine and reached for her handbag on the seat next to her, she saw movement in her rear-view mirror and turned around. A large black vehicle had stopped behind her, blocking her exit.

Frowning, handbag in hand, she got out and locked the Crown Vic. The other driver slid out of his vehicle and approached her.

"Detective Inspector March?"

"Yes."

"Excuse me, could I see your identification, please?"

A little annoyed, Ellie fished out the wallet and held it up. The man took it from her hand, gave it the same careful inspection it had received from the commissionaire in the booth, then passed it back.

"Thank you, ma'am. I'm Sergeant Dominic Lambert." He tugged at a lanyard hanging around his neck to pull out his RCMP identification card. "If you wouldn't mind coming with me, I'll take you to your meeting with Assistant Commissioner Merrick."

"I don't understand. He asked me to meet him here."

Lambert nodded. "He's been on the Hill all morning and sent me to bring you there. If you wouldn't mind?" He walked around the rear of his vehicle, a Lincoln Town Car, and opened the back door on the passenger side.

Ellie followed, puzzled. Lambert wore a black business suit with a crisp white shirt and red tie, and he had a calm athleticism Ellie had seen before with law enforcement professionals who had a military background. His blond hair was cut short, and the grey eyes that met hers as she got into the Town Car were cool and appraising.

Lambert slid behind the wheel and drove out onto the street. He kept both hands on the wheel at ten o'clock and two o'clock, and he checked his mirrors every ten seconds. He wore a simple gold wedding band on the ring finger of his left hand and a large watch on his right wrist.

"Do you work with the assistant commissioner?"

"Yes, ma'am."

"With the National Division?"

"The assistant commissioner will be able to answer all your questions, ma'am."

"What's he doing on Parliament Hill?"

"I should probably concentrate on my driving, ma'am."

Ellie gave up and sat back, looking out the window. It wasn't every day she was told to fuck off so politely. If Merrick was on Parliament Hill as opposed to out here at NHQ it probably meant he'd been participating in briefings with senior personnel, likely the RCMP commissioner and perhaps the minister of public safety. Presumably he had something of substance to tell them, and hopefully he'd share it with her so she could get on with her own damned investigation.

After a few blocks she checked her watch and saw that it was now two minutes before ten o'clock. She'd arrived at Leikin Drive almost fifteen minutes early, and now it was apparent she'd be late for their meeting. Some of the Mounties she'd previously dealt with were sticklers for punctuality, but in this instance the schedule was in Merrick's hands rather than hers. That was fine, but she wouldn't allow him to shorten the length of their meeting and brush her off simply because he'd been called away to something else on Parliament Hill.

She took out her cellphone and speed-dialled Patterson. The Lane post-mortem was supposed to begin now, and she wanted to make sure there'd been no complications.

"Scott, it's Ellie. How's it going?"

Patterson laughed without humour. "Started at nine, so we got here an hour late."

"Christ. Any preliminary findings?"

"They did x-rays and the MRI first thing this morning. Dave's looking at the pictures now. Guy's elbows were both shattered pretty bad. I don't know if he would've been able to hold a paintbrush steady after that if he'd lived. The kneecap was a total write-off, and the skull was shattered like an eggshell. Pretty vicious stuff, Ellie."

"Keep me posted." She ended the call and put away her phone, thinking about what Patterson had said. Lane had obviously been tortured by someone with a mean streak who'd swung his weapon with a great deal of fervour. Nothing tentative at all, from the sounds of it. Either a professional, or someone with a passionate hatred of Darius Lane.

They were northbound on Merivale Road, heading for the Queensway. Traffic was running smoothly, but it would still be a while before they reached the Hill. Fingering the handle of her handbag, she was glad she'd decided to dress more formally this morning. She wore a black suit jacket and skirt set she'd bought after receiving her promotion in the spring, along with a white blouse and black pumps with two-inch stacked heels. The clerk in Nordstrom who'd rung up the suit had complimented her on the choice, explaining that many women were unaware of the difference between business professional and business casual attire. Pants, she said while running Ellie's credit card, were not normally considered business attire in the strictest sense. Perfectly acceptable as business casual, of course.

Ellie was instantly thankful she'd bought her new pantsuit at a different store without having to endure the fashion seminar.

Did she really think a collection of law enforcement males would know the difference between business professional and business casual, much less care? Hardly. If they looked at her legs, which were fine but not exactly attractive, they'd damn well see business professional legs or to hell with them.

She didn't really give a lot of thought to her appearance, when it came down to it. She wore no makeup other than a moisturizing lipstick, because her lips tended to chap. Her high cheekbones were littered with freckles that came out in summer sunlight. Her shoulder-length brown hair had a mind of its own. She normally didn't pay much attention to how she looked, but this morning's choice of the skirt suit and new shoes had been deliberate. Look professional, feel professional, act professionally.

The world according to Nordstrom.

They stopped at a traffic light just before the on-ramp to the Queensway. Lambert glanced over his shoulder. "Ma'am, are you carrying your service weapon this morning?"

"Yes."

"Do you carry a backup, ma'am?"

"Not today."

He held out his hand. "If you don't mind, ma'am, I need to secure your weapon before we arrive."

"Secure it?"

"I'll lock it in the centre console, right here." He pointed. "I'll be waiting in the vehicle for the duration of your meeting, so it'll stay safe. I'll return it to you when I take you back to Leikin Drive. Ma'am? Please?"

Sighing, Ellie reached under her jacket and unclipped her holster.

Down the rabbit hole we go, my dear, she thought.

chapter SIXTEEN

The Town Car eased up to the curb and stopped at the side entrance of a large, brown sandstone building at the corner of Wellington and Metcalfe Streets. Lambert got out and circled the car to open Ellie's door for her. As she got out, another athletic-looking male in a dark suit and red tie, an RCMP identification lanyard around his neck as well, emerged from the doorway and gestured her forward. Ellie looked across Wellington Street at the imposing sight of the Parliament buildings before following him through the heavy wooden double doors.

She showed her identification and badge to the commissionaires at the security desk, signed in, and was escorted by the nameless officer up to the fourth floor. He took her into a large conference room with a high ceiling, tall windows, and an enormous oval conference table.

"Please have a seat," he said, pulling out a chair at the table for her. "The assistant commissioner will be right in." As Ellie sat down, he walked over to a side table. "Would you like something? Tea, coffee, juice, or water?"

"Coffee, please. Black, one sugar." Ellie looked around. "Excuse my ignorance. Which building is this?"

"Langevin Block, ma'am. Here's your coffee." He set a cup and saucer down in front of her. "Help yourself to anything else you'd like."

She watched him leave, closing the door silently behind him. She opened her handbag and removed her notebook and pen. She wrote down the date and time. The door opened and two men came in. One was short, young-looking despite his dishevelled salt-and-pepper hair, and clean-shaven. He wore a black suit, blue dress shirt, and no tie. The other man was older and heavier. He wore an Ottawa Police Service uniform with a medal pinned to the left breast below his badge, and he carried his hat tucked under his arm. Ellie put down her pen and stood up.

"Thanks for coming," said the younger man in the black suit. "Glad to finally meet you in person. I'm Danny Merrick."

Ellie shook Merrick's hand. He was Ellie's height and small-boned, but his grip was firm. There was something familiar about his looks that Ellie couldn't quite place at first. She took in his uncombed grey hair, his high cheekbones, small brown eyes and friendly smile, and realized he bore a resemblance to Richard Gere, the American actor.

"This is Deputy Chief Ross Carrière of the OPS," Merrick went on. "Chief, Detective Inspector Ellie March, OPP." Short and round-headed, Carrière shook her hand with a grim nod.

"Ross is in charge of operational support," Merrick said. "He's been assisting our investigation off the Hill. Ellie is the OPP case manager, Ross, as I mentioned, and she'll be coming to you for whatever she needs."

Carrière handed Ellie a business card. "Call the bottom number. At any hour."

"Thank you."

Merrick walked him to the door and showed him out.

"He has to brief his chief in ten minutes," Merrick explained, coming back to the table. He sat down and leaned back. "Sorry about the change of venue, but it couldn't be helped." He looked around at the portrait of Queen Elizabeth II on one wall and the large map of Canada on another. "First time here?"

"Yes. What can you tell me about my investigation?"

Merrick nodded. "I think first I should take a few minutes to explain in more detail what we're doing, and why. Is that all right with you, Ellie?"

"Fine."

"As you may know, our Protective Policing Service extends protection to the governor general, the prime minister," he ticked them off on his fingers, "Supreme Court and Federal Court judges, cabinet ministers, and foreign dignitaries while they're in Canada. We also secure Parliament Hill, Rideau Hall, and the Supreme Court." He raised an eyebrow. "The average taxpayer may also assume we protect members of Parliament and senators, but the truth is, only while they're on Parliament Hill or one of the other designated sites. Otherwise, they come and go the same as you and I."

"Is that what you're in charge of?" Ellie asked. "The Protective Policing Service?"

"Actually, no." Merrick shifted in his seat. "I used to be, though. In fact, when I first transferred to National HQ as a commissioned officer I was assigned to Jean Chrétien's protection detail." He smiled. "Interesting times, believe me. After he left, I was appointed officer in charge of the Executive Protection Service and then was AC for two years. Now they've got me in charge of something known as Special Projects."

Ellie frowned.

"I know," he said. "That's usually where the old and useless go to die. In this case, let's just say that I'm the head janitor. My people clean the toilets and mop up the messes." He sat forward suddenly. "Never mind that. Let me go over what we've been doing since we were read in."

"Please do," Ellie said, beginning to take notes. He glanced at her notebook but said nothing. Apparently she hadn't violated security protocol with her intention to write stuff down.

"We're coming at this from every possible angle," he said. "To begin with, we have a team interviewing other members of the Social Affairs, Science, and Technology Committee that Senator Lane participated in. There are fourteen of them, including the chair and deputy chair. Plus, the speaker and the clerk of the Senate, and the Liberal house leader. We've interviewed each of them twice, so far. We're asking them about Lane, and we're asking them about themselves. If Lane was compromised, were others as well? This line of investigation is ongoing and sensitive, as you can imagine."

"What sort of committee work was he doing that could have led to a security breach?"

Merrick grimaced. "I can't be specific. But," he held up a hand as Ellie opened her mouth again, "I can say this much. As you can tell from the name, the committee's mandate covers a whole range of subjects from aboriginal affairs and cultural issues to housing, employment, and health and welfare. Senator Lane's first contribution was to co-author a report on social inclusion in Canada, which was completely innocuous as far as we're concerned. He was currently sitting on a committee studying this country's readiness to respond to a biological crisis. A virus attack, to be specific." He stopped talking and stared at her.

"Oh. I see."

He sat back again. "I've also got a team looking for a money trail. We're going over all the bank information and co-ordinating with FINTRAC to see if there were payments from known sources of terrorist financing that ended up in his accounts." He was referring to Canada's financial intelligence unit, the Financial Transactions and Reports Analysis Centre, which, among other things, received reports of suspicious transactions from banks and other financial institutions.

"Another team's co-ordinating with CSIS and CBSA," he went on, referring to the Canadian Security Intelligence Service and the Canada Border Services Agency, "to come at this from the opposite direction. They're looking for known individuals who may have either entered the country or been resident here and made contact with the senator before his death. Another team's canvassing Colonel By Drive where Lane's condo was located, plus restaurants, convenience stores, and everywhere else they can think of between his home and the Hill. He was a walker, he went everywhere on foot, and the number of places he could have met one of these contacts is almost infinite. As you can imagine," he smiled faintly, "no one's slept since the call came in, and we don't expect to sleep for the next twenty-four hours at least."

"What else?"

At that moment the door opened. A man looked in at Merrick and said, "He's here."

Merrick stood up. "All right."

The man stepped into the room, and when Ellie saw who was following him, she finally understood the full nature of the challenge faced not only by Danny Merrick but by her, as well.

chapter SEVENTEEN

"You must be Detective Inspector March," he said, shaking her hand. "I'm sorry to interrupt, but I really wanted to meet you."

"I'm honoured, sir," Ellie said, at a loss for words. For a moment, all she could think of was that he was a lot taller in person than he looked on television.

"Please, let's sit down for a minute." The prime minister grabbed a chair and sat down between Ellie and Merrick. "Danny just finished briefing me, and I know you have a lot to do and not enough time to do it in, so I won't take long. Kathleen spoke highly of you, so I feel confident you're going to find whoever did this horrible thing to Darius."

"Thank you, sir," Ellie said, sitting down. She was surprised that the premier of Ontario would know about her, then realized Commissioner Moodie would have included the case manager's background when briefing her on the case.

"Not to be an armchair detective, Ellie—is it all right if I call you Ellie?"

She nodded.

"Not to be an armchair detective, and while I understand the urgency in checking for a national security breach, I personally don't see how Darius could've been murdered as part of some kind of terrorist activity." He shrugged, a gesture reminiscent of his father. "But you know the times we live in, and how necessary it is to be vigilant."

"Yes, sir."

"Having said that, I expect it's going to be you and your team that will find Darius's killer and bring him to justice, rather than Danny."

Ellie nodded again.

The prime minister leaned back, crossed his legs, and clasped his knee with both hands. He wore a navy pinstripe suit, a pale blue dress shirt, and no tie. His black hair was tousled, as though he'd been absent-mindedly running his hand through it. He looked so young, Ellie thought. She could see both his father and his mother in his calm, open features.

"Darius was one of my first appointments after the election," he said. "There were several Senate vacancies, and I thought, well, we've got former NHL hockey players in there, why not a Canadian painter?"

Ellie glanced at the door, where the RCMP Protective Service officer stood, hands clasped in front of him, eyes riveted on her.

"Actually," the prime minister continued, "Darius was one of my favourites, going back to when I was a kid. Have you seen *The Fire in a Boy's Heart*?"

"No," Ellie admitted. "Not yet."

"You must. It's hanging in Rideau Cottage now, but when my father bought it, he put it in a bedroom at Harrington Lake. The bedroom I stayed in when I was there. I was ten or eleven at the time, but that picture meant a lot to me. It showed a young boy standing in a sunburned field," he moved his hand around, as though tracing the painting in the air, "with an autumn tree line in the distance painted to look as though the horizon were on fire. A projection of the boy's inner passion." He smiled faintly, dropping his hand to his lap. "You can tell I majored in literature. Anyway, the more I looked at that painting as a kid, the more I thought I was that boy. The determination in his face. I think of it often." He shrugged again. "Having said that, a painting wasn't the reason I decided that Darius should be appointed to the Senate."

Ellie said nothing. Unable to sleep last night, she'd run a Google search on Darius Lane and had read a number of archived news articles about his social activism. She was interested to see what the prime minister would mention.

"He became very outspoken on social issues over the past decade and a half," he said. "Because of his own experiences, he advocated for adequate housing for the homeless and better funding for food banks and missions, all the things he'd seen first hand. Letters to the editor, then guest editorials in the *Globe and Mail*, appearances before city council here and in Toronto, speeches at fundraisers and special events. He practically talked himself into a seat. I just made it official. And it was a no-brainer he'd go right on the committee."

"Did his social views make him enemies?" Ellie asked.

"His political opponents on the right can be just as passionate and just as loud as Darius, but no. Not the kind of enemies you're thinking of."

"Are you aware of any specific threats he may have received?"

"No, Ellie. I'm not." He glanced at Merrick. "She's very good at what she does, isn't she?"

"Yes, sir," Merrick said, looking at Ellie with amusement. "Interrogation is her specialty, as I understand it."

Ellie blushed. "Sorry, sir."

"Don't be." The prime minister stood up and held out his hand. "I'm glad we talked. I feel a little better about things, having met you."

"Thank you, sir." Ellie stood up and shook his hand.

"You know, my office is right below this room, two floors down. Another time, maybe you can drop in and see it. I don't spend a lot of time there, but we could make arrangements and I could show you around."

"I'd like that, sir."

"Danny." He turned and shook Merrick's hand. "I'll expect you at four o'clock?"

"Yes, sir."

Ellie watched the prime minister leave the room. As the door closed behind the Protective Service officer, she looked at Merrick.

He smiled. "No pressure, Ellie."

chapter EIGHTEEN

A new day meant a new Bishop, who hummed to himself as he drove, tapping a light rhythm on the steering wheel as they left behind the hobby farm belonging to arson victim number four, Dr. Gordon Roberts.

"That didn't get us very far," Kevin said, looking out the window of the black motor pool Crown Vic as Bishop ran a stop sign and turned left onto County Road 5.

Dr. Roberts had proven to be elderly, soft-spoken, and completely baffled by the fire that had burned down his brand-new horse barn, destroying his collection of antique buggies along with it. He knew of no one who bore him any malice and could think of nothing he'd done to attract the attention of someone who liked burning things down for kicks.

"Yeah, the old dude's pretty fuzzy." Bishop chuckled, eyes on the road.

Kevin took out his sunglasses and slipped them on. The road was damp and covered with puddles from last night's hard rain that had broken the humidity with cooler air. "What's so funny?"

"Just thinking of you moonlighting as a clown at kids' parties."

"Yeah. Ha-ha."

"You really think you can learn shit about the offender mind-set or whatever the fuck by teaching yourself sleight of hand?"

Kevin shrugged. "We'll see."

Bishop glanced over. "C'mon, Kev. That's a reach, even for you."

Kevin stared at the trees hugging the road on his side.

"You know you're dying to tell me all about it," Bishop prodded.

"Yeah, and you're just dying to listen to me go on and on."

"Why not? Nothing better to do in the next fifteen minutes." It would take them about that long to reach the Wierdsma farm on Visser Road, the scene of the third barn fire.

Kevin sighed. "Okay, you asked for it. It has to do with how to take advantage of the way people habitually think to perform what they call cognitive illusions."

"Cognitive illusions. Christ, Kev."

"I read an article online a few months ago about Teller, the famous magician. He was a participant in a study researching the neuroscience of magic."

"Yeah, so?"

"It's when you create an illusion by diverting attention and fooling a person's normal reasoning processes."

"Misdirection," Bishop said. "I get it, Kev."

Kevin nodded. "It's actually very interesting. There are two kinds of cognitive illusions, overt and covert. Overt illusions are when you direct someone's gaze away from what you're doing, like telling your beautiful assistant wearing almost nothing to go fetch you something from the prop table."

"Mmm hmm."

"Covert," Kevin pressed on, "is a lot more difficult to pull off. It relies on what psychologists call change blindness."

"Change blindness. I've heard of that before."

Yeah. It's what happens when something has changed right in front of you, and you didn't notice. I start by holding up the seven of spades, divert your attention for an instant, switch cards to the seven of hearts, and you don't notice the difference because you didn't see the switch and your mind takes it for granted that it's still the same card while I go on with other stuff."

"Weird, but let's say it's possible."

"Or you drive by the same black Chevy van parked in a driveway on the way to work every day, and it takes you a week to notice it's now a dark blue Ford van with a different licence plate."

"That wouldn't happen, pal. Not with a vehicle."

Kevin shrugged. "Not everyone's as sharp as you are, JB. There's something called the Vanishing Ball trick, a very basic beginner move that you've seen before. The magician tosses a ball up into the air and catches it over and over, then makes it disappear in mid-air."

"Sure, I've seen that one before."

"He follows the ball up in the air with his eyes and head, over and over, while running through his stand-up comedy routine, and the audience can't help following the ball with their eyes, up and down, up and down. Suddenly it disappears half-way up, or it seems to. In fact, he just doesn't throw it that time, he keeps it in his hand and makes the throwing motion and pretends to watch it with his eyes again. The audience is so used to seeing the ball go up, they're sure it did this time, too. This is an example of a cognitive illusion that takes advantage of our brain's tendency to detect a pattern and then race ahead to predict the same outcome once too often. We could swear we saw the ball go up again, even though it didn't."

"And you figure this is going to make you smarter how, again, exactly?"

Kevin sighed. "I don't know, JB. I'm still thinking it through. But I have to say, something was off with the Pool kid, yesterday. Something I didn't pick up on."

"He's a punk, but I didn't see jack shit to give us probable cause on the truck or the dump he's livin' in."

"Yeah, I know." Kevin frowned. "We were so damned busy making sure the dog wasn't coming off its chain, and checking out the medical weed, and feeling sorry for his father that our attention was moving in six different directions at once."

Bishop thought about it for a moment. "Could be."

"I didn't get the same feeling when we were talking to Lennon."

"He's a son of a bitch, but I have to agree with you on that one." Bishop swung out to pass a tractor pulling an empty hay wagon. "We'll see if Wierdsma recognizes one of them from the pics. Hopefully he's got more of a clue than Roberts. Christ, that guy. Hopefully he was a little more focused when he was holding a scalpel in his hand than he is now."

Last evening before going home, Bishop had prepared a photo array to show around during their interviews. The array contained photographs of twelve men. Ten were fillers, non-suspects, while an eleventh was a photograph of Patrick Lennon and the twelfth was a photograph of Jeremy Pool. All twelve photos were taken from drivers' licences so that they all had the same look and feel.

After printing off the photographs, he put them in separate brown envelopes. A witness would be handed each envelope in no particular order. While they examined each picture, Kevin used his cellphone to record the process. Normally the photo array procedure was conducted at the detachment office so that it could be videotaped, but when it was done in the field like this, Kevin activated the video mode on his cellphone to record it.

The hope was that one of the arson victims could identify either Lennon or Pool from the array and give them some kind of connection between victim and suspect that would move their investigation in a promising direction.

Roberts, unfortunately, had drawn a blank on all the

photos.

Visser Road was a narrow lane off County Road 5 that was lined with old cedar rail fences and scrub brush. They passed two homes before reaching a small cinder block building with a sign over the door that said, "Wierdsma Cheese Factory and Store." The neon "Open" sign in the window was illuminated. They rolled past the building and turned into a long driveway that led to the farm. Kevin looked at tall silos, large barns, black-and-white Holstein cattle grazing in a pasture, and a well-kept brick farm house with a detached two-car garage, sheds, and other outbuildings. Unlike the Lennons, whose farm seemed to be functioning at a level not far above subsistence, Wierdsma was obviously running a successful large-scale operation.

When they knocked on the kitchen door, Mrs. Wierdsma told them her husband was in the barn. Using an intercom system, she called him in.

Peter Wierdsma was short and stout, in his early sixties, and his handshake was crushing. When Kevin apologized for interrupting his work, he made a face.

"Don't think of it," he said, his voice carrying a light Dutch accent. "I have a cow that wants to calve, but she can't make up her mind exactly when she wants to do it. Anyway, my son is there. How can I help you?"

"We're following up on the barn fire," Kevin said. "We have a few questions."

"That's fine. I hope you didn't want to see what was left, because I tore it all down and hauled away the mess to the dump as soon as they said it was okay. But I can show you where it was."

They followed him through the dooryard and across the lawn, skirting a white board fence at the front of a small corral. Inside the corral was an old, cross-looking pony that eyed Bishop as though measuring him for a kick. Wierdsma stopped at the far corner of the fence and leaned on the top board.

"Out there," he said, pointing at the field beyond. He glanced at the pony and added, "It was the barn we kept him in. I'll build something new in the fall. He belongs to my daughter, so even though he's very mean and likes to bite, she loves him and I have to take good care of him."

Kevin walked around the corner and leaned back against the fence. It was nothing more than an empty field, maybe an acre in size, enclosed by a page wire fence. Between the corral and the field was a drainage culvert, about three metres deep and lined with large stones, with a steady flow of water running at the bottom. There was no sign of the former barn. A slight breeze moved against his cheek. The air was much more pleasant than it had been yesterday.

Bishop took a set of envelopes out of his jacket pocket. "Would you mind looking at some pictures for us?"

"Sure, be glad to."

"The person who burned down your barn may not be in here, Mr. Wierdsma. You may not recognize anyone, so don't feel like you have to."

"Sure sure, that's okay."

"After you look at a picture, turn it over and check off either Yes or No as to whether you know the person or not." Bishop handed him a pen. "Put the date, which is the sixteenth today, and write the number of the picture. There are twelve, so the first one is one, then two, and so on as you look at them. Then initial in the space and put it back into the envelope. Sound okay?"

"Yah," Wierdsma drawled, "not too too complicated."

As Wierdsma took the first envelope, Kevin began recording the process with his cellphone. Bishop kept his eyes averted as the photograph came out of the envelope, so he wouldn't know which picture Wierdsma was looking at. Wierdsma worked his way methodically through the twelve photos and shook his head. "No. I don't know any of them."

"Never saw any of them before, in town or something?"

"No. Not that I know of."

"Okay, no problem." Bishop stuck the envelopes and pen back into his jacket pocket.

Kevin put away his cellphone and leaned on the fence. "You have dogs, Mr. Wierdsma. I heard them barking when we came in the yard."

"Yah. Two collies. They live in the house with us. They were barking that night, for sure."

"So tell us what happened. Walk us through it."

Wierdsma shrugged. "What's there to say? I was working on the account books in my office, which is next to the kitchen. My son was away visiting with friends, my daughter was on the computer in her bedroom, and my wife was listening to the radio in her room upstairs, one of her religious programs. Her father was a minister in the Dutch Reformed church, you know, and she had a strict Calvinist upbringing." He smiled faintly. "I myself came from a secular family, so I had to learn how to be religious before she would marry me. A long time ago, now." He tilted his head. "It wasn't so hard. You do what your heart tells you to do."

"So she was upstairs," Kevin prompted, "and you were downstairs in your office?"

Wierdsma nodded. "The dogs started barking at the back door, and they wouldn't stop, so I went out to see. They were going crazy, so I took them outside with me. They both ran right over here, up to the edge of the culvert, and barked at the field. When I caught up to them, I saw the barn was on fire. I went back and got in my truck and drove over."

Bishop frowned. "Out on the road?"

"No, no. If you go behind the corral and the shed, back there, I have a bridge goes over the culvert." Wierdsma gestured with his arm. “I drove that way.” He ran a hand over his balding head. “As I crossed the bridge, I looked at the road. I saw red lights, tail lights, going away from here very fast, driving toward the highway.”

“That’s all you saw?”

Wierdsma sighed. “Yah. Too bad, huh? Maybe I could have seen the guy running to his truck if I’d been earlier. Seen him with my headlights. But I was too late for that.”

“You told Detective Constable Carty at the time that the pony was in the barn.”

“Yah, that’s right. He likes to break the fence posts at the back of his field and get into the pasture for the cows, so he gets put in the barn at night to make sure he doesn’t disappear. This guy must have let him out before he set fire to the barn. Myself, I would have to think twice. Just joking. Of course. Anyway, he obviously didn’t want the pony to burn, so he let him out first.”

Back in the dooryard, Kevin handed him a business card. “If you think of anything else, please give me a call, Mr. Wierdsma.”

“I will.”

They turned around as the kitchen door opened and a slim blond woman walked out. One of the garage doors began to rise, revealing a small red Sunfire parked inside.

“My daughter, Lizbeth,” Wierdsma said. “Going to work.”

In her twenties, she wore black polyester pants, a blue golf shirt and a Walmart vest with a name pin that said “Liz.” She embraced her father. “What are you doing, Papa? Goofing off again?”

“These men are detectives with the police. They were asking about the barn fire.”

“Detective Constable Walker,” Kevin said. “This is Detective Constable Bishop. Did you see or hear anything unusual that evening before the fire, Liz?” He remembered only a very brief interview report in Carty’s file, to the effect that she'd been in her room with her headphones on, and had seen or heard nothing at all, not even the dogs barking.

She shook her head, folding her arms, standing close to her father. "I can't believe someone would do something that mean."

"You don't know anyone who might want to cause your family problems?" Kevin asked.

"No. Mama and Papa are the nicest people you'd ever want to meet. Who'd want to do something like this to hurt them?"

Glancing at Bishop, Kevin asked, "Liz, would you mind looking at some photographs?"

"Sure, if it would help."

Kevin took her aside as Bishop went to the Crown Vic for another set of envelopes. They followed the same routine as with her father. She looked at the first nine photographs and handed each one back with a shake of her head and a clear "No."

When she looked at the tenth, she paused, frowned, and turned it over. About to fill out the information on the back, she shook her head and turned it over again.

"This one," she said. "I know this guy."

"All right," Bishop said. "Fill out the back, show it to the camera, and give it to me. I'll get you to look at the other two, as well."

Liz held up the photograph so that Kevin could record it with his cellphone, then returned it to the envelope and gave it to Bishop.

She then looked at the last two, but didn't recognize either person.

"So, number ten." Bishop said. "Tell us what you know about the guy."

Kevin lowered his cellphone to belt level but kept it running. The photograph she'd reacted positively to had been taken from the driver's licence of Jeremy Pool.

chapter NINETEEN

"I saw him several times at work," Liz said, folding her arms and squinting against the sunlight. "He kept coming through the checkout with only one item. Know what I mean? You're expected to make eye contact and try a little small talk with customers, but for him I made an exception. He gave me the creeps."

"In what way?" Kevin asked.

Her face coloured. "You know. Plus, he acted very immature. He reminded me of a couple of freshmen I knew when I was a senior at college."

"Where did you go?" Kevin asked.

"Calvin College. In Grand Rapids, Michigan. My mother went there, and my two older sisters."

Kevin glanced over at Wierdsma, who was watching his daughter with a mixture of pride and concern. He was getting the sense that they were a close-knit family.

"So this guy," Bishop said, "what did he say to you?"

"Oh, I don't know." She strolled back toward her father. "The first time I noticed him, you know, when I realized I'd seen him in the store before, he said something about the blouse I was wearing, that it matched my eyes. Because it was blue, I guess." She rolled the eyes in question at Wierdsma. "All that time and money to get a math degree and go to teachers' college, and I have to stand at a cash register and make small talk with people like this."

"Patience, *mijn engeltje,*" Wierdsma said.

"When was the last time you saw him?" Kevin asked.

"About a month ago. I was greeting at the front door, handing out shopping carts. He came from the checkouts and said, 'oh, there you are' or something like that. I'd just come back from break and didn't see him, I guess, when he came in." She frowned. "He wouldn't leave, kept standing around making all these silly little comments, then asked me what I was doing after work."

"What'd you say?" Bishop asked.

"I told him to please leave the store or I was going to call the manager."

"How'd he take that?"

"He grabbed my arm. He said, 'come on, let's have some fun. I've got weed.' Words to that effect."

"Then what?"

"I said, 'leave me alone or I'm calling the police,' and he left."

"I remember this," Wierdsma said, his voice rising. "You came home and told Mama about it right away. You were very upset."

"When did this happen exactly, do you know?" Kevin asked.

As Liz was shrugging Wierdsma held up his finger. "Wait, you know what? That was the same day as the fire. That afternoon!"

"Are you sure?" Kevin asked.

"Yah yah, of course I am. It's because I'm thinking about this as I'm catching the pony and taking him around to the barn. I'm thinking about this stupid pony and how Lizzy still loves this horrible beast even though she's grown up, and then I think of this thing earlier in the day and how much it upset her. Her mother teaches her not to date Canadian boys—"

"Papa!"

"—what, it's not true? Then this thing happens,

someone burns our barn, and it's like the whole world's upside down. *That's* how I remember when it happened."

"And you haven't seen him since, Liz?"

She shook her head.

"Have either of you seen an older model Ford Ranger truck, light blue with a white aluminum cap, either on your road or elsewhere nearby?"

"Not that I've noticed," Wierdsma said. "We get cars coming to the store all the time." He looked in the direction of their cheese factory at the edge of the road. "Who pays attention to them?"

"What about you, Liz?"

"No. Sorry."

Kevin gave her a business card. "If you see this person again, or the truck I described, please call."

"You think he's the one who burned down our barn?" she asked. "Because I wouldn't talk to him?"

"It's possible." Kevin thought of something. "Liz, do you know Brenda Mason? She's younger than you, eighteen. Lives on Forfar Road."

"No. Never heard of her. Is she connected to this guy somehow?"

"I thought you might be friends with her."

"No, I never heard of her."

"Okay. Thanks for your time, both of you." Kevin shook Wierdsma's hand and nodded at Liz. "We'll be in touch."

Back in the Buick, Bishop started the engine and grinned at Kevin. "We just pulled a rabbit out of our hat, didn't we, Mister Magic Boy?"

"Could be." Kevin buckled his seat belt. "But we still don't have anything solid putting him here or at any of the other scenes. Especially Spencer Farm."

"Yeah, well, forget that one and accept the fact we're cleaning up Carty's back files while he's out working our homicide for us." Bishop turned around in the dooryard and drove out onto the narrow road, rolling slowly past the cheese factory and store.

Looking across Bishop, Kevin saw a blond woman watching them through the window of the store. She looked like an older version of Liz Wierdsma. A sister, no doubt.

"I can begin to see some connections here, Kev," Bishop said, accelerating away. "Kid's got a hang-up with girls. His peep show with the Mason chick gets busted and he burns the barn down to cover his getaway, then this one tells him to hit the road and he comes back at night for payback, and probably a fuck-you jerk-off to go with it."

"He gets into the road rage altercation with Crane," Kevin said, "and goes back that night for payback, and the same here. Gets angry because he's rejected, and burns their barn down as revenge."

"Those three definitely fit around his neck real good," Bishop agreed. "The only one I don't get is Roberts. What the fuck's he got against antique buggies, for chrissakes?"

"You're right," Kevin said. "That one still doesn't fit."

chapter TWENTY

Ellie had just convened the afternoon team meeting in the detachment conference room when all hell broke loose and Patterson charged out, followed by Sisson, Bishop, Martin, and Merkley. Something was happening along the river west of Brockville and the crime unit was being scrambled along with ERT, FIU, and all available Traffic units. Left in the room with her were Carty, Kevin, and Leung.

Carty made a quick call on his cellphone and hurried out, saying he had to meet someone in town and would be back in an hour.

Ellie got up and poured herself a cup of coffee from the urn on the side table as Kevin slipped out to the front to see what was going on. She added a spoonful of honey, stirred, and looked at Leung.

"Looks like we'll have to reschedule this, Dennis."

Leung nodded, slipping his tablet back into its protective case. "No problem."

Ellie watched him remove his glasses and polish the lenses with a handkerchief. Today he was wearing an olive-coloured suit with a green and grey repp tie, a pale yellow shirt, and a cordovan belt and slip-on shoes. His watch was a vintage Bulova model, and his ring was sterling silver with a green peridot stone. He was, she decided, quite the fashion plate.

"How are you finding it here, Dennis?" she asked. "Getting adjusted?"

He smiled. "I think so. It's very different."

"It's been what, two months?"

"Yes, nine weeks. I like it, though."

Ellie sipped her coffee. Leung came across as someone who never complained no matter what he actually felt. She was aware that his departure from Toronto had not been voluntary, and she was interested to know the specifics. She hadn't had time to ask Patterson about him, so she decided she might as well see what he was willing to tell her about himself.

"You were with AGCO," she said.

"That's right."

"Did you like it?"

His face brightened. "Very much." The Alcohol and Gaming Commission of Ontario was responsible for the regulation of casinos and other gambling activities operated by the OLG, the Ontario Lottery and Gaming Corporation, a provincial government body. The AGCO's Investigations and Enforcement Bureau, which policed the casinos and slot machine facilities, operated under the direction of the OPP. Leung had been one of the resources assigned there.

"Why were you transferred out?"

He blinked at the directness of her question but did not break eye contact. "A conflict of interest arose that I was not aware of until it was brought to my attention by my commander."

"Oh? What kind of conflict of interest?"

He sighed. "A cousin of mine was arrested and charged with running an illegal gambling operation in Chinatown."

"That doesn't sound very good, Dennis."

"No," Leung agreed. "My mother's family is very large and I don't have much to do with most of them. I hadn't seen this particular fellow since I was a boy, but I couldn't deny the familial connection. The investigation was long and very uncomfortable, and I was glad when it was over. They were satisfied I had nothing to do with him or his gambling business, but obviously I had to be re-assigned. It was either here or Rainy River." He shrugged. "I didn't want to go up north."

"You have a family, don't you?"

"Four girls. My wife is a bank manager. She was able to find a job in Brockville, although not at the managerial level. Not yet, anyway."

Kevin came back into the room. "So here's what's happening. Mona's been investigating a series of boat thefts and break-ins at the marinas along the St. Lawrence this summer."

"Right," Ellie remembered, "she works with the marine patrol."

Kevin poured himself a cup of coffee. "Yes. Bishop's been helping her, since he covers property crime. So apparently some guy waltzed into the marina at Butternut Bay this afternoon, hooked up to somebody's twenty-nine-foot yacht, and drove off with it."

"Oh my goodness," Leung said.

Kevin nodded. "Real dumb. The boat owner was in the marina office at the time. He took off after his boat while his wife called it in. The thief towed it out onto the 401 eastbound and ran for it."

"What happened?"

"Apparently he didn't secure the hitch properly. He lost control about a kilometre down the highway and the boat trailer came loose. It flipped and shattered the boat all over both eastbound lanes. A hundred and fifty grand, shredded into junk. He got off at the Highway 2 exit and now he's holed up in someone's house just off Hallecks Road."

"Oh oh."

"Yeah. He has two hostages, an elderly couple. A complete and total screw-up. They're going to be down there for a while."

Ellie drained her coffee and poured another cup. "I think I'll step outside for some air. Want to join me?"

"Sure," Kevin said.

"Mind if I tag along?" Leung asked, standing up. "I need a smoke."

Ellie nodded. She'd intended to talk to Kevin in private, to find out how he was coming along since making the decision to remain with the crime unit, but she didn't want Leung to feel excluded. She led the way to the rear exit of the building and across the back parking lot to a picnic table used by detachment staff for breaks and lunch when the weather was good. There was no one out here right now, so they made themselves comfortable.

Leung offered her a cigarette. She was tempted, but shook her head.

"How did it go in Ottawa?" Kevin asked.

"Strange," she said, then realized from his tone how out of the loop he was feeling. "Did Tom have a chance to fill you in on the autopsy findings?"

Kevin shook his head.

Ellie glanced at Leung, who also shook his head. "It was on the agenda for this meeting," she said. "Cause of death was blunt force trauma to the upper right side of the head."

"So it definitely wasn't from the fire?"

"No." Ellie turned to face Kevin, who was sitting beside her on the bench seat. "According to Dave Martin, there was no soot in the lungs, no searing in the air passages, and the lab will likely find no carbon monoxide in the blood. So he wasn't breathing when he was set on fire. Plus, the victim's skull was fractured, and the fragments were forced inward. Apparently when a body burns in a fire, there's fragmentation of the skull from the heat, but the fragments tend to fall outward, which was not the case in this instance, confirming an ante-mortem blow."

"So the motive for the fire was crime concealment," Kevin said.

"It seems so. Time of death is estimated at about six o'clock Monday morning. The injuries to his elbows were already several hours old." She shook her head. "We're looking at a probable scenario where he was captured and tortured in Ottawa, then transported down to Elgin and tortured some more while taped into the office chair. Eventually he gave up whatever it was his kidnapper wanted to know."

"Before the shot to the head," Kevin said, "which was the killing blow, right?"

Ellie nodded.

Leung lit his cigarette and exhaled away from them. "What about the murder weapon? Any idea?"

"They believe it was a twelve-inch wrecking bar, the kind made from hex bar stock."

"That's pretty specific."

"Yes. They found evidence to suggest the weapon had edges consistent with a hexagonal bar rather than a round one, and the width of the hex surface suggests a twelve-inch length."

"Nasty stuff," Leung said. "I can't imagine the pain." He glanced at Kevin. "I've never attended an autopsy before."

"Consider yourself lucky."

"You have?"

"Once." Kevin looked at Ellie. "Let's just say it wasn't my finest moment."

"They take some getting used to," she said. She drained her coffee cup and set it aside.

Leung glanced at Kevin and then looked away, tapping ash from his cigarette into a coffee can left on the table for the smokers to use.

"What do we know about Lane's bank records? Any indication of payoffs?"

Ellie shook her head. "Zip. No large expenditures

suggesting he was being blackmailed, no payments coming in suggesting he was being bribed in exchange for classified information connected to his Senate duties. No sign of any secret accounts, no suitcases under the bed filled with cash, nothing out of the ordinary."

"Interesting." Leung dropped the remainder of his cigarette into the coffee can.

"The RCMP did a full workup on his timeline Saturday night and Sunday morning," Ellie went on. "Lane spent Saturday night at his condo on Colonel By Drive in Ottawa and was seen Sunday morning on his daily walk along the canal by several witnesses. He likely spent the afternoon working on a painting in his condo, and then went out for dinner at a restaurant in the market called the Twisted Pear. He was with a woman who hasn't yet been identified. He paid his own bill with his debit card, and the woman paid for hers with cash. They left the restaurant together on foot, and that's the last trace of Darius Lane until his body was discovered yesterday morning."

"No ID on the woman?" Kevin asked.

"Not yet."

"And they have no idea where he went after the restaurant, if he spent more time with the woman, and how he got down to Spencer Farm?"

"That's right. And Ident found zero in his condo in terms of fingerprints, DNA, signs of a struggle, et cetera, that could help."

OPP Forensics Identification Services had executed a search warrant on Lane's condominium this morning, and according to Dave Martin it had produced nothing useful.

"What about the vehicle at the farm?" Kevin asked.

"Looks like it was a 2014 Mercedes Benz Sprinter cargo van, going by wheelbase and vehicle length measurements, plus the tire tread marks, which matched two-hundred-dollar Michelins available for Sprinters. When Dave sent the info to the Mounties, they pulled a list of Sprinters in

Canada, ran it against their lists of known or suspected terrorists, and got no hits. They compiled a list of vendors who sold that model of tire, ran that list against their terrorist database, and again came up negative. A check of land border systems for crossings between Canada and the United States for such a vehicle in the past three months also gave them nothing. Meanwhile, Bill Merkley's going to be looking at all the vans on the list in the National Capital Region."

"What about Lane's Senate committee work, Ellie?" Kevin asked.

"According to the government website, the Senate reported on Canada's preparedness to respond to a pandemic outbreak of the flu virus in 2010, but apparently they're now working on an updated report that focuses on deliberate attempts to introduce viruses into the population and the role of the intelligence community in government preparedness."

Kevin's eyebrows went up. "That's why everyone's so worked up."

Leung nodded. "Their potential security breach."

"I think it's a fair assumption." Ellie looked at him. "How much do you know about his personal contacts, Dennis? Friends, associates, neighbours? Any insight into who the woman was that he had lunch with?"

Leung shook his head. "Apparently the circle was small when it came to Senator Lane's social interactions. But tomorrow I'm going to talk to Dr. Charlie Stewart in Perth. He's the art professor who helped get Lane back on his feet in Kingston. I'm hoping to get more in-depth information on friends and enemies, if there were any."

Ellie nodded. She felt a sudden urge to go with him, to get out and get busy on the case, but she said nothing. Instead, she turned to Kevin. "I understand you and Bishop have come up with a good lead on the barn arsons."

"That's right." Kevin described their interview with

Wierdsma and his daughter, and the connection to Jeremy Pool and two of the other fires. "We're just not seeing a link right now with the most recent one, the Roberts horse barn, is the only thing."

"Or to the Lane case, I take it?"

"No," Kevin admitted.

Ellie turned back and put her elbows on the picnic table. Across the parking lot, she watched the back door open. Merkley stuck his head out, saw them sitting at the table, and started toward them. He walked with a slight limp, she noticed, and was about thirty pounds overweight. The breeze flipped his straight brown hair into his eyes. He raked it aside and shoved his hand into the pocket of his jeans.

"I thought you left with the others," Ellie said when he reached the picnic table.

"Bathroom emergency." He shifted his large brown eyes to Kevin. "I've been working the phone, doing some digging of my own into your barn arsons, Kev."

Kevin nodded. "Find something useful?"

Merkley grinned. "You want to believe it. You're going to find this very, very interesting."

chapter TWENTY-ONE

"Thanks again for coming in this evening, Dr. Roberts," Kevin said, setting a cup of coffee down on the corner of the desk in the interview room as Bishop closed the door behind him. The stocky detective stood in the corner, arms folded, and gave the old man his best cop stare as Kevin dropped a file folder onto the desk and sat down. The hostage-taking incident had been resolved several hours ago and Bishop had not been needed. Once Kevin called him with the information Merkley had put together, he'd wasted no time returning to the detachment office.

"Now that you've had a chance to call your lawyer," Kevin was saying, "we're going to ask you a few more questions."

"Edward said I have the right not to answer." Roberts sipped the coffee and winced as it burned his lips.

Kevin looked at his frail body, the well-groomed red hair that had thinned and whitened with age, the liver spots on his scalp, face and hands, the beige cardigan sweater, khaki pants, and topsider shoes that were expensive when new but were now old and well worn. He felt vaguely sorry for the old man.

"Your lawyer's correct, Dr. Roberts, but I think it's in your best interest to take this chance to explain the situation from your side. The barn that burned down, how much did it cost to build?"

"It wasn't cheap, I'll tell you that."

"It had six stalls, correct?"

"Yes, it did."

Kevin flipped open the file and picked up the top sheet of paper. "It's my understanding that a traditional wood barn like yours can cost around fifty dollars a square foot to build new. If a six-stall barn works out to be twenty-four hundred square feet, which I believe yours was, then it would cost at least a hundred and twenty thousand to build. Does that sound like about what you paid?"

Roberts glanced at Bishop. "About that, yes."

"How did you finance it, Dr. Roberts?"

"The same way we all do, son. I went to the bank."

"Which bank gave you the loan?"

"Oh, the usual one."

Kevin frowned. "Isn't it true, sir, that your regular bank turned you down? You had to try two others before you found one willing to give you the money?"

Roberts examined the backs of his hands. "That's confidential information I'd rather not share, if you don't mind."

"You put up your house and farm as collateral, didn't you?"

"I don't think I need to answer these questions."

"Are you in financial difficulty, Dr. Roberts?"

Roberts frowned at a knuckle.

"You were an orthopaedic surgeon, weren't you?"

"Yes, I was."

"You retired from practice nine years ago."

"Yes."

"Right before the economic downturn. How did your investment portfolio make out?"

"Fine," Roberts snapped. "How about yours?"

Kevin smiled. "Dr. Roberts, on what I make I can pay my bills and have enough left over for lunch, and that's about it. You got hit pretty hard though, didn't you?"

Roberts sighed. "Who have you been talking to?" When Kevin didn't respond, the old man shook his head. "Gerald, probably. He doesn't like me very much."

Kevin continued to look at him.

"I watched everything we had," Roberts said, "all our equity, melt away to nothing in six months. It was devastating. Our portfolio still has only recovered about a quarter of what we lost, if that. After nearly a decade. With interest rates almost zero and earnings only very slowly ramping back up, it's hard to regain any of that lost ground."

Kevin shuffled through the file and pulled out a stapled report. "You kept your buggy collection in the barn. Thirty-six of them altogether, is that right?"

"Yes. Horse-drawn carriages, sleighs, doctors' buggies, cutters. A few of them I restored myself. It was my hobby, when my hands were still sound and functional."

"Worth fifty-four thousand dollars, as I understand it."

"I believe that's reasonably accurate."

"Why were they in the new barn? You moved them only a short time before the fire, didn't you?"

"The shed they were in leaks. The roof needs repair, and I was starting to see some minor water damage. The new barn wasn't ready for the horses yet, so I put my collection in there until I could get the money, well, until I could have the shed roof done and the work finished on the new barn so the horses could go in there."

"I understand you tried to sell the collection."

"Oh? Where did you hear that? Gerald again?"

"According to our information, you received an offer and turned it down."

Roberts frowned at Bishop, who stared back at him.

"He low-balled you, didn't he?" Kevin asked.

Roberts bared his teeth. "Yes."

"Offered you fifteen grand for a collection worth more

than three times that amount."

"I don't want to even think about it. Anyway, the collection's gone, so it's all moot now, isn't it?"

Kevin plucked an eight-by-ten photograph from the file folder and set it down next to Roberts's coffee cup. "This is your grand-daughter?"

The old man looked at the photo, a colour shot of a teenager on a horse. She wore a black top hat, a black jacket with tails, white riding pants, and black boots. "Yes. Melissa."

Kevin tapped it with a finger. "She's an equestrian. She competes in dressage, I think they call it. That's an incredibly expensive sport, isn't it, Dr. Roberts?"

"So's hockey."

"That jacket she's wearing," he tapped the photo again, "is called a shad belly coat. Eight hundred bucks. The top hat's another four, the pants almost that much, and the boots are a grand, easily. Just what she's wearing in this picture costs two thousand five hundred dollars, and she's still a growing girl who'll need a whole new outfit before long. She's a member of the Ontario Horse Trials Association, which costs money to join, and she travels all over the country competing in trials to qualify for events like the Pan-Am Games, which she barely missed the last time. We all know how expensive it is to travel these days. And the horse," he pointed again, "is worth sixty grand on its own, isn't it?"

"You've apparently done your research."

"Your daughter, Emily, works as a nurse in Brockville."

"Correct."

"She's separated from her husband now, isn't she? Gerald Brown?"

"Yes."

"I understand he works in construction. Carpentry. So even when they were still together they really couldn't afford all this, could they?" He moved the photograph with the tip of his finger. "You've been paying for most of it, haven't you?"

"I've been helping. It's her dream to ride in the Olympics. I'd like to see that happen before I shuffle off this mortal coil."

Kevin put the photograph back in the file folder. "You're boxed into a financial corner, Dr. Roberts. You mortgaged the house to build the new barn, thinking you could board out some of the stalls to generate income, but you defaulted on the mortgage payments and now it's all coming down on your head. The insurance on the buggy collection pays you more than the low-ball offer you got, and when you put that with the insurance on the barn, it's just about enough to get you out from under, or at least buy you some time. So you read in the newspaper about the fire up on Visser Road, where the pony was chased out of its barn by the arsonist before he torched it, and it gave you the idea. You bought some road flares at Canadian Tire and used one to start your own fire. Didn't you?"

A tear rolled down the old man's cheek.

"You set that fire yourself, didn't you, Dr. Roberts?"

"No," the old man whispered, head down. "It's not possible."

"We can prove you bought the flares, and we can prove you had a motive. The money tells the story, Dr. Roberts. You set that fire yourself, didn't you?"

"I can't..."

"You're a man of honour, Dr. Roberts. You're respected in the community, and your life has been filled with remarkable accomplishments. Don't tarnish who you are and what you've done over the years by lying now, by trying to evade responsibility when you know you have to own up to it. You set that fire, didn't you?"

"Yes," Roberts whispered, eyes closed. "I did. I'm sorry. I'm so very, very sorry. I didn't know what else to do. I had nowhere to turn. I was desperate, and I love that girl very much. I had to make her dream come true. I'm so, so sorry."

"I know," Kevin said, closing the file folder. "I know you are."

chapter TWENTY-TWO

Ellie stared at her cellphone and fought the battle once again. She should call; she knew it was her obligation to stay in touch, to make the effort, to demonstrate that she cared. She dreaded the calls so much, though, that she kept putting them off. Now the time between them was becoming so long that it was obvious she was avoiding them.

She poured a little more Jack Daniels over the ice in her glass and looked out over the lake. Off to the right, the sun had dropped behind the tree line and the sky was rimmed with colour. It was a beautiful evening sky, but she was having trouble seeing it because her mind was elsewhere.

Eight months had passed since she'd last visited her adoptive parents. Paul and Mary March lived in an assisted-living facility in Richmond Hill, a town in York Region that was part of the Greater Toronto Area. Paul had been moved to the long-term care wing in January to receive the attention he required now that his Alzheimer's disease had advanced beyond the point that Mary was able to continue looking after him. She herself was now showing signs of dementia as her eighty-fifth birthday approached, and Ellie had found that their weekly telephone calls had become long, disjointed, and repetitive.

Although she did not give her time to others as freely as did someone like Kevin Walker, who devoted every off day to his girlfriend and her two children, Ellie believed she was not a selfish person. Her own two girls would disagree, of course. Their dislike of her was painfully well documented. Her focus on her career and the long hours on duty had taken their toll.

When it came to Paul and Mary, they'd explained to her at a young age that she was adopted and that while they loved her very much, they were not her natural parents. She remembered it very clearly. It had been a summer day a few weeks before she'd entered Grade One. Kind and gentle souls, they'd tried their best to explain this strange adult concept of child adoption. She remembered taking the news solemnly, as though they'd told her she was a strange being from another planet whose welfare had been placed in their willing hands by civil servants from some alien civilization in another galaxy.

She'd endured the inevitable schoolyard teasing without complaint and had never shed a tear over her unknown natural mother and her inexplicable abandonment. She'd developed a strong sense of loyalty to Paul and Mary, who'd treated her well and given her everything a little girl might want, within their limited means. But when the time had come to accept a scholarship to university, she'd left them behind with no hesitation and had never looked back.

She loved them. There was no question about that. She just didn't spend a lot of time thinking about it.

Except for moments like this one, when she knew she should call Mary and spend the next hour listening patiently to her rambling, circular stories that were no longer securely anchored in reality.

As she stared at the cellphone on the deck railing beside her it began to vibrate, startling her. She looked at the call display and picked it up. "March. How are you, Jack?"

"The usual. Expecting company, Ellie?" Jack Riley lived in a ramshackle farm house up at the corner where Tamarack Lane, on which her cottage was located, intersected with Lake Road, which led to civilization. "The usual" meant that he was sitting on his front porch sipping the illegal potato vodka they both pretended he didn't make, watching the world go by.

"No, I'm not. Why?"

"Just saw a big black Lincoln Town Car turn down your way. Government plates. Driver and one passenger in the back. Figured you were the only one on the lake might rate a visit from the feds."

"Thanks for the heads-up."

"Come up and have a glass with me, later."

"I'll have to take a rain check on that, Jack." She ended the call and heard tires crunching the gravel in the lane out front. She got up and walked down the deck steps.

As she headed around the side of the cottage, the Town Car pulled into the parking space beside her Crown Vic. Sergeant Dominic Lambert got out and opened the rear passenger door for Danny Merrick, who looked around for a moment, a bemused smile on his face, then saw her and grinned.

"Good evening, Ellie. What a beautiful spot!"

She stopped and folded her arms. "Assistant Commissioner Merrick. To what do I owe the pleasure?"

He strode past her down the path along the side of the cottage, eyes on the lake. "Gorgeous. Absolutely gorgeous. I always wanted a cottage, but I don't think I'd ever have the time to do it justice." He stopped and grinned over his shoulder at her. "This is beautiful. You're very lucky."

"What can I do for you?"

He gestured toward the Town Car. "Where would you like Dom to put this stuff?"

Lambert had popped the trunk of the Town Car and stood there with a banker's box in his arms, waiting for instructions.

"What's that?"

"The results of our threat investigation," Merrick said.

"Two boxes, everything we've been able to declassify for you and your team. Electronic files on disc, and hard copies for your convenience. Where would you like Dom to put them?"

Ellie waved at the short wooden boardwalk running along the front of the cottage. "There is fine."

"I'd rather put them inside, ma'am, if that's all right with you."

"Kitchen door's around the far side," Ellie pointed. "It's unlocked."

As Lambert disappeared with his load, Ellie frowned at Merrick. "Are you saying you're all done?"

"Let's sit down for a moment, Ellie. I'll walk you through it."

She led him back to the deck. He gawked at Ridge Ballantyne's lodge next door, then followed her up the steps and leaned on the railing. "Can I get you something to drink?" she asked, pointing to her whisky bottle.

"Beer, if you have it."

"Glass?"

"No, thanks."

Lambert had left the banker's box on her dining table. She tipped the lid and looked at neatly-labelled files. The kitchen door opened and Lambert came in with the second box. She closed the lid and moved toward the fridge.

"Are they okay here on the table, ma'am?"

"My office is in there," Ellie pointed. "On the desk, if you don't mind."

"Yes, ma'am."

As he took the box into her spare room, Ellie opened the fridge and took out two bottles of beer. "Can I get you something to drink, sergeant?"

Lambert came out and picked up the box on the kitchen table. "No thanks, ma'am. I have water in the car."

"Please stop calling me ma'am."

"Yes, ma'am." He disappeared into the spare room and

came back out empty-handed.

"We're on the deck," Ellie said. "Just through here." She went out the sliding patio door and handed a bottle to Merrick, who had settled into one of her Adirondack chairs. She opened hers and sat down in the other chair. "You were saying?"

Merrick opened his beer and took a long drink. "Ah, man. I haven't slept in thirty-eight hours and I'm not exactly sure what I ate or drank in that time, but this tastes good." He smiled. "We found no evidence to indicate that Senator Lane's death is in any way connected to an individual or group that poses a threat to the national security of this country. We don't believe he was giving up classified information, either voluntarily or involuntarily, nor was he assassinated as a terrorist act, either by a lone wolf or a radical cell operating in Canada." He glanced at his watch. "Our commissioner has informed the minister of public safety and the prime minister that we're turning our findings over to you for use in your investigation. The premier should be calling your commissioner right about now."

"So you're saying the terrorist angle is out?"

Merrick nodded. "Unless new evidence comes to light, we're reasonably satisfied that Senator Lane did not release sensitive material or compromise his senatorial position in any way." He smiled. "Now that the experts in national security have finished butting in, it's time for the experts in homicide investigation to bring this case to its successful completion."

Ellie glanced over her shoulder as she heard the kitchen door close. "I said he could join us."

"He'll wait in the car."

"He might enjoy the view."

"He's a former sniper, Ellie. He's very good at waiting."

She let it go. A slight breeze coming off the lake pushed

hair into her eyes. She brushed it aside. “So everything’s there, in those boxes?”

“Yes. Your people were very co-operative, and we appreciate it, believe me. You now have copies of our own lab reports, transcripts of all our interviews, our analyses of his financial and phone records, whatever could be declassified.”

“Redacted, no doubt.”

He smiled at her over his beer. “Well, we are the federal government, after all.”

“Any leads for me, Danny?”

He shrugged. “He lived what you could call a small life, Ellie, despite his prominence as a public figure. He didn’t own a computer, for example. He has a website and an e-mail account that are managed by a staffer in his office on the Hill, but that’s it. No Facebook, Twitter, or what have you. No cellphone; his only telephone contacts once again were through his office and were almost exclusively handled by the staffer. No driver’s licence, as you know, and no credit cards, just a debit card that he used on occasion. He left a very small footprint.

“We did manage to identify the woman Lane had lunch with on Sunday, just before he dropped off the radar. Her name’s Rosa Battaglia. She carried Lane’s paintings in her gallery in Ottawa at one time. According to her, the lunch meeting was an attempt on her part to convince Lane to do business with her again. Something about a commission with a corporation in Victoria. She claims he left the restaurant without saying goodbye, and that’s the last time she saw him.”

“All right.” She watched him finish his beer and twist the empty bottle around in his hands. “Want another one?”

He closed his eyes and sighed, obviously tired. The light was fading rapidly, and in profile his resemblance to Richard Gere seemed even more pronounced. He sat slumped in the big chair, his navy suit rumpled and his short grey hair sticking up as though he'd absent-mindedly finger-combed it before getting out of the car. He opened his eyes and blinked. "It's so nice here. I shouldn't but I'll have one more, thank you."

Ellie stood up. "Would you like something to eat?"

He smiled up at her, handing her his empty bottle. "That's very nice of you, Ellie, but I'll get Dom to stop somewhere on the way back. I can't stay very long."

In the kitchen, Ellie was reaching for the handle on the fridge door when her cellphone began to vibrate. She took it out, looked at the call display, and answered.

"March. Good evening, sir."

"I've got news for you, Ellie," Commissioner Moodie said. "I've been informed that the RCMP's completed their national security threat assessment with a negative finding. They've agreed to provide you with everything they have—well, everything they can clear for release—right away."

"Yes, sir. Assistant Commissioner Merrick is here right now, actually. At the lake. He and his driver just dropped off their reports."

"All right, very good. Then I won't keep you. Please pass along my best to Danny, will you?"

"Yes, sir."

"Good night, Ellie."

"Good night, sir."

When Ellie stepped back out onto the deck, Merrick gave a little start and sat forward. She handed him a beer and said, "Dozing?"

"Smelling the water. I love the smell of water. It's not salt water, but it still smells terrific."

She sat down beside him and uncapped her beer. "Where are you from?"

"Moncton."

"How long have you been a member of the RCMP?"

"Since 1984." He tipped his bottle and swallowed. "This is your one chance to interrogate me, Ellie. I'm too damned tired to be evasive."

She gave him a faint smile and looked out across the lake, which had now grown dark. Behind her, the photosensitive porch light had come on, gilding the deck with faint illumination. It was that transition time when there was still some light overhead in the sky, but the trees on the horizon were black silhouettes and the immediate surroundings were visible as shapes without detail. A brief bridge between illumination and darkness.

Ellie was aware that she was seen by others as aloof and disinterested, but the truth was that, like any other experienced law enforcement professional, she had an abiding curiosity about people. As an interrogator, she'd enjoyed the process of worming information out of suspects. When she was out in public during her off-hours she was an inveterate people-watcher. At the mall she'd buy a coffee and sit on a bench for half an hour just to practise her observational skills, a trick she'd learned from an old friend and former colleague, Tom Faust. If the opportunity presented itself to ask someone a question about themselves, she rarely let it pass. Since Danny Merrick was offering her carte blanche, she thought she might as well take him up on it.

"Parents?"

Merrick chuckled. "Much different than yours, Ellie. For better or for worse, mine were both media stars in the small pond that was the Maritimes of the sixties and seventies."

Ellie frowned. "Different than mine?"

"Well, we ran your background, of course."

"I see. Go on."

Merrick closed his eyes and leaned his head back against the wide slats of the Adirondack chair. "My father was Fred Merrick, long-time weatherman for the local TV station. Everyone in the region knew his face and that famous baritone voice. We couldn't go anywhere when I was a kid without people stopping him to ask for his autograph. Why someone would want a weatherman's autograph is beyond me, but that's the power of celebrity, I guess. He loved it. It's what got him up in the morning, the knowledge that people knew who he was and thought it was wonderful to have him notice them, even for a few seconds. One year he was grand marshal for the Santa Claus parade, and he was drunk for a week afterward celebrating that particular high."

"He drank?"

"Like a fish. And slept around. And loved it when local restaurants tore up the bill in exchange for a mention on the air. He was a force to be reckoned with, Fred Merrick was."

"And your mother?"

"His polar opposite. Her name was Marie-France Leblanc. She was a reporter for the Acadian activist newspaper *L'Evangeline* until it went under in 1982. She was the niece of Emery Leblanc, who was editor-in-chief of *L'Evangeline* until 1962. In person she was quiet, shy, and unassuming. In print she was a lioness, fierce and courageous. I was very, very proud of her. Much closer to her than to my father."

"Are they still living?"

"My mother is. My father's liver gave out almost twenty years ago."

"Siblings?"

Merrick smiled, eyes still closed. "I was essentially raised by my sisters. My mother, you see, spent most of her time on the road chasing stories, and I've already explained why my father wasn't much use as a parent. Louise was ten years older than I, Sylvie was eight years older, and Annette seven years older. They got me up in the morning and off to school, made my lunches and gave me hell if I didn't eat them, cooked supper, made sure I did my homework, and did their damnedest to keep me out of trouble." He looked over at Ellie and winked. "That part wasn't too hard. I was a pretty easy-going kid. I had to be, the only boy in a crazy family with three older sisters."

Ellie said nothing, sipping beer. Once a subject begins to talk, silence can be one of the interrogator's most powerful tools. Some grow uncomfortable and feel a need to explain themselves more clearly, while others will use it as a tacit cue to wax poetic. Merrick, for his part, grinned at her obvious use of the technique and looked up at the darkening sky.

"Sylvie was the joker in the family. She seemed to think I was her own personal source of amusement. I've always been a heavy sleeper. I was hard to get up in the morning, and it was an ongoing battle to get me out the door before the school bus got there. One morning I woke up and discovered she'd sneaked in during the night and put one of Annette's dresses on me. She'd painted my fingernails this hideous bright pink and put lipstick and eye shadow on my face. I had to scramble like hell to get it all off before the bus got there."

Ellie laughed.

"Another time she slipped an open bottle of cheap perfume into my backpack before handing it to me as I went out the door, and of course it tipped over when I got on the bus. My schoolbooks, homework, pencil case, and everything else reeked like hell. I took a lot of flak in the schoolyard for that one." He sighed. "But she was the best baker in the family, and she always had something fresh for me to eat when I got off the bus at the end of the day. Chelsea buns, apple muffins, and the most incredible butter tarts you ever tasted. Of the three, she was the one who really wanted to spoil me."

Ellie drained her bottle of beer and put it down on the deck beside her.

"She's fifty-seven now. It's hard to believe. Divorced from her husband, and her children all grown up and moved away. She's a school superintendent in Prince Edward Island, getting ready to retire. Life is a very, very strange trip, Ellie. Very strange."

"It is that," Ellie agreed.

"Of the four of us," he said, "only Louise and Annette had good marriages. Sylvie fought constantly with her husband, and as for me," he leaned forward and looked over at her, "let's just say that my marriage went pretty much the same way yours did. For people like us, career comes before everything else." He suddenly stood up. "On that note, I should leave. Thanks for the beer. And for listening."

Ellie got to her feet and followed him down the stairs and around the side of the cottage.

"You've been very professional," he said. "I admire the way you handle yourself."

"Thank you."

He stopped in a circle of light from a motion-activated spotlight that had come on as they approached. "If I could make a suggestion?"

"Of course."

"We didn't feel comfortable with the answers we were getting from Battaglia. She ended up being of zero interest to us from a security perspective, but my people got some weird vibes from her. We think there's a past history you might want to look at more closely."

"I'll keep it in mind."

He held out his hand. "It's been a pleasure, Ellie."

She shook his hand, nodding.

"Keep me in the loop, in case something comes up that we need to know."

"Will do."

He smiled. "If you need a fresh set of eyes and ears and you want to bounce something off me, don't hesitate to call. I'm a pretty good listener, too."

"I'll keep it in mind," she said again.

"Please do."

She watched him walk away into the shadows. After a moment, the dome light came on inside the Town Car and she saw him get into the back seat and close the door. Before the light dimmed down again, he looked over at her and touched an index finger to his temple in an informal salute.

She nodded back as the engine gunned to life and the car eased away. When the red tail lights had disappeared down the lane, she shook her head and walked slowly back down to the deck.

He was good, she had to admit. He was very, very good.

She couldn't help but like the guy.

chapter TWENTY-THREE

As Bishop turned into the long cratered driveway of the Pool residence on County Road 8 the following morning, Kevin could see right away that the Ford Ranger was not there. Bishop slowed the Crown Vic to a crawl in front of a large pothole, cursing.

"There," Kevin said, pointing up the driveway.

Sitting in a lawn chair in front of the house was Larry Pool. He wore a blue plaid long-sleeved shirt, jeans, and sandals. Wraparound sunglasses slowly turned in their direction as Bishop took his foot off the brake and eased up the driveway. There was no sign of the dog as they parked at the side door of the house and got out.

"Looks like he's conscious, anyway," Bishop said as they walked around to the front yard.

"Good morning, Mr. Pool," Kevin called out, approaching the lawn chair. "We're detectives with the OPP. Is your son Jeremy home at the moment?"

The sunglasses slowly tipped up. "No." It came out as a moist whisper, as though from a long way away.

"Can you tell us where he is at the moment? We need to talk to him."

"In town."

"When will he be back, Mr. Pool?"

"Soon. He promised me lunch."

The lawn chair in which Pool sat was one of the old

canvas kind with little pockets stitched into the arms to accommodate beverage containers. An open bottle of beer stuck out of one of the pockets, but Kevin could see that it was almost untouched. Behind the lawn chair was a walker with a little wicker basket tied to the front with dirty white shoe strings. The basket held a small box of tissues and other odds and ends.

"Where was your son last Sunday night?" Bishop asked.

"I don't know. With me, I guess."

"How about taking off the sunglasses while you're talking to us?"

Pool's chin dropped. He slowly reached up and removed his sunglasses. His eyes were closed. They looked pinched and tiny. "I don't see too good in the light."

"That's okay," Kevin said. "Put them back on."

Bishop folded his arms across his chest. "So which is it? Was your son here with you last Sunday night, or you don't know?"

Back on Pool's face, the sunglasses tipped up toward the detective. "What day is it today?"

"It's Wednesday," Bishop replied, impatiently.

Pool thought for a moment, then shook his head. "Sorry. I ... can't remember."

"What about May 16, June 4, and June 24? Can you remember if he was here on those nights?"

"Sorry."

"Have a lot of problems remembering stuff, do you?"

Pool's right hand fluttered on his thigh. "Sometimes. But I remember back pretty well for the most part. It's just when I'm drinking, I have problems."

"Are you drinking this morning?" Bishop asked.

"Not really. Don't feel too good. Just wanted some sunshine."

Kevin heard the shortness of breath and fatigue in his voice. "How long have you had MS, Mr. Pool?" Kevin asked.

"Twenty years. I was ... twenty-one."

"That's a long time."

"Yeah." Pool hesitated. "My wife left me when I found out."

Kevin exchanged looks with Bishop. "How old was Jeremy then?"

"Two."

"It must have been hard, raising him by yourself with your condition."

Pool's mouth twisted, and he made a huffing sound. "Yeah."

Kevin had a sudden thought. "Did he leave home for a while? Take off somewhere?"

"Yeah. He was up in Ottawa. For a couple of years."

"Oh? When was that?"

"A while ago. He dropped out of Grade Nine."

"How long's he been back?"

"Four years or so."

Kevin thought about it. If Jeremy had bummed around in Ottawa as a teenager, he'd probably run into problems with the authorities up there from time to time. It would explain his attitude and his apparent disinterest in being questioned by the police.

"He acts like there's something wrong with him," Bishop said. "Is he on meds of some kind?"

"He's bipolar. He takes something for it."

"Does he like to burn stuff?"

"The garbage. I got a permit. And wood in the stove. In winter."

"How about other people's barns? He like to burn them, too?"

The sunglasses stared at Bishop.

They turned at the sound of tires in the driveway. It was the Ford Ranger, with Jeremy Pool behind the wheel. As they watched, it bounced up the driveway into the yard, where it stopped next to Bishop's Crown Vic. The dog stuck its head outside the open back window over the tailgate and barked at them.

"Here he is," Pool said. The relief in his voice was almost pathetic.

As Jeremy got out from behind the wheel, Bishop made a beeline for him, his hand under his jacket.

"Secure that dog, right now."

"He won't hurt you," Jeremy said.

"I said, secure the damned dog right now." Bishop moved his jacket so the kid could see that his hand was near the butt of his service weapon.

"All right, all right. Jesus Christ." Jeremy grabbed a leash from the cabin of the truck and snapped it on the German Shepherd's collar, then dropped the tailgate and led the dog around to the back of the house. Bishop followed, keeping him in sight. Kevin drifted away from Larry Pool toward the truck, watching Bishop.

Jeremy came back without the dog, arms at his sides, head down. He walked around the house to his father. Bishop followed close behind.

"Are you okay, Larry?" Jeremy asked, darting a glance at Kevin. "Are they bothering you?"

"What's going on, Jeremy?" Pool began trying to struggle to his feet.

"He needs to come with us to answer some questions," Bishop snapped, looking at Jeremy. "Want to come along nicely, or should we discuss it first?"

"Hang on," Kevin said to Pool, grabbing his walker. He pulled it around and helped the man to his feet. "We need to ask Jeremy some questions about barn fires in the area. We think he knows some things that can help us."

Pool shrugged off Kevin's hand. "He doesn't know anything, you ... bastards." He reached for his walker and missed, staggering.

Kevin grabbed his arm and kept him upright.

"Leave my boy alone," the man slurred. Spittle flew from his mouth and landed on the front of his shirt.

"Stop." Jeremy stepped forward and pushed at Kevin to get him to move aside. He grasped Pool's wrists and guided him to the walker. "Go inside, Larry. I'll take care of this."

"They think they can come in here and..."

"I know. I'll go with them and answer their questions. Just settle down and go inside. Take a nap."

"Think they can push us around..."

"They can't." Jeremy took Pool's elbow and got him started across the lawn. ""It'll be all right. I'll go with them and be home later. Don't call Terry, all right?"

"I'll call anyone I want. Call a lawyer ... goddammit."

"Whatever. Just don't call Terry. You don't need any more."

"Just a mickey ... until you get home."

"I said no, Larry."

Kevin and Bishop followed them around to the side door. Kevin held the screen door open while Jeremy guided Pool inside. They got him settled in his recliner chair, then Jeremy went to the refrigerator and brought him a bottle of spring water.

"Drink that. Don't call Terry. I'll be back, later."

Pool slumped in his chair, eyes closed, his chin damp with saliva.

Jeremy looked at Bishop with ill-concealed venom. "Let's get out of here and get this over with."

chapter TWENTY-FOUR

They kept Jeremy in the interview room for nearly three hours without breaking him. He waived his right to counsel and responded to their questions in a calm monotone, but he gave them nothing on which to build their case.

Because it was an investigative detention based on their reasonable suspicion that Jeremy was implicated in the three barn arsons predating the Roberts and Spencer Farm fires, they knew they were working under a time limit beyond which the detention might be deemed unreasonably long. If they didn't soon place him under arrest, any admission Jeremy did make might subsequently be viewed by the court as tainted. The problem was, however, that they weren't getting anything from him that would give them reasonable and probable grounds to arrest him for the arsons. If they didn't come up with something soon, they would have to cut him loose.

They tried to force an admission that he liked to look in people's windows after dark, that he had anger issues that boiled over when he drove, and that he'd stalked Liz Wierdsma at her place of work and her home. In each case Jeremy calmly avoided saying anything that might implicate himself. It became maddeningly obvious that he knew how to handle himself while under police questioning.

It was close to noon when they finally huddled with Patterson and Crown Attorney Susan Mitchum. Everyone agreed that they would have to let Jeremy walk.

Before having put Jeremy into the Crown Vic back at the Pool house, Bishop had done a pocket search which turned up a prescription bottle in Jeremy's name for lithium carbonate. When asked about it, Jeremy would only say that it was prescribed to him by a doctor in Smiths Falls and that he was supposed to take it three times a day. He refused to say what it was for. Suspicious, Bishop had stopped in at the lab and arranged for a sample to be tested. At the detachment, he ran a quick Google search and learned that lithium carbonate was a common medication to treat bipolar disorder. It was supposed to be particularly effective in treating the irritability and aggression that might characterize the manic episodes of the disease.

Once the decision had been made to release Jeremy, Kevin went back into the interview room and waved him out. "I'll give you a ride home," he said, pointing the way down the hall.

Bishop met them at the security door and tossed the bottle of prescription medication to Jeremy. "Don't forget these."

When Kevin raised an eyebrow, Bishop shrugged. "They're legit."

Out on the highway, Kevin felt the worm of suspicion still crawling around in his head. He glanced over at Jeremy, who was staring out the side window, his face impassive. He was clearly not well. He was taking medication for bipolar disorder, and his body language and affect radiated distress. If he was responsible for burning down those barns, he had to be stopped. The fact that he'd chosen barns without livestock that weren't worth much, or in the case of the Wierdsma fire, had chased out Liz's pony before burning the structure, suggested he was more unwell than dangerous. But it *was* dangerous to burn down a barn, and clearly against the law. Kevin's concern was not so much a matter of whether to bring down the full weight of the law on Jeremy's shoulders but *how* to bring it down.

"Your father told us you spent a few years in Ottawa," he said. Jeremy didn't respond. Kevin pursed his lips. "Did you get in trouble up there? Get arrested?"

No response.

"We'll find out," Kevin said.

Jeremy stared out the windshield. "Leave me alone."

They were the last words Kevin was able to coax out of him for the rest of the drive. Jeremy got out of the car, slamming the door, and walked into the house without looking back. Kevin watched the dog bounce around at the end of his chain for a moment, then executed a K-turn in the yard and drove back down the cratered driveway.

As he turned out onto the road he glanced at the dashboard clock and cursed. He was running late, and Janie was going to crucify him again.

chapter TWENTY-FIVE

"Bologna?" Kevin asked, putting Caitlyn's empty plate and juice cup into the dishwasher and coming back to the kitchen table. "What's wrong with bologna?"

"It's yucky," Brendan said, making a face.

"No, it's not." Kevin moved the plate with its uneaten sandwich back in front of the boy, who sat with his arms folded, a stubborn expression on his face. "You eat it all the time. It tastes really good."

"No, it doesn't. It tastes like yuck."

"Let's go," Janie announced, hustling into the kitchen. "Why are you guys still dicking around in here? Time to go. Now."

Kevin picked up Brendan's plate. "Do you want this in a doggie bag to go, Brendan?"

"Brendan's a doggie!" Caitlyn chirped, watching her mother bustling around the kitchen, searching for something. "Woof! Woof!"

"No, I'm not!" Brendan cried.

"Enough!" Janie burst out. "Get your shoes on and get out into the damned car, now!" She snatched up a piece of paper that had been hidden behind a loaf of bread on the counter. "Jesus!"

As the children ran from the kitchen to escape their mother's wrath and put on their shoes at the side door, Kevin grabbed a plastic bag from a drawer and dumped

Brendan's sandwich into it. The little devil would wait until they were a block from home before complaining about his abandoned lunch, and Kevin intended to be prepared for it.

"Are you sure you're okay to take them to Mom's?" Janie asked, sarcasm unmistakable in her voice.

"Sure. No problem."

"No emergencies you have to rush off to? No dirt bags to interrogate first?"

"No, Janie," Kevin replied calmly, "it's okay." She hadn't hidden her anger when he'd gotten to the house half an hour later than he'd been expected. He followed her out of the kitchen and down the stairs to the side door, clipping his service weapon onto his belt and grabbing his sports jacket from a hanger. "Can you call me after your appointment? Tell me how it went?"

She slammed out the door without answering and made a beeline for Kevin's motor pool Fusion, where the children were horsing around instead of getting into their assigned seats and buckling up. Kevin locked the door behind him and hurried past the Grand Cherokee, which was blocked in the driveway by the Fusion. He had no idea what Janie's appointment with her doctor in Smiths Falls was for, if it had anything to do with her chronic headaches or something more serious, but he *did* know that if he didn't get moving in the next thirty seconds she was liable to take another run at him, and he really didn't think he had the energy to absorb it right now.

Life with Janie was definitely a challenge these days.

"I've got this," he said, touching her lightly on the shoulder as she bustled Caitlyn into the back seat on the driver's side and struggled with the seat belt buckle. "It's okay."

She clicked the buckle into place and turned on him. "One of these days, Kevin."

He watched her march off to the Grand Cherokee.

She slammed the door and gunned the engine into life. "Hands and feet," he said, and carefully closed the door on Caitlyn.

Brendan's legs were sticking out from the back door on the passenger side. The boy lay flat on his stomach, poking under the front seat.

"Brendan, please," Kevin begged, "your mom needs to get going. Please get out of there and sit down. Okay?"

"Look at all the stuff under here!" The boy's right arm emerged, twisted up over his back, holding up Bishop's discarded Fudgsicle stick. "Can I have one of these?"

"Brendan, *now*." Kevin put his hands on the boy's hips and gently pulled. He came out stiff, like a horizontal human plank. Kevin turned him so that he was vertical and got him sitting down in the seat. As he pulled the seat belt out, he saw that the boy held something in his left hand.

"Look what I found," Brendan said, giving it a shake.

Kevin clipped the seat belt into place and held out his hand. "Let's see."

Brendan surrendered it, a serious expression on his face.

It was Jeremy Pool's prescription bottle of lithium carbonate, still more than half full.

chapter TWENTY-SIX

"So you talked to this Stewart guy on the phone," Ellie said, glancing over at Leung in the passenger seat of the Crown Vic. "How did he sound?"

"Amused," Leung said. "Saddened."

"Amused?"

"To be talking to the police. An eccentric, retired academic with not a lot of exposure to the harsher side of life." Leung shrugged. "He sounded genuinely fond of Lane. Which puts him in a very small minority, as I understand it."

They were driving to Perth to interview Charlie Stewart, the retired professor of art history Leung had made arrangements to see today. Ellie had also arranged for later meetings in Ottawa with Lane's parliamentary assistant and Deputy Chief Ross Carrière of the Ottawa Police Service, so she'd decided to combine her two meetings with Leung's so that they could take care of them together.

After a few kilometres she said, "Tell me about your family, Dennis. You said your wife works in a bank."

"Yes. Her name's Lily."

"And your girls?"

"May's twelve, Lucy's ten, Lan's eight, and Meilin's six."

"Sounds like a full house."

Leung laughed. "Very much so."

"Are your parents still alive?"

"Yes. In China my father was a surgeon in the rural community where he and my mother lived, but when they emigrated from Guandong Province in 1974, he couldn't get a licence to practise here in Canada. He and my mother have a herbal remedy store in Toronto. In Chinatown. They're in their seventies now, and my brother Lee works in the store with them, but my father's still as sharp as a knife. If you're interested in natural remedies, he knows more than anyone else in Canada about them, I guarantee. Ask him a question, and you'll have to settle in for a lecture that could go on all afternoon." The pride in his voice was evident.

"What does he think of you being a police officer?"

"He approves, but it's a constant source of entertainment for him. When I got the assignment to AGCO, I never heard the end of it."

"Why is that?"

"Well, because of the stereotype, Ellie. Asians are considered to be pathological gamblers, aren't they? He tells all his friends not to talk to me, because I'll report all their secret gambling activities and they'll get arrested. He never tires of the joke."

"What about now?"

"He thinks I'm working undercover to bust Triad human trafficking along the St. Lawrence corridor. I say to him, 'Ah Pa, I'm just a regular detective constable. They don't pay me enough to work undercover,' but he doesn't believe me. He likes his version of my career a lot better than mine."

Ellie thought she heard a note of regret in the soft laugh that followed this statement. Today Leung was wearing the same charcoal suit he'd worn on Monday, this time with a white shirt and black tie. From the corner of her eye she saw him fiddling with the ruby-and-diamond ring on his right hand.

"That's nice," she said. "Your ring."

"Thank you." He held it up. "It's zircon. I always wanted a ruby ring, but who can afford that on our salaries, right?"

"It doesn't look synthetic. It's very attractive."

"Oh, it's not cubic zirconium, it's the mineral zircon. A real gemstone. Worth more than the synthetic, but still not too much."

"I don't know much about jewellery," Ellie said.

"That's all right. My father's an expert on the supposed healing properties of minerals. Zircon is referred to as a stone of virtue because it is thought to provide spiritual balance and grounding."

"You figure you need that, do you, Dennis?"

He laughed, more freely this time. "I wear it to show a little bling, Ellie. Who wants to look like a typical, boring flatfoot? I don't think that's very grounding, spiritually speaking, do you?"

Charlie Stewart lived in a beautiful stone cottage on a side street in Perth, a town of about six thousand people in Lanark County about eighty-five kilometres southwest of Ottawa. Leung had to knock three times before Stewart opened the door. He removed the pipe from his mouth with a flourish and waved them inside.

"I'm just in the back. Come on through; don't worry about your shoes. This place has seen a lot worse from the soles of my feet than anything you're likely to track in. Back here." He led them down the hall and through the kitchen into a solarium at the rear of the house that looked out onto a large back yard. Ceiling fans turned slowly overhead. Despite the bright sunlight it was cool in here, as cool as the house itself had been. Ellie caught a glimpse of a central air conditioning unit at the back corner of the house. Leung introduced her, and Stewart held out his hand.

"Pleased to meet you, Inspector," he said, vigorously

shaking her hand. "Dennis gave me the impression you're the big wheel on this thing, so I'm honoured to answer all your questions. Sit down, please."

Ellie chose a wicker chair with a floral seat cushion. Leung eased himself into a matching rocker across from her as Stewart slid down onto the settee and began pouring tea into three small cups.

"I know the Chinese have a different approach to the tea ceremony than the Japanese, who are positively obsessed with the whole thing, but I thought I'd pour for us even though I'm the elder, and by quite a long shot, at that. A sign of respect for the enormous responsibilities you carry in your jobs."

As Stewart set a cup of tea down at Leung's end of the table, Dennis lightly tapped it with his finger before picking it up.

"Ah, yes. You're very welcome. My pleasure." Stewart watched them sip their tea, then swallowed his own. "Can I get you something cold? We've got fresh lemonade, or soda if you prefer. No alcohol in the house, but you probably don't imbibe on the job anyway. Inspector? Dennis?"

Leung glanced at Ellie and said, "I think we're probably fine for now. We don't want to keep you too long. We just have a few questions about Darius Lane."

"So you said on the telephone." Shoving the pipe back into his mouth, he leaned back in the settee and fingered his bushy white beard. He wore sandals, faded blue jeans, a white cotton shirt turned up on his forearms, and an unbuttoned grey vest. The fringe of hair around his head was as frizzy and white as his beard. His bare toes were bony and yellow, but thankfully the nails had been carefully trimmed. His lips were thick and dark, his nose was a bony hook, and his eyes were milky blue. He stared at Dennis with a slight smile bending up the corner of his mouth opposite the pipe. "Ask away, by all means."

As Leung drew breath to frame his first question,

Stewart removed the pipe and grinned at Ellie. “Do you like this patio set? It’s antique, you know.”

“It’s lovely,” Ellie replied.

“It’s a Bar Harbor set made by the Whitney Reed Factory of Boston, Mass, in the first decade of the nineteen hundreds. Original oxblood stain. Came from a Cape Cod estate held by the same family for over a hundred years. Cost me four thousand dollars.”

“It’s beautiful,” Ellie repeated.

“Reminds me of home. I’m from Waltham, Mass, you know. Native New Englander. But I’ve been in Canada since 1971. And yes, I was a draft dodger. Absolutely. But I’m a Canadian citizen now. Been so for quite a long time. Cut me and I bleed maple leaf red.”

“When did you first meet Darius Lane?” Leung interjected, anxious to get a word in edgewise.

Stewart looked at Leung for a long moment, then abruptly smiled. “I first met Darius in the back yard of an apartment house on Victoria Street in Kingston. Well, it was across the fence, technically speaking. A four-foot board fence that divided my back yard from his. I had a dog, a Bouvier des Flandres. Big fuzzy fellow. My girl friend at the time joked that Richard and I—that was the dog’s name—looked like brothers. I suppose she had a point; my hair and beard were as black and frizzy back then as his coat. Well, the previous tenants next door made such a fuss about Richard that I had to fork out the money to pay some guy to put up the fence. Good fences make good neighbours, as Frost said. But anyway, you don’t give a damn about the fence. I’d seen Darius coming and going for about a month or so, but on this particular day I looked out my upstairs bathroom window and saw him outside in the back yard in front of a bed of peonies, trying to paint. I had no idea he was a painter; I thought he was just some guy.”

A woman walked into the solarium from the kitchen

carrying a silver serving tray filled with bottles and glasses. She set the tray down on the table in front of Stewart and smiled.

"You brought us refreshments," Stewart said.

"Of course."

Stewart waved his hand. "This is my wife, Sunny. Sunny, meet Detective Inspector March and Detective Constable Leung from the OPP. They're here to ask me about Darius Lane."

"Yes, I know." Sunny smiled tentatively at Ellie. She was tall and willowy, somewhere in her middle fifties, and deeply tanned. Her blond hair was shoulder length and bleached at the tips. She wore cut-off shorts and one of Charlie's cotton shirts loosely knotted over a red spandex crop top.

Stewart grabbed a bottle and an opener. "This is birch beer soda," he said, uncapping the bottle. "Anyone? No? I'll keep this one for myself, then. We have root beer, black cherry, and ginger ale. Dennis?"

"I'll try a ginger ale," Leung replied.

"Ellie?"

"That would be fine."

Sunny uncapped a bottle of ginger ale and poured it into a glass, then handed it to Ellie. When Stewart had served Leung, Sunny nodded to Ellie and disappeared back into the kitchen.

"Former student," Stewart said, swallowing soda. "Third time lucky, I guess. Next year's our twenty-fifth anniversary."

"Congratulations," Leung said.

"Thank you. So he's smearing acrylic paint all over this canvas in these big, frenetic brush strokes and I'm thinking, 'This guy must have the killer hangover of all time, if this piece is any indication'—by this time I'd come out into my back yard and I was watching him over the fence. I figured maybe his psychiatrist told him painting was good therapy or something and he was giving it the old college try. But the more I watched the more I could see the confidence in his strokes, the complete lack of hesitation as he worked on his palette to mix his colours and I thought, 'Now wait a minute, Charlie. This guy actually knows what he's doing. He's got something specific in mind here that he's working out on the canvas.' I must have stood there for forty-five minutes at least, not saying a word, just watching over his shoulder as he worked on that picture."

Stewart smiled enigmatically and shoved the pipe back into his mouth, the stem clattering against his back molars.

Leung nodded. "Go on, please."

Stewart pulled a box of wooden matches from his pocket, relit his pipe, and dropped the spent match into a glass dish on the table between them. "Well, that was pretty much it. After three-quarters of an hour he suddenly stood up, hurled his brush and palette tray over the back fence into the next fellow's yard, turned around, saw me, and told me to fuck off and mind my own business. Then he went back inside, the canvas still sitting there on his easel, and I didn't see him for another week. Meanwhile the canvas sat out there the whole time, and the rain gradually ruined what he'd done."

Ellie said, "I understand he was difficult to get along with."

Stewart laughed. "Oh, yes. The next time I saw him was in a discount store down at the far end of Princess Street. He was buying these plastic jars of crappy acrylic paint. The stuff kids use. I was behind him in line and I said, 'I believe we're neighbours.' He just looked at me—you could smell the booze coming out of every pore on his body—and he didn't say a word. So I said, 'A friend of mine's a sales rep for a big art supply distributor. I've got a lot of tubes of pigment and jars of linseed oil you're welcome to have. Unless you prefer the acrylic.' He just paid for his junk and took off without a word. But that afternoon I went down to the basement and filled a box with this stuff, and some really nice brushes and a couple of canvas panels, and took them over. At least he said 'thank you' before he slammed the door in my face."

Stewart puffed out smoke and leaned forward to set the pipe down in the glass dish. "I just kept going over. Cindy, my first wife, would make up these casseroles and baked rolls and stuff, and I'd take them over. Eventually he asked me in for a drink. His apartment was upstairs, at the back. A single room with a shared bathroom in the hall and a tiny kitchen just inside the door. When he opened the fridge to put in Cindy's tuna thing, or whatever it was, I could see there was almost nothing inside. There was a bare mattress on the floor, a beat-up old armchair he'd probably brought in from the side of the road, and the rest was his work. Do you know what I mean? Canvas after canvas, leaning in piles against the wall. The kitchen table was covered with materials and whatnot. I asked if I could take a look, and he just shrugged. He was pouring himself a drink. I didn't ask for one. I walked up to a stack of canvases and flipped through them. I was surprised by what I was looking at. I said, 'There's some very good work here,' and he said, 'You think so?' I thought he was being sarcastic, but when I looked at him I saw it wasn't so. Not at all. He was anxious for approval.

"I explained what I did for a living, that I was a professor of art history and conservation at Queen's, and that I wasn't just giving him a lay opinion. I said, 'What I see here is a rather stunning example of romantic modernism. Do you know what I mean by that?' He shrugged and said, 'You tell me.' So I said, 'The treatment of these subjects, this night landscape, this city street, the back yard, it all conveys a very distinct sense of significance in the commonplace. Imbuing the ordinary with great mystery. And the sense of inevitable failure that's essential to the romantic sentiment. Art as a failed instrument of social salvation. The loneliness of seeing things the way no one else sees them.' When I finally came up for air, he shook his head and smiled at me for the first time. I'd made a friend."

"You helped him get through rehab to control the alcoholism, didn't you?"

"Yes. My father was an alcoholic. That's why I never consume the stuff myself. Whenever I wasn't on campus I tried to spend some time with him. You know, policing the booze, talking about his work, keeping him focused on stuff other than taking that next drink. Cindy didn't like him, and it was a source of friction between us. Well, one of many. But I could see he was making progress. His painting got even better over the next year or so, he started eating proper food and sleeping at night instead of whenever the booze knocked him out, and he talked more and more to me about his past in Toronto, his studies at OCA, the failed showing at the Isaacs in 1961, his stubborn insistence that the ordinary held great significance, and his hatred of op art and pop art and all the facile stuff that was still very popular then despite the fact that the sixties were well behind us by that time.

"I found him a part-time job framing pictures in a downtown gallery run by an old girlfriend of mine. He washed dishes in restaurants and swept floors in an office building, and for the next three years spent all his earnings on his rent, food, and canvases and paint.

"Of course, his work was up and down. Some of it was junk, so those canvases quickly got recycled. Some of it was incredible, though, and I convinced him to set a few pieces aside. It was all building up, of course, to the series of paintings that told us both he'd reached a level that was as good as anything I'd ever seen in contemporary art."

"Oh?" Leung frowned. "Are you referring to *The Fire in a Boy's Heart*?"

"No, no, no!" Stewart grabbed his pipe and rapped it

sharply against the edge of the dish, emptying its spent coals. "Well before that. Quite a bit before that." He took a pouch of tobacco from his pocket and refilled the bowl of his pipe, lighting it with quick, sharp movements that betrayed his sudden irritation. "That piece is fine, it's wonderful, but its reputation is rather inflated by the fact that a prime minister of Canada bought it and hung it at Harrington Lake. No, I'm talking about a series of nudes and portraits he painted in 1977. His definitive work."

Leung frowned. "A series of nudes."

Stewart stared at him for a moment. "You're confused," he said suddenly, "and I understand why. The paintings I'm referring to were never shown. Never sold. Darius held on to them, kept them private. I was lucky enough to see them a few times before he moved from Kingston, and of course he'd talk about them at length. Then he had a falling out with the model, the paintings disappeared, and he never mentioned them again. Not in my hearing, certainly, and never in any interviews he gave after he became prominent."

"How many paintings are we talking about?"

"No idea, but I saw at least half a dozen. There might have been more."

"What do you think happened to them?"

"Not sure." Stewart fidgeted. "After he went up to Ottawa he moved around a bit, and had another period of homelessness, so God only knows. I just pray he didn't destroy them in a drunken rage one night. He did that sometimes, you know. Some remarkable work was lost to us that way."

Everyone was silent for a moment. Ellie watched Leung jot a few notes in the notebook on his lap. She said to Stewart, "You said there was a falling out between Lane and this model?"

Stewart nodded. He picked up his pipe, then changed his mind and put it down again. "They started a relationship not long after she began modelling for him. She was a former art student of mine who was doing an MFA and was modelling on the side for extra money. She was twenty-two and he was thirty-eight. It went on for six months or so, then she got involved with someone else and broke it off. He didn't take it very well. The police were called a couple of times because of all the shouting and things breaking in the middle of the night. This wasn't next door to me, I should explain. By this time he was living in a two-bedroom apartment on Johnson Street. Anyway, to make a long story short, after the relationship ended the paintings disappeared and he moved on to other things."

"*The Fire in a Boy's Heart*," Leung said.

Stewart tipped his head to one side, as though acknowledging a student's good guess. "*Now* we can talk about the monster painting."

Leung said, "You were the gallery director, weren't you?"

"Interim director." He looked at Ellie. "We're referring to the Agnes Etherington Art Centre, in case you're not very familiar with Kingston or the Queen's University campus. It's a lovely facility, a nineteenth-century house willed to the university to be used as an art gallery. It contains over thirteen thousand works in its permanent collection, some going back as far as the fourteenth century. It was my privilege to serve on an interim basis in 1979 while they were conducting a search for a permanent replacement for the previous director. I hardly felt I was taking advantage of my position to arrange for several of Darius's works to be included in exhibits of local artists during that time. I encouraged him to attend other events at the centre, introduced him to people, and just generally talked him up. He began to circulate a bit in that circle, and despite being a taciturn son of a bitch people started warming to him. He sold a few pieces and things got better for him. Then in 1981 Trudeau bought his now-famous painting, and things were never the same."

"He moved to Ottawa not long afterward, didn't he?" Leung asked.

Stewart fingered his beard. "He did. The Gibson Gallery ran an exhibit of his work, playing up the Trudeau angle, and suddenly the collectors were taking an interest. The money started flowing, and Walter Gibson convinced him to move up to the capital. He rented the upstairs of a rowhouse on MacLaren Street and went to work for Gibson. The commissions came in from all directions, and his bank account went through the roof. In 1984 he became an RCA, and suddenly he was everybody's darling. The critics couldn't stop talking about him, and the collectors were lining up for whatever fell off his easel."

"RCA?" Ellie asked.

"Royal Canadian Academy of Arts," Leung explained. "He was elected as a member in 1984." To Stewart he said, "Why did he leave Gibson?"

"Well, he was with him for sixteen years." Stewart frowned. "The old man finally retired and sold the studio. Darius was drinking again by this time, unfortunately, and it went from bad to worse. The new owners dumped him; he got arrested a couple of times for disorderly conduct; he sank all his money into a big house in Rockcliffe and promptly lost it; and then eventually he ended up in the streets again. The rise and fall of Darius Lane."

Stewart watched Leung writing in his notebook and added, "That's about as much as I know of the Darius Lane story. If you want background on how he met Constance Spencer and put his life back together one last time, you'll probably want to talk to Madeleine Menzies. She's been the one working with him over the last few years. Her gallery's called The March Hare. In the Glebe somewhere."

"I see," Leung said. "Thanks."

"It's our understanding," Ellie said, "that Lane was approached by someone just before his death about a possible commission. A woman by the name of Rosa Battaglia, who runs a gallery in Ottawa. Do you know anything about her?"

Stewart snorted. He stared at her as though she were a very dull student indeed. "What? Haven't we been talking about her this entire time?"

"I don't understand."

Stewart clapped a hand on his knee. "Good lord, did I not make it clear? It was she and her husband, John Scott, who bought Gibson out and promptly dumped Darius out into the street. Which was completely predictable, of course. Darius and Rosa fought like cats and dogs whenever they saw each other. They had some epic battles over the years, believe me. Burton and Taylor stuff. Over the top."

"They knew each other, then? Before Battaglia and her husband bought the gallery?"

Stewart stared at her for a moment, lips parted, then he raised a hand. "I'm very sorry. I haven't told the story very well at all, have I? You see, when I talked about that series of nudes which marked the turning point for Darius and the model he had the fling with that year in Kingston, in 1976? That was Rosa Battaglia, of course. The one and only."

Leung sat forward. "She was the model? For this mysterious series of paintings?"

Stewart nodded slowly, a wise expression on his face. "She broke his heart. He never forgave her. They never fell out of love, I don't think, but I know one thing for sure."

"What's that?" Leung asked.

"They hated each other with a passion."

chapter TWENTY-SEVEN

After Kevin had dropped the kids off at Barb's house in Brockville, he drove up to the detachment office and found Bishop at his desk doing paperwork on the Roberts arson case.

"Carty's idea," the stocky detective groused, pushing his shirtsleeves up higher on his biceps. "Seconded by Patterson and Mitchum. They want everything done pronto so they can process the old guy before he changes his mind on a guilty plea."

Kevin made a face. "I have to go up to the Pool house first; then I'll come back and give you a hand."

"Pool? Why?"

Kevin held up the prescription bottle containing Jeremy's medication and gave it a shake. "He lost his meds in my car."

"Big fucking deal. We're supposed to get the kid's interview report done this afternoon too. Take his shit up to him later."

Kevin shook his head. "Better not. He's already missed a dose, and I don't want us to be liable if he does something and it gets blamed on the meds."

"Come on, he could miss a whole frigging day and it wouldn't matter."

"Better safe than sorry." Kevin slipped the bottle back into his pocket.

"Just don't take all day." Bishop curled his lip at the monitor in front of him. "This shit doesn't get done all by itself."

When Kevin arrived at the Pool residence, he saw that there was already a vehicle parked at the top of the driveway behind Larry's Ford Ranger. He pulled up behind the car and got out, looking at the Government of Ontario and Community and Social Services logos on the door. He heard voices coming from the back of the house, angry and strident, punctuated by the steady barking of the dog.

As he walked around the house he encountered a tense, confrontational standoff. Jeremy Pool stood beneath the large Manitoba maple tree with a red plastic gas can in his hand. Larry lay on the grass nearby, propped up on one elbow, head down, vomit drooling from his mouth. Confronting them was a woman in her forties, short brown hair, brown suit jacket and skirt, a clipboard and file folder held protectively to her chest.

"What the fuck more do you want from us?" Jeremy was screaming. "Can't you leave us alone?"

"You're not helping your father's case in the slightest!" the woman shouted back.

"Ma'am!" Kevin called out, hurrying forward, "OPP. What's going on?"

"This young man's not helping his father's reassessment in the slightest! The ministry—"

Jeremy lunged forward, sloshing gasoline from the can at her.

The woman shrieked, dancing backward. The gasoline slopped on the ground, missing her.

"You cut his benefits back just because I had a part-time job!" Jeremy yelled. "We're starving out here—"

"If you wouldn't feed him alcohol all the time—"

Kevin was still a good twenty metres away from them, and as he hurried across the back yard, it seemed to happen in slow motion. Jeremy lifted the gas can over his head, poured gasoline over himself, and flicked a lighter. With a puffing sound, the gasoline vapours ignited. Jeremy was covered from the waist up in a coat of fire.

The woman screamed and ran off in the direction of her car.

Cursing, Kevin stripped off his jacket and covered the remaining distance between himself and Jeremy in a blind rush. He caught Jeremy in his jacket and tackled him to the ground. Gripping him in a tight bear hug, he rolled back and forth, back and forth, back and forth.

After an eternity, he stopped. Jeremy lay on top of him, shrouded in Kevin's smoking, ruined jacket. Kevin could feel the boy's chest shuddering, and he could hear a faint racking sound. Kevin stared up at the sky for a minute, aware of a searing pain in his chest and neck. He must have been burned.

Was the kid all right?

He rolled his head to the side, wanting to ask the woman for help. No, he could hear the sound of a car speeding away, down on the highway. She hadn't stayed.

Was his cellphone in his jacket? Yes; it was probably fried.

No. He remembered putting it into his pants pocket. Front right.

He moved his right arm. Pain rippled up his forearm. He groped in his pocket and, after a bit of a rest, pulled out the phone.

God, he thought, *this damned thing better still work.*

The sun went behind a cloud, and it got dark. The phone slipped from his fingers, but he forgot to try to find it again.

chapter TWENTY-EIGHT

Ellie and Leung picked up sandwiches to go and ate on the way from Perth to Ottawa. They both agreed that Rosa Battaglia was now definitely a person of interest in their case, but Leung wanted to talk to Madeleine Menzies, the owner of the March Hare Gallery, before approaching Battaglia. He wasn't really sure which woman might have been more interested in getting her hands on the Lane nudes Charlie Stewart had described as being so important, but if it was Rosa Battaglia he would prefer to make a move only when he'd gathered as much information as possible about her. Of the two, she was the one who was known to have fought with Lane in the past, according to Stewart.

They passed through Kanata on Highway 417 and crossed the railway bridge between Eagleson Road and Moodie Drive that was dedicated to the memory of OPP Constable John F. Montgomery, who died in a motorcycle accident while on duty in 1931. As they reached the merger with Highway 416, Ellie's cellphone buzzed. She keyed the hands-free device. "March."

"Ellie, it's Scott." Patterson's voice sounded stressed. "Are you still in Ottawa?"

"On the Queensway right now. You're on car speaker with me and Dennis. What's up?"

"We've made an arrest for the earlier barn fires. The suspect is a twenty-two-year-old named Jeremy Pool."

Ellie glanced at Leung, who nodded. "We recognize the name. Kevin mentioned him yesterday."

"He's confessed to the first three fires," Patterson said, "but swears he had nothing to do with Spencer Farm. Bishop's doing a follow-up, but if you and Dennis are chasing a lead up there, keep going. I don't think this kid is good for it."

Ellie glanced at the clock on the dashboard. "Would Kevin be able to meet us up here in an hour or so? There are a couple of interviews Dennis needs to do in the city this afternoon, and I should get back down there with you."

"Uh, that's another reason I called. Kevin went out to the Pool residence but there was an incident. The kid set fire to himself, and Kevin was burned putting the flames out."

"Oh my God," Ellie said. "Is Kevin all right?"

"Second-degree burns to his upper chest, the right side of his neck, and on his right forearm. I'm here with him right now at the Smiths Falls hospital. They're telling me he won't need to be admitted. Tough bastard. They're treating him as we speak. When he comes out I'm sending him home."

Ellie sensed between the lines that Patterson had already argued the point with Kevin and won. "Is anyone else available this afternoon?"

"I'm sorry, Ellie. Yesterday's insanity has put us in a hole this afternoon. I've got Carty working on that other thing while I'm up here with Kevin and Bishop. Help's coming, but not until tomorrow morning."

Patterson was referring, of course, to the boat theft that had turned into a prolonged hostage-taking incident. The crime unit would be dealing with the aftermath of that one for days. Ellie needed to sit down with Patterson and decide which additional resources to add to the Lane case while Carty and the others were temporarily drawn away on the other thing. However, she felt a sense of momentum growing in their investigation following the interview with Charlie Stewart, and she was hesitant to let the rest of the day slip away.

"All right. Dennis and I will continue on up here this afternoon. We'll meet with Lane's assistant and the OPS, and then do another interview before we come back down." She touched the brakes and changed lanes to avoid a slow-moving tractor trailer in front of her. The Parkdale Avenue exit, which would take them to their Parliament Hill meeting with Lane's assistant, was coming up in another kilometre. "Are you sure Kevin doesn't need to stay in the hospital overnight?"

"The doctor said no and Walker said hell no, so I guess that's a no."

"All right. Keep me informed."

Ellie ended the call and left the Queensway, following Parkdale Avenue north to the Sir John A. Macdonald Parkway, which ran along the river. After passing two bridges that led across the river into Gatineau, the Parkway merged with Rideau Street. Ellie drove a few blocks up to Vittoria Street where she turned left at the Confederation Building and drove back to a parking lot reserved for vehicles on Parliament business. She threw an OPP placard on the dashboard and they got out.

Ellie led the way along the crest of the hill, following a paved pathway behind the West Block. They reached an oval area in the centre of which was a large bronze statue of the late Prime Minister Lester B. Pearson. A few tourists stood nearby, cellphones in hand, taking selfies and admiring the view of the river behind them.

Ellie walked over to a man sitting on a bench by himself. He was eating a sandwich and reading a bound report of some kind on his lap. Seeing the Parliament Hill identification card hanging around his neck on a red lanyard, she held up her badge and identification and said, "Are you Gilles Morin?"

The man looked up at her and nodded. He put the sandwich down on a paper bag next to him on the bench, pulled a bookmark from the back of the report and stuck it in at the page he'd been reading, set the book aside, put the remnants of his sandwich into the paper bag, wiped his lips and fingers on a napkin, and stood up, offering his hand.

"Detective Inspector March." He shook her hand and looked at Leung.

"This is Detective Constable Leung," Ellie said. "Thank you for meeting with us. We won't take up much of your time."

Morin shook Leung's hand as Ellie sat down on the bench next to his report. The title on the red-and-white cover was *Libérer l'innovation pour stimuler la mise à l'échelle et la croissance* which, when Ellie applied her high school French, translated as *Freeing Innovation to Stimulate Growth and Understanding*, or something like that.

"I've already spoken to the RCMP twice," Morin said. "There isn't any new ground to cover."

He sat down next to her and put the report back on his lap. He was somewhere in his early forties. His oval-shaped head, round silver-framed glasses, receding hairline, and prominent teeth gave him the appearance of a mild-mannered turtle, but his thick neck and muscular upper body suggested he lifted weights in his spare time. He wore a navy polo shirt, neatly-pressed khaki trousers, and expensive-looking cordovan slip-ons. Everything about him projected a sense of crisp efficiency.

"We appreciate that," Leung said, moving to stand on Morin's right, out of the direct sunlight. There was no room for him to sit on the bench, but he didn't seem to mind. "We're interested in anything you can tell us about Senator Lane and how he conducted himself." Leung took out his notebook and pen. "I don't really know much about senators and what they do."

Morin smiled humourlessly. "They do pretty much whatever they feel like doing."

"Was Senator Lane around the office very much?"

"Not really." Morin tilted his head to one side. "But that might give you the wrong impression. He put as much time into his responsibilities as any other senator. More, in most cases."

"I see." Leung wrote something down.

"He sat on the Social Affairs, Science and Technology Committee. He attended all the meetings. He presented reports that he wrote himself in longhand and I typed and printed for him. He met with other committee members outside the chamber to lobby support for his various positions, and he did all the other things you'd want an unelected representative of the public to do on the taxpayers' dollar."

"How did he get along with his colleagues?"

Morin shrugged. "He was *not* popular."

"Did he have political enemies?"

"He had political opponents." Morin adjusted his glasses. "Some of them disliked him rather intensely. As his parliamentary affairs advisor, I experienced it first hand, believe me. But it's ludicrous to suggest that someone on the Hill took their detestation of the senator to such an extreme. It's just not a rational consideration. I told the RCMP that. Now I'm telling you."

Leung said nothing, his eyes briefly dropping as he continued to write in his notebook. Then he frowned and said, "Did he receive threats?"

"Hunh." Morin's lips peeled back. "I gave them copies of the letters. At least one a week, sometimes more. The occasional phone call."

"What was the nature of the threats?"

"They varied. 'Bloodsuckers like you will be squashed under the heel of capitalism.' I liked that one. 'Go back to the dumpster you crawled out of before you get a .44 between the eyes.' That one was written in red Sharpie with drops of red paint that were supposed to look like blood. 'Be careful crossing the road because I'm going to run you over with my truck.' That sort of thing."

"You reported these to security?" Ellie asked.

"They all get sent directly to the RCMP, each one. What they do with them I don't know. I never hear back. They're all time wasters, in effect."

"Was there anything recent," Leung asked, "that gave you cause for concern?"

Morin shook his head. "As I've already told the others, nothing. This whole thing is absurd. He was like a lightning rod for the one per centers and their cronies who oppose social reform to address the problems facing the homeless and the poor people in this country, yes. He was so contentious and argumentative that he himself threatened to start fist fights in town hall meetings or even in the corridors outside the chamber, more than once. He always wanted to fight. It was crazy. He had no political sophistication, which I guess was his strength, really. He argued from the heart. Lots of people on the Hill wished—prayed—he'd just go away and never come back. But not like this. God, no."

"He didn't mention to you any conflicts he might have had over the past week that happened off the record? Something other than a letter or phone call or in a meeting?"

"No. Nothing."

"Does the name Battaglia mean anything to you?"

Morin thought for a moment. "No. I don't know anyone by that name."

"You're sure?"

Morin frowned. "Having a superb memory for names and faces is part of what I do, sir. When I say the name is unfamiliar to me, you can take it to the bank."

"All right." Undisturbed by Morin's acerbity, Leung looked at Ellie.

She stood up. "Thank you for your time, Mr. Morin. We appreciate your candour."

"No problem." Morin rose and held out his hand to her. "In fact, candour is something I learned to appreciate while working for Senator Lane. He was the most candid human being I've ever met."

"So I understand." She watched him pick up his sandwich bag and walk away.

"Nothing," Leung remarked, putting away his notebook and pen.

"No." Ellie took a deep breath and let it out slowly. Morin had added nothing at all to what they'd seen in the RCMP report summarizing their interviews with him during their threat assessment. The meeting had ended up being nothing more than another box checked off on the list of things to cover.

As Leung headed back toward the car, Ellie paused in front of the statue of Pearson. The fourteenth prime minister of Canada sat upright in a comfortable office chair, his legs crossed, his hands folded, his bronze stare taking in the city that sprawled before him. She looked at his cap-toed lace-up shoes, his cuffed trousers, his wide-lapelled jacket and his trademark bow tie. Although he'd died two years before she was born, she'd learned about him in school and was aware of his reputation as an international leader who'd won a Nobel Peace Prize for his work in creating the United Nations peacekeeping force. He was said to have had a casual and friendly nature, not unlike the current prime minister who was expecting so much of her.

Lowering her gaze, she followed Leung back to the car.

chapter TWENTY-NINE

Their meeting at OPS headquarters was short and to the point, much as Ellie had expected it to be. Deputy Chief Carrière greeted them, repeated to Ellie his support, and passed them off to Inspector Ted Worthy, in charge of their Major Crimes Unit. Worthy added his own pledge of assistance and introduced them to Detective Constable Susan Brannigan, explaining that Brannigan would assist them in any way possible. With that, he hurried off to another meeting.

"Sorry," Brannigan said as the conference room emptied out. "It's a really bad day around here. One of our constables was seriously injured in a traffic accident this morning in Barrhaven."

"I'm very sorry to hear that," Ellie said.

"It's a head injury," Brannigan said. "We're waiting for him to come out of surgery. Everyone's pretty stressed."

"How did it happen?" Leung asked.

"He was responding to a fender bender at a busy intersection. Someone ran a red light and front-ended his cruiser."

"That's terrible."

"The driver's elderly. She's on life support. It's a disaster all around."

Leung spent a few minutes giving Brannigan an overview of the Lane case. He then explained what they might need from her in terms of interview rooms, recording equipment, and other arrangements should they need to question someone in more formal settings. He mentioned Rosa Battaglia and Madeleine Menzies as persons of interest they wanted to talk to, explaining that they'd just gotten the names this morning and hadn't had a chance to run them yet.

Brannigan led them out of the conference room to her desk in what was a typical detectives' bullpen in a typical police organization—noisy, cluttered, and disorganized. She found them chairs, got them seated around her desk, and tapped in her password to log back on to the computer network.

Several searches yielded Rosa Battaglia's cellphone number and home address, the address and telephone number of the Scott Gallery on Sussex Drive in which she was a partner with her husband, John Scott, and a long list of parking tickets and traffic violations, including speeding and unsafe lane changes. She'd paid every ticket and fine without an appeal, so there were no outstanding warrants on her record.

Leung called the gallery number. It rang four times and went to voice mail. The recorded message said that she was out of town on business and the gallery would be open tomorrow. He tried the cellphone number and it immediately went to voice mail.

"How about Menzies?" he asked Brannigan, who turned back to her computer screen.

Madeleine Menzies operated the March Hare Gallery on Bank Street in the Glebe district and lived in a house just around the corner from it on Third Avenue. She answered her cellphone on the second ring and told Leung she'd be at the gallery until five o'clock.

The gallery was located on the west side of the street between Fourth Avenue and Fifth. It occupied one half of a two-storey brick tenement crammed into the middle of the block between two other similar buildings. The other half belonged to a tobacco and magazine store. The doors to each half of the building were side by side; Ellie found herself reaching for the door of the tobacco shop when Leung gestured discreetly. She preceded him into the gallery.

It was much deeper than it was wide, she realized as she walked slowly across the open floor. Everything was white plaster and pale oak. The lighting was bright but without glare, and the displays were organized in such a way as to show as many pieces as possible without creating a sense of clutter. Ellie glanced at abstract paintings in bright colours, rural Canadian landscapes, and stuff someone's kid could do (or may have done). She paused by a display in the middle of the floor that featured a piece of plywood with random chess pieces and a scattered geometry set, a semi-circular thing made of glass and wood with more chess pieces, and a large Boston fern inside a pyramidal wooden frame.

"My God," she said, "I've killed more of those than I care to think about."

"I beg your pardon?" The woman standing next to Ellie smiled uncertainly. Her well-shaped teeth were as white as her short, gel-spiked hair.

"The fern. I was talking about the fern." Ellie reached into her jacket pocket for the wallet containing her badge and identification. "Is it real or fake?"

"Real. The artist, bless her heart, replaces it every second day. There's a florist the next block down. I'm Madeleine Menzies, and you must be," she peered at Ellie's ID through tinted, black-rimmed glasses, "Detective Inspector March." She straightened and shook Ellie's hand.

Leung badged her as well and said, "Thanks for seeing us." He pointed at a large painting that was hanging on the far wall. "I see you have a Lane on display."

Menzies nodded. "It's the only one I have left."

"Impressive," Ellie said, strolling over to look at the painting. It measured about a metre across and nearly two metres high, and was hanging in an expensive-looking gilt frame. It was a portrait of a mature-looking woman sitting in a large wicker chair. She wore a tweed suit and a white blouse with a collar pin at the neck. Her hands were folded in her lap, and her legs were crossed at the ankles. She was looking down and to the left, as though thinking about something very sad. There was an odd quality to the painting, as though the woman were being seen as a reflection on the surface of a calm sheet of water. It was a little unusual but very moving, Ellie thought.

"That's Connie," Menzies said, beside her again.

"Ah," Leung said. "Senator Constance Spencer?"

"Yes." Menzies adjusted the green plaid scarf around her neck and folded her arms. "You said on the phone you're investigating Darius's murder."

Leung nodded. "Is there somewhere we can talk?"

"There are some chairs in the back," Menzies said, tugging at the cuff of her denim dress. "We might as well sit down."

"It might be a good idea to lock the front door," Leung said.

"If someone comes in while we're talking, Detective Leung, I'll probably have a heart attack. We don't get walk-ins, except for people who want to buy cigarettes and pick the wrong door."

Ellie trailed behind, looking around, as Leung followed Menzies around a false wall on which were hung a series of paintings of dogs running through tall grass and across a rocky meadow. Menzies had arranged wooden chairs against the back wall, and they sat down here. Menzies took the one at the end where she would be able to see around the false wall in case anyone actually did walk into the gallery. Ellie picked up the middle chair and moved it so that she could sit facing Menzies. Leung settled down on the gallery owner's right and opened his notebook on his knee.

"We'd like to ask you a few general questions about Darius Lane if you don't mind," he began. "We talked to Professor Stewart earlier today, and he gave us a pretty good idea what Lane's life was like in Kingston before he moved up here."

"And now you want all the Ottawa gossip," Menzies said, crossing her legs.

"How long did you know him?"

"I first met Darius fourteen years ago." She gave him an odd little smile and looked up at the high ceiling above his head. "He called me an infuriating bitch and threw a half-eaten slice of pizza at me."

"Goodness."

"Yes, well, it got better after that. More or less."

"I hope so."

"It was Connie who brought him in that day. She and I hadn't met at that point. She'd called Rachel Watson in Toronto—she's a very close friend of mine, and her gallery makes a hell of a lot more money than this one does, believe me—and Rachel gave her my name. Rachel knew Darius by reputation of course, but she wasn't really in a position to handle him. She told Connie she'd be better off trying someone local and mentioned me. So Connie called, we talked, and I agreed to meet with her and the artist."

Leung frowned, adjusting his glasses. "So you met Darius Lane through Senator Spencer, is that what you're saying?"

Menzies looked at him sideways, her mouth curling up, and she suddenly slapped him on the knee. "You look like a man who needs a cup of tea. I need a cup of tea. If you're looking for the whole story, I'm going to need tea." She looked at Ellie. "Would you like tea, too?"

"I'd prefer coffee," Ellie replied, "but don't go to any trouble."

"It's no trouble." Menzies pulled a cellphone out of the pocket of her dress and speed-dialled a number. "Jenn, it's me. Could I get two large green teas"—she looked at Leung—"is that okay? Anything in it? No, both neat, and a coffee"—she looked at Ellie, who said, "Black, a teaspoon of honey."

Menzies repeated this and then asked, "Is Rudolph working today? Oh, good. Send him on down, that's a good girl."

She ended the call and put the phone away. "They're a few doors up. It'll only be a minute."

"We appreciate it," Ellie said.

"No problem. Did you like the dogs, Detective Leung?"

Leung shrugged. "They're okay, I guess."

"I saw him frowning at the pictures on the other side of the wall," Menzies said to Ellie. "The artist's a primitivist. They refer to it as naive art or folk art, but I prefer the term primitive. If it was good enough for Henri Rousseau, it's good enough for Ginette Lafleur. She's ninety-six and lives in a hunting camp north of Renfrew."

"Interesting."

Menzies laughed. "The smallest canvas lists at eight thousand. Her work has brought in more than a hundred thousand so far this calendar year. I've been showing her for six years now, and that's what she generates every year. We have about a dozen clients who are dedicated collectors of her work. I don't particularly like it myself, but it's not about me, it's about matching repeat buyers with the artists they like."

Leung shook his head, smiling.

The front door opened and a young man walked in with a tray of hot drinks and a paper bag. Menzies waved him on back. He was tall and skinny, in his early twenties, and his black jeans looked as though they'd been spray-painted on. He traded the tray and the bag to Menzies for a folded-up ten-dollar bill, blushed furiously, and hurried out.

Menzies watched him all the way up to the front and out the door, then motioned for Leung to grab the empty chair next to him and bring it around where she could put down the tray and the bag. She tore open the paper bag, which contained paper napkins and half a dozen lemon squares dusted with confectioner's sugar and maple sugar crystals. "You have to try one of these," she said to Leung, grabbing a square. "They're incredible."

He sampled one, and when his eyes widened, Ellie accepted Menzies's offer and took a bite. "You're right," she said, "they're delicious."

"Rudolph," Menzies said, helping herself to another one.

"He baked these?"

Menzies nodded as she swallowed. "He's a pastry chef. When he's not minding the cash register and making deliveries."

"He's very good." Ellie accepted a paper napkin from Menzies and dusted the sugar from her fingertips.

"He's engaged to my daughter. She owns the café. I've told him he's on probation." Menzies sipped her tea and looked at Ellie over the rim. "His parents are somewhat doltish, and I've explained to him that I won't have any of it leaking into my family. I expect to see an artist's sensibility, a great sense of humour, and complete and utter loyalty to Jenn."

"How's he doing?"

"He's on probation," she repeated, as though it were all quite obvious. "But you didn't come here to talk about him, now, did you? You want to hear about Connie and Darius."

"If you don't mind," Ellie said.

"Oh, I don't mind at all."

chapter THIRTY

"Darius Lane was a drunk," Madeleine Menzies said. "That's understood, isn't it?"

Leung nodded. "We're aware he had a chronic problem with alcohol."

"He was a drunk," she repeated firmly. "He preferred being drunk to being sober. There were long stretches when he made absolutely no effort to clean himself up. Same thing with the homelessness. There were times when he'd just as soon sleep in a doorway or a back alley as in a nice warm bed. It's a state of mind most of us can't relate to. I know I sure as hell can't."

"He was homeless when you started showing him, wasn't he?"

"That's right." She sipped her tea. "But the interesting thing is, it neither added to nor subtracted from the value of his work. Every now and again you'll see a novelty act, an artist or performer who gets brief attention because they're out on the street and trying to make something of themselves. Their work will sell a bit, then the novelty wears off and they disappear back to wherever it was they came from. Not so with Darius. His work sold, and sold well consistently, because it's absolutely stunning. People actually paid very little attention to his lifestyle or his back story. Other than the Trudeau thing, of course. I take it you're aware of *The Fire in a Boy's Heart*?"

Leung nodded.

"Good. I'd rather talk about his later work." Menzies smiled when she saw Leung's eyes drift over to the portrait of Constance Spencer. "Yes, like that. You take one look at that portrait and you know how much he cared for her, don't you?"

"Yes."

Her smile faded. "And yet he almost never showed any sign of affection, never said 'I love you,' never bothered trying to cross that gap between a man and a woman that exists when they come together at that stage of life." She winced and hid her mouth behind the cup for a moment as she drained the last of the tea and set it aside. "Sorry. I get carried away. My point is just that he was a hard man to love, never mind like, and yet Connie loved him."

"How did they first meet?" Leung asked. "Do you know?"

"Of course I do." She raised an eyebrow at him. "I heard all about it from both sides, and oddly enough, the stories matched. You're aware he lived for a while on MacLaren Street while he was showing at Gibson's and making a lot of money. Apparently he didn't drink for a while, painted some okay stuff, became an RCA, and life was good. Then old man Gibson retired, and everything went to shit. Pardon me."

Leung turned a page in his notebook. "As we understand it, his gallery was purchased by Rosa Battaglia and her husband, John Scott."

"Yes. I bought this place from her when she decided to move up in the world. Well, I bought it from her husband. She ran the gallery, but he paid for everything."

"I wasn't aware of that." Leung flipped the page back and scribbled a note.

"I don't know her all that well," Menzies said, looking at Ellie. "Darius would go on and on about her when he was particularly soused. It got rather dreary."

"There was a falling out between Lane and Battaglia," Leung prompted.

"Yes. Once she'd put herself into the big leagues with Gibson's gallery, she didn't want a drunk hanging around who might say the damnedest things at the least appropriate times, so she turfed him. They had a big argument a few days after her grand re-opening. He showed up for some event she was having. This is the gallery down on Sussex, right? Across from the American embassy. She'd taken down four or five pieces of his work and put them away in the back room. He flew into a rage. She slapped his face, and he slapped hers back. She went into the stock room and came out with his pictures. She took them outside, propped them against the wall along the sidewalk, and stuck a 'Free' sign next to them. Apparently it was a busy day. They disappeared in about thirty seconds and were never retrieved."

"Oh my God," Leung said.

Watching him shake his head as he took notes, Ellie thought Leung was probably wishing he'd been walking down Sussex Drive that particular day.

"After that, he started hitting the bottle pretty hard. He got kicked out of his MacLaren Street apartment, lost his money in bad investments, and ended up on the street."

"This would be in the year 2000, right?"

"Yes. It went on for two years." Menzies adjusted the scarf around her neck. "His work from this period is particularly hard to find. He bought cheap paint and canvas boards from the dollar store, the eight-by-ten boards you can get for a buck, and spent his time painting around the Market and Parliament Hill. He traded them for food. There was a guy up on Rideau Street, past King Edward, who had a pizzeria. He'd give Darius a slice of pizza and a Coke for one of his pictures because he felt sorry for him. Didn't have a clue about art or who Darius was or any of it. Apparently he threw most of them out."

"Oh no," Leung whispered.

"Well, he didn't care like you or I would. He just felt sorry for this homeless old guy who took his artwork so seriously, and he felt like helping out a little." She shrugged at Ellie. "There was a story about it years later, when Darius started into his social activism thing. They interviewed the guy, and he still didn't have a clue who Darius was. He admitted that he threw most of the paintings in the garbage and gave the rest to various people. He didn't know who. He didn't really care. It wasn't important to him. He was a lot more interested that Darius seemed to have made something of himself and now wanted to help other homeless people."

"So when he was painting on these dollar store boards," Leung said, "that was when he met Constance Spencer."

"That's right. When Connie met him, he was hanging around the Hill." She smiled. "That was in January 2000. A cold morning, according to Connie. She and her assistant were walking past the Centennial flame on their way to her office, which was in the Victoria Building across Wellington Street. They both had coffees in their hands, and here's this gruff-looking old man in a grubby duffel coat sitting next to the flame on a fold-up stool, painting on one of those damned eight-by-tens on his knee. He had a satchel open on the ground next to him, in the snow, with his paints and brushes and so on in it.

"Connie, being Connie, stopped for a look. She could see right away it was something extraordinary, and she was really surprised. She said something nice and he growled at her. Like a dog. Never looked away from what he was doing, never stopped working, just growled. Her assistant got nervous and started walking away but Connie, again being Connie, asked him if he would like to have her coffee, which she hadn't yet touched. He shrugged, reached out with the brush still in his hand, took the coffee, drank some of it, put it down in the snow next to him, and went back to work."

Leung smiled, too busy listening to take notes.

"She tried to get him to talk, but all he'd say was that if he didn't get this picture finished in the next half hour he wouldn't eat until tonight, so would she please mind pissing off now?" Menzies shook her head. "But Connie was never one to quit. Every morning on her walks after that she looked for him. Three days later she saw him doing a painting of the Library of Parliament and stopped again. He apparently remembered her, because this time he didn't growl. Just gave her a glance and kept on painting. She looked over his shoulder and was excited again by what she saw. You have to remember, although she was a career politician, she'd minored in Fine Arts as an undergrad, many years before, so she understood talent and experience when she saw it. Impulsively, she offered him a hundred dollars for the picture when it was done."

Leung's lips formed a soundless *oh*.

"Exactly. He told her off, in no uncertain terms. Went up one side of her and down the other, all the while still working away without missing a beat. When he finally came up for air, Connie handed him a business card and said, as calmly as you please, 'If you bring it to my office across the street when it's finished I'll gladly pay you whatever you think it's worth, or accept it as a gift, or trade it for more coffee. Your choice.' "

Leung laughed.

"She had nerve, our Connie." Menzies fingered her spiky hair. "And she was stubborn, too. Stubborn as hell, when she wanted something."

"Did Lane take her up on her offer?"

"Oh, yes. But it was because of her damned business card, not because of her. It identified her as a Liberal senator, of course, and he happened to be an admirer of Jean Chrétien, so he brought the painting over when it was done in order to talk politics with her. Social politics, of course. Why the 'little guy from Shawinigan' wasn't doing more to stand up for the little guys sleeping in the street just a few blocks from his doorstep. Connie postponed a rather important meeting to give him an hour to vent his spleen on the subject. Then he jumped up and was heading out when she said, 'Wait a minute, I haven't paid you for your painting.' 'Keep it,' he says. 'It was warm in here, and you didn't interrupt me once. That's rare.' 'For a woman?' she said, trying to be smart. 'Good lord no, for a politician. They all want to talk and not listen.' She noticed he hadn't signed the picture and asked him to do so, which he did, then off he went. She didn't recognize his name and had her assistant look it up. Once she saw that he was actually an RCA, she realized he'd had quite a career. She said it explained how articulate he was for a street person, how well-informed he was, politically speaking, and why his work was so incredible, even on cheap dollar store canvas boards."

She sipped her tea. "The point I'm trying to make is that she was hooked by him, right away. He had this damnable charisma you couldn't miss despite the bad-smelling clothes and the greasy hair. And they were only five years apart, age-wise. She was fifty-eight and had never married. Career politician, as I said."

Leung nodded, writing something down. Ellie was amused by the intensity of his interest, which reminded her of Kevin and his insatiable curiosity.

"That winter Connie kept tabs on him as much as she could," Menzies went on. "He was staying in the mission on Nicholas Street some nights, when it was really cold, but he hated the shelters and would sleep in a stairwell if he could get away with it. Anyway, she had him over to her office several times, gave him lunch, bought him a change of clothes and a new parka, and they became friendly. To call them friends at that point would be a stretch on Darius's part, because he didn't make friends, it wasn't part of who he was as a person, but Connie was able to get him to lower the barriers more and more and treat her as a human being instead of an annoyance or an obstruction to his work."

"Was he drinking at this point?" Leung asked.

"No, he wasn't. He told her later that when they met, he hadn't had anything to drink for more than four months. He kept away from it right through that first spring and summer they were together, with one or two brief lapses."

"When did they start living together?"

"Not for another two years, actually. But that first April he stayed in her apartment for a week." Menzies smiled at Leung's puzzled look. "She had to fly out west for some kind of Senate committee business, I forget what. She talked him into using her condo while she was gone. Stocked it with groceries, gave him a duplicate key and two hundred in cash for any expenses he might have, and convinced him she was worried about break-ins while she was gone. Talked him into house-sitting for her. He reluctantly agreed."

"Remarkable."

"When she got back he was already gone, but he'd stayed there the entire time. The place was spotless, the plants were watered, the dishes were done and put away, and he'd left a thank-you note on the dining room table. It explained that he'd used the money she'd left to buy canvases and paint, good stuff this time, and he'd done three pictures for her to say thanks for the week of peace and quiet. They were waiting for her in the living room. One was a view of Parliament Hill from her balcony, the second was a self-portrait he'd done using the bathroom mirror, and the third was that incredible portrait of Connie hanging over there, which he painted from memory."

"Wow." Leung shook his head, impressed.

"Wow is right. She kept all three at the condo until she passed away. Darius didn't want them, so we put them up for sale as part of her estate. The landscape went for eighty-five thousand and the self-portrait brought in one-twenty."

"Wait." Leung wagged his pen. "Is that the one where he's in his undershirt, shaving? With the little cut on his chin?"

Menzies nodded.

"My God, it's incredible. I love that painting."

"You've done your homework, haven't you?"

"I've looked at his work online." His eyes travelled back to the portrait of Constance Spencer. "To actually see it in person, though..."

"As soon as his estate is settled, that portrait of Connie is going to break the record for his work, I'm sure." She eyed it sadly.

"So there were two years between the time she met Darius Lane and when they moved in together," Leung said. "Where did he stay during that time?"

Menzies poked a finger toward the ceiling. "Here, as a matter of fact. I gave him a room upstairs. An apartment, actually. He painted in the living room. Turned it into a studio."

"This would be the period between 2002 and 2006," Leung said, "when he began the series of paintings featuring street people done with religious undercurrents, is that right?"

Menzies nodded.

"Including his *Madonna and Child*, so called?"

"Yes." Menzies saw the blank look on Ellie's face and said, "It's a painting of a priest kneeling by a homeless woman. She has a small dog in her arms. A reviewer recognized the allusion to the Madonna and Child and suggested the Church might not be very pleased. The painting got stuck with that nickname. Darius didn't like it at all because it lowered the work to the level of a parody in the eyes of some critics. It made him furious."

"Was there much interaction between Lane and Rosa Battaglia?" Ellie asked.

"None at all while he was living here. He seldom went out."

"What about the husband, John Scott?"

Menzies shook her head. "Scott never bothers with the artists. Thinks they're dilettantes and sponges. I doubt that Darius exchanged more than a few sentences with him."

"What can you tell us about him? John Scott, I mean?" Leung asked.

"They met at university, Rosa and John. He was doing an MBA at Queen's while she was getting her MFA. She was working as an artist's model on the side to make extra money, and got into a relationship with Darius, who was still in Kingston back then. They didn't get along, to put it mildly, and she ended up walking out on him and taking up with John."

Leung glanced at Ellie. "It was John Scott she left Lane for?"

Menzies nodded. "Turns out they were both originally from Hamilton. I've heard it said that his family name is actually Scotti and that both their families have some kind of connection to the Mafia down there or something, but that's not the sort of thing you ask questions about over cocktails and hors d'oeuvres, is it? Anyway, he'd done a business degree at McMaster's and had come up to Kingston to do his Master's. I always got the feeling he was there to keep an eye on Rosa for some reason, but that was just me, I guess."

"John Scott and Darius Lane didn't get along," Ellie said.

"No. As I said, John hates all artists. He thinks they're all a bunch of leeches, fakes, and drunks, and he doesn't mind saying so. He's really an obnoxious loudmouth, when it comes right down to it. A creepy and rather scary loudmouth."

"And yet he's fronting all this money for art galleries and the rest of it."

"For Rosa's sake. It's her thing, even if it's not his. And she works at it twenty-four/seven. Makes money, which keeps John happy. The only thing that makes him happy, as far as I can tell."

"Did he ever argue with Lane, confront him, anything like that?"

Menzies shrugged. "No. As I said, they were seldom in the same room together."

Ellie looked at Leung with a question in her eyes. He nodded and said, "There's one other thing I'd like to ask you about, if you don't mind."

"Not at all," Menzies replied.

"This morning, Professor Stewart told us about a series of paintings Lane did in Kingston when Rosa Battaglia was posing as his model. Do you know anything about them?"

She turned her head sideways and stared at him for a moment. "What did he say, exactly?"

"Well, uh, not much," Leung replied, caught off guard. "Just that they were a series of nudes and portraits painted in 1977, and that they are said to have marked his turning point as an artist. The paintings in which he discovered himself, so to speak. They were never shown, never sold, and may not still exist."

"I see." Menzies stared at the wall for a moment. "He said he'd actually seen them, himself?"

"Yes."

"Interesting."

Leung frowned. "Why is that?"

Menzies shrugged. "I sometimes wondered whether they were just part of the Lane legend, an urban myth or something. Rumours had circulated, of course, but Darius never talked about them. He refused to discuss that period of his life with anyone. If they do exist, they'd be worth a few pennies, believe me. Collectors would be lined up down the street, cheque books in their hands, waiting to outbid each other."

Ellie put her empty coffee cup down on the floor beside her chair. "If they surfaced, would they be sold through here?"

"I would certainly think so," she replied, tight lipped. "I had a long-term agreement with Darius. At his request. Once he saw I could sell his work with little problem, he wanted it that way so he didn't have to bother with the business side of it at all. I've already spoken to my lawyer, and she assures me the estate has to honour that agreement. So that means I have right of first refusal for any other works of his that are considered part of his estate. If Charlie Stewart says they were never sold, then, yes. They should come through me."

"You discussed these paintings with your lawyer?" Leung asked.

"No, no. Not them specifically. Just any other canvases that might emerge as part of his estate. In general. Like I said, I didn't really believe the Kingston nudes actually existed."

"Okay." Leung clicked his ballpoint pen and looked at Ellie.

"We appreciate your time," Ellie said, standing up. "Tell Rudolph he has a future as a pastry chef. Hopefully as a son-in-law, too."

Menzies stood up and shook hands with her. "Time will tell."

"I'll call if I have any follow-up questions," Leung said, putting his notebook away.

"No problem." Menzies shook his hand and showed them up through the gallery to the front door. As she held it open for them, she caught Leung's eye. "Do me a favour, will you?"

"If I can." Leung stopped in the doorway. Out on the sidewalk, Ellie turned back to listen.

"Catch the person who did this to Darius, will you? This horrible thing?"

"That's our intention, Ms. Menzies."

She ran the tip of her finger under her eye to clear away a tear. "He was an irascible old bastard, but I was very, very fond of him."

"I understand," Leung said, joining Ellie out on the sidewalk.

chapter THIRTY-ONE

It was Janie who answered the door when Ellie knocked a few minutes after eight o'clock that evening. Her grey track pants and t-shirt were spattered with spaghetti sauce and splashed with bath water. She flung open the door, nodded, and stomped back up the stairs. As Ellie stepped inside she could hear Janie yelling at Caitlyn to get back into the tub and at Brendan to get back into bed.

Ellie stopped at the top of the stairs. The kitchen was on her left, the tiny dining room was straight ahead, the corridor to the bedrooms was on her right. The living room was accessible either through the kitchen or the dining room. She could hear the television and thought that Kevin might be in there, so she went straight ahead, not wishing to risk the kitchen with Janie on the warpath and the housework apparently not yet done for the evening.

She found Kevin in his recliner, feet up, eyes closed, television remote in his hand. He wore an unbuttoned short-sleeved shirt that exposed the bandages on his chest, neck, and forearm. Redness extended up the left side of his face, but from where she stood Ellie could see no blistering there. As she looked down at him, his eyes opened.

"Oh, hi."

"Don't let me disturb you. I just wanted to see how you were doing."

"Fine. I'm fine. Just a sec." He fumbled with the remote

and muted the volume.

As he struggled to sit up in the recliner, she put out her hand. “Stay there. Just rest, I won’t be long. What did the doctor say?”

Kevin put the remote down on the side table and picked up a half-empty bottle of water. “Just superficial second-degree burns on my chest and first degree on my neck. I’ll be back in tomorrow. Won’t need to miss any time.”

“You should take a couple of days,” Ellie said, sitting on the arm of the couch across from him. “Give yourself a chance to heal.”

“I’m okay. Did you hear anything about the kid?”

“They upgraded him from serious to fair late this afternoon, and it looks like he may recover,” Ellie replied. “He’s given a statement, and so has Carol Borowski.”

“Who?”

“The woman from Community and Social Services who was there this afternoon when you got there. She’s Larry Pool’s case worker. He’d missed an appointment for reassessment of his medical condition, and she went out to investigate. Apparently the alcohol abuse is an ongoing problem.”

“I didn’t get the impression she was handling it very well.”

“She’s been suspended while they review her whole case load, apparently. The only thing in her favour at this point is that she called it in and stayed with you until the paramedics got there.”

“She did? I thought she took off. I’m a little fuzzy on the details.”

“She claims she drove down the road until she could get reception on her phone, called 911, then came back.”

Kevin shook his head. “Whatever. You said the kid gave a statement. What did he say?”

“He confessed to the Mason, Crane, and Wierdsma fires. Said he had nothing to do with Roberts, which we now know is true, and the same for Spencer Farm. He doesn't always take his medication. When it runs out, he waits for a while before getting a refill, because of the cost. He's got a lot of problems."

"Maybe now he can get help. Maybe he and his father both can."

Ellie said nothing to this, knowing that Kevin felt bad for Jeremy Pool, despite the fires he'd set and the damage he'd caused. He was that kind of police officer.

"You did a brave thing," she said after a moment. "Trying to save his life like that."

Kevin tried to smile. "I didn't think about it. It was one of those things."

"Are you in a lot of pain?"

"It's not bad," he replied. "They gave me extra-strength acetaminophen. It seems to be helping." He tried the smile again, this time with more success. "I broke my collarbone a few years ago. That hurt a hell of a lot more than this does."

"Okay."

He took another drink of water and set it aside. "I learned something interesting about burn treatment. After Jeremy stabilizes, they'll have to do what they call debridement, which means removing infected or dead skin from the burn wounds."

"Sounds lovely."

"There are pharmaceutical products they can use to break down the dead tissue, or they can remove it surgically, or apply wet bandages and lift the pieces up on them." He licked his lips. "Here's what's interesting, though. Another option is to use bottle fly maggots."

Ellie looked at him. "Maggots."

"Interesting, huh? The maggots only consume the dead tissue." He shrugged and then grimaced. "Damn, it does hurt. Anyway, they don't offer maggot treatment at Smiths Falls. It's a little too unorthodox for them, I guess."

"I don't see why it would be," Ellie said, dryly.

"I know," he said, catching her tone, "it's just me. I can't help it. Stuff like that I just find interesting. How did Dennis make out today in Ottawa?"

"Good. We made progress." She filled him in on the interviews with Charlie Stewart and Madeleine Menzies.

"Dennis did a good job on the victimology," Kevin said.

"Agreed. He's very thorough. Now the next step is to talk to Rosa Battaglia and her husband, John Scott. I think we're getting very close to the answer." She made a face. "I wanted you up there this afternoon working with Dennis. But this happened, instead."

"He and I can pick it up again tomorrow."

Ellie paused, looking at the muted television. The department had followed protocol and contacted the provincial Special Investigations Unit this afternoon to report Kevin's incident, as required when an injury occurs during an interaction between police and a member of the public. The signed statements of Carol Borowski, Jeremy, and Kevin were then faxed to the SIU, and several long hours had passed while they waited for word to come back on whether the independent civilian agency would launch an investigation.

When the response finally came, they were able to breathe a collective sigh of relief. Given that all the statements agreed Kevin's actions had not contributed to Jeremy's suicide attempt and that no criminal charges against Kevin would be contemplated, the SIU had advised that they would not be investigating the incident. The way was cleared for him to return to work.

"I understand the doctor said you could return to duty as long as you're up to it. You're taking the antibiotics he gave you, right?"

Kevin nodded. "I've got a great immune system, anyway. I'm not prone to infections."

"Mmm. I understand you talked to your rep before you left the hospital."

"Yeah. He talked about me taking sick leave and the paperwork and a bunch of other stuff, but he knows me better than that."

Ellie raised an eyebrow.

"We play hockey together. He's seen me take a puck in the face and show up for work the next morning like nothing happened."

"This was on the job, Kevin, not on personal time."

"I know. But he and I talked to Patterson before I left the hospital. I'm going back in tomorrow."

Ellie held up a hand. "All right, all right. I give up."

Janie appeared in the kitchen doorway. "What a circus around here. He's worse than the kids. Can I get you a coffee or something?"

"No, I'm fine, thank you." A little self-consciously, Ellie pushed strands of hair away from her face.

"I've got some openings on Friday," Janie said immediately, "if you want to stop around. A quick trim would do you good."

"Thanks, Janie, but I don't think I'll have the time."

"Suit yourself. I don't bite." She disappeared back into the kitchen, where plates rattled and drinking glasses clinked together as she began to load the dishwasher.

Ellie turned back to Kevin, who was watching her with amusement.

"Don't believe her," he whispered. "Her bite's a lot worse than her bark. But she'd do a really nice job on your hair."

"I'll think about it." She looked at him, realizing that they hadn't had much of a chance to talk in several months. He'd done a very good job in the Hansen investigation last winter, and she'd been much less upset than he was when his former mentor with the now-defunct Sparrow Lake Police Service turned out to be involved. She'd talked to Scott Patterson a few times since then, and Patterson admitted that the young detective's status within the crime unit remained fairly low. Carty had emerged as the alpha dog, his military experience showing in his job performance and cool demeanour, while Kevin's progress seemed to have stalled.

"How are you finding things these days?" she asked.

"At work? All right. When Dennis came in, Patterson put him on violent crimes. I'm still helping out on that, and I'm backing up Bishop on property. Patterson calls me his utility player. He's not smiling when he says it, though."

Ellie jumped as something crashed to the floor in the kitchen. Janie swore, and something else banged.

"I'd better get going," she said to Kevin.

"Good idea. I don't have an extra helmet that would fit you."

She patted his arm and stood up. Once again she decided that the dining room was the safer route to take and, waving to Kevin, walked quietly through the door.

She paused at the kitchen door, considering whether it was wise to say a polite goodbye to Janie, but she was crouched in front of the dishwasher, cursing softly at something or other that seemed to be wedged inside. Ellie decided that discretion was the better part of valour. She let herself out the side door, closing it quietly behind her, and walked on cat's-feet down the driveway to her car.

chapter THIRTY-TWO

When Dennis volunteered to do the driving up to Ottawa the next morning, Kevin didn't argue. Despite assuring Scott Patterson and Tom Carty that he was fine and that it was a waste of resources not to let him contribute to such a high-profile investigation when it was just gaining momentum, the truth of the matter was that he hadn't slept well last night and he felt a little beat up today.

Thankfully, the redness on the side of his face had faded a little, to the point that it looked like an uneven patch of sunburn. Effectively, it was no more serious than that. The burns on his chest were somewhat worse, though, and it had been painful when Janie replaced the dressings for him before breakfast. She'd been surprisingly gentle and sympathetic, and Kevin had appreciated the break from Hurricane Janie. Just the same, even her careful fingers had not been able to avoid causing Kevin some serious moments of discomfort. At the breakfast table, he took three acetaminophen tablets with his orange juice before joining Caitlyn and Brendan in a heaping bowl of Froot Loops.

At the detachment office he'd sat in on a brief huddle with Leung, Carty, Patterson, and Ellie before heading out the door. Mark Allore had been slated to join the investigation full time, but his arrival had been delayed by a court appearance that was taking longer than expected, so Carty reluctantly agreed that Kevin should accompany Leung up to Ottawa. His reluctance, Kevin believed, had less to do with his health than with Carty's opinion of his abilities.

On the way, Leung filled him in on what he'd discovered about the background of Rosa Battaglia's husband, John Scott. "The gallery owner, Madeleine Menzies, said something about his real name being Scotti and that he was from Hamilton. Turns out both his family and Battaglia's have known connections to the local Mafia down there. The ones from the south of Italy."

"Sure," Kevin said, "the 'Ndrangheta. I've read about them."

"From Calabria. Anyway, Scott started his own real estate business from scratch and now he's worth eight figures. According to Bill Merkley, he doesn't seem to have any active connection to his family in Hamilton, business-wise. Neither does Battaglia, for that matter."

Kevin nodded. He remembered reading a news story a year ago about a combined special forces enforcement operation in Hamilton that led to the arrest of several members of this organization for drug trafficking and weapons offences. While their activities occasionally flared into violence—and arson, Kevin suddenly remembered—they normally preferred to operate well under the radar with modest, discreet dealings. He wondered if John Scott, a.k.a. Scotti, might be operating so far under the radar that intelligence hadn't picked up on him before now.

"Wasn't there a house fire or a car bombing down there not too long ago involving one of the 'Ndrangheta families?"

"Yeah, but not involving either the Scottis or Battaglias. Still," he glanced at Kevin, "fire's fire. Right?"

"I guess so."

When they reached Ottawa, Leung took the Nicholas Street exit off the Queensway only to discover that traffic had been reduced to a single lane because of ongoing construction. It took forever for them to crawl northward past the Ottawa Mission, and to work their way down into the Byward Market area, where they left the car on the rooftop level of a parking garage and walked three blocks to Rosa Battaglia's gallery on Sussex Drive, across from the United States embassy building.

The gallery was closed and the lights were off. Kevin looked through the front window. The art on display looked interesting, but unfortunately their person of interest was nowhere to be seen. He and Leung walked down to the end of the block and rounded the corner onto Murray Street. A narrow alley ran behind the buildings facing Sussex Drive. They walked up until they reached the rear entrance to the gallery. Leung pounded on the door with his fist, but no one responded. Kevin took a few pictures of the layout with his cellphone, and then they went back to the car.

Behind the wheel, Leung shoved the keys in the ignition and took out his notebook. Looking up the contact numbers for Rosa Battaglia that had been included in her file, he dialled the gallery number first. After four rings it went to voice mail. He tried her cellphone number and it went immediately to voice mail.

Next on their itinerary was Rosa Battaglia's home address, which turned out to be in Rockcliffe Park, an exclusive neighbourhood in the east end of the city along the Ottawa River. Leung turned off the Sir George-Etienne Cartier Parkway onto Princess Avenue, a narrow, two-lane street without sidewalks that circled above Rideau Hall, the official residence of the Governor General of Canada, and Rideau Cottage, where the prime minister and his family currently lived while 24 Sussex Drive, the official residence of the prime minister, was being renovated.

At a Y-intersection Leung stopped and eased left onto Lisgar Road, passing an enormous gated estate that sat between the branches of the Y.

"Look at that place," Leung said, frowning at some kind of crest on the stone gatepost.

"Wait," Kevin said, "that's the crest of Norway. I know what this place is. It's Crichton Lodge, the residence of the Norwegian ambassador."

"Man." Leung shook his head. "I knew I should've gone into foreign affairs instead of law enforcement."

"Roger that."

They both gawked through the trees and shrubbery, trying to catch a glimpse of the mansion, until Kevin nudged Leung's arm and pointed. "Bike."

Leung forced his eyes back to the road and eased around a cyclist who had just emerged from the next driveway. The house from which he'd come, a two-storey family home with attached garage, was modest compared to the place next door, but Kevin suspected it was probably worth well over a million dollars.

Leung pulled up at a stop sign and slid around the corner onto Mariposa Avenue. The streets continued to be narrow and lined with trees on either side, as though they were driving in an actual park instead of a city neighbourhood.

"This is like another world," Kevin said. "There are no sidewalks, Dennis. On any of these streets."

"People up here are too damned rich to walk." A black passenger van with red diplomatic licence plates passed them, the driver giving them a quick once-over as they drew abreast of each other. The two passengers seated behind him ignored them. "See what I mean? Everybody's got a driver. Their kids probably get chauffeured door to door on Halloween."

They followed Mariposa past the campus of Ashbury College, the exclusive private school. "Did you know," Kevin said, "it costs sixty thousand dollars a year to board your kid at that school? Can you imagine that?"

"Wow." Leung took an extra look, then frowned at Kevin. "How do you know all this stuff?"

"I do a lot of reading."

"You must have a lot of free time, brother."

Kevin shrugged. "That's why God invented bathrooms, Dennis. You might as well do something useful while you're in there."

Toward the end of Mariposa Avenue, Leung turned left onto Acacia Avenue and pulled into the circular driveway of a very large, single-storey home made of stone and brick. They eased up behind a Mercedes parked near the front entrance and got out. A man in a dark suit tossed a briefcase through the open driver's door onto the passenger seat of the car and turned to look at them through Wayfarer-style sunglasses.

"Are you John Scott?" Leung asked, holding up his identification and badge.

"Who wants to know?" The man closed the car door and leaned against it. He took off his sunglasses and put them in his inside jacket pocket.

"I'm Detective Constable Leung, OPP, and this is Detective Constable Walker. Are you John Scott?"

The man was tall and slender, and his iron grey hair was thick and wavy. The cuff of his suit jacket had pulled up to reveal a large wrist watch, and he wore a large diamond ring on his right hand that made Leung's bling look like a child's costume jewellery. "Yes, I am. What can I do for you?"

"We'd like to ask you a few questions about your wife, Rosa Battaglia," Leung said. "Do you know her current whereabouts?"

Scott shrugged. "No clue. Sorry."

"We need to talk to her about the murder of Darius Lane," Leung said. "Do you know when she'll be back?"

"Never, hopefully."

"This is where she lives, isn't it?"

"Not any more." Scott rolled his eyes. "Look, she's gone. I threw her out three weeks ago."

"Where's she staying, Mr. Scott?"

"I have no idea. Probably a hotel downtown, since she burned all her bridges with her friends a long time ago. Now, if you'll excuse me." Scott pushed away from his car and reached for the door handle.

"If you don't mind," Kevin said, "we need to ask you a few questions as well. What was your relationship with Darius Lane?"

Scott opened the car door. "My relationships are something you'd probably better talk to my lawyer about. Call my office and they can give you her name and number. Have a nice day, gentlemen."

"We're aware of your family background, Mr. Scott," Leung said. "Your father's name is Antonio Scotti, isn't it? Little Tony?"

Scott closed the car door again and slowly turned around. He leaned back against the car, studying Leung. The corners of his mouth rose. "Go on. This should be good."

"What was your relationship with Darius Lane?"

"I didn't have one. I barely knew the guy. He was an asshole, like most of the *artistes* Rosa hangs around with."

"When was the last time you saw him?"

"Hell, I don't know. A couple years ago now, I think. When Rosa opened the Sussex Drive place after I bought it from Gibson. She threw Lane out. It was hilarious, actually. She tossed all his stuff onto the sidewalk, and people walked off with it. One of her finer moments, I thought."

"And you haven't seen him sincc?"

Scott sighed. "Are you going to keep asking the same question, or do you have anything else? I've got meetings all morning and I don't want to be late."

"How's your business doing these days, Mr. Scott?"

"It stinks, thank you very much. Which is why I can't afford to miss any meetings this morning."

“Do you have any business connections to your family in Hamilton, Mr. Scott?” Leung asked.

Scott smiled. “Ah. There we are. The question you were working up to.”

Kevin shifted his weight. “Please answer it, Mr. Scott.”

Scott took out his sunglasses, but didn’t put them on. He looked at Kevin for a moment, as though trying to decide how seriously to take him, then pointed the sunglasses at Leung. “You’ve got nerve, asking me that question. But what the hell. You caught me in a decent mood this morning. The answer is no, I don’t have any business dealings with my *family* in Hamilton. I’m what you’d call a self-made man.” He slipped on the sunglasses. “Now, if you’ll excuse me.”

Leung straightened. “Do you have any of Darius Lane’s paintings in your possession?”

“No, I don’t.” Scott opened the car door and rested his hand on the top edge. “We did have one; Rosa had it hanging in a guest room. But she sold it about a year ago, so no. No Lanes. She’s the one who’s into art, Detective. I’ve got no use for it, myself.”

“I take it you and she are separated. What happened?”

“That’s personal and has nothing to do with Darius Lane.” He swung the car door open and got in.

“This is a murder investigation,” Kevin said. “At this point, everything has to do with Darius Lane.”

Scott shut the door, started the engine, and lowered the window. “I explained this to the Mounties. Infidelity’s part of her genetic makeup, apparently. I put up with it for years, but I just got tired and said enough’s enough.”

Leung bent down and put his hand on the chrome window sill. “Had she resumed her relationship with Darius Lane?”

Scott glanced down at Leung’s hand. “Detective, if you don’t mind.”

Leung removed his hand but continued to stare at Scott

through the open window. "Was she involved with Darius Lane again?"

Scott shook his head impatiently. "You're way off base. Lane was an old man. Rosa's a cougar, for chrissakes. Can't keep her hands off the young guys."

"You're aware that she and Lane had a dinner meeting last Sunday? Shortly before Lane's murder?"

Scott rolled his eyes. "So they told me. The Mounties. God knows why she'd think he'd do business with her again after all this time."

"She had some kind of commission in the works?"

"I don't know. I never paid any attention to what she was doing, I just kept track of the books and made sure she was making money. That was the whole point of the place, right?" He stepped on the accelerator and revved the engine, giving them a broad hint that he was about to leave.

"Just one more thing," Leung said. "Do you know anything about a series of portraits Lane painted years ago when Rosa was his model?"

Scott frowned up at him. "What do you mean? Back in Kingston, before we were married?"

"Yes. Do you know anything about those paintings, Mr. Scott?"

"Nope." His eyebrows went up. "She was his model; this was back when we were still in school. I guess that's what you're talking about. Why?"

"Do you know what became of those paintings?"

"Not a clue. Now, if you don't mind." He began to raise the window.

"Did your wife know about those paintings? Where they are now?"

"You'll have to ask her."

Kevin leaned down. "When your wife and Lane fought, was it ever physical?"

Scott just caught the question as his window closed. He

looked at Kevin, hesitated, and lowered the window again. "That's a hell of a question to ask."

"Did it get physical?" Kevin pressed. "Slapping, hitting?"

Scott snorted. "When Rosa gets into a fight, she gives a lot better than she gets, believe me. I've got the scars to prove it."

"Do you think she's capable of having killed Darius Lane if she thought the stakes were high enough?"

Scott stared at him for a long moment. Then he shifted the car's transmission into drive, accelerated out of his driveway, and roared off down the street.

Leung shook his head. "Okay, that was interesting."

Kevin clapped him on the shoulder, a little out of breath as the adrenaline rush from the encounter crested and began to recede. "Let's go find Rosa Battaglia before I keel over from exhaustion."

chapter THIRTY-THREE

They sat in the car for a few minutes while Leung recited Rosa Battaglia's phone numbers to Kevin. As they left Scott's driveway and drove down Acacia the way they had come, Kevin called the cellphone number. It went straight to voicemail.

"We'd better start calling the hotels downtown to see if she's staying at one of them," he said.

Leung turned right onto Mariposa Avenue. A man on a bicycle passed them going the other way. He wore a spandex cycling outfit and a helmet. A black unmarked Suburban followed him, trailing along like a security detail.

"Wasn't that the Governor General?" Leung frowned into his rear-view mirror.

"Could be. I've read that he's an avid cyclist." Kevin punched in the number for the gallery. The call was answered after two rings.

"Scott Gallery."

"Hello, am I speaking to Rosa Battaglia?"

"Yes, this is she." The voice was low and brusque. "To whom am I speaking?"

"Detective Constable Kevin Walker, Ontario Provincial Police. We'd like to talk to you about Darius Lane. Will you please remain at the gallery until we get there?"

"Look, I'm not open. I'm here to pick up a few things, and I'm waiting for an important call from a client. Then

I'm leaving again."

"We're about fifteen minutes away." Kevin glanced at Leung, who nodded. "We appreciate your co-operation, Ms. Battaglia."

"I already talked to the RCMP about this. I don't have anything more to say."

"Your co-operation is greatly appreciated," Kevin repeated.

The voice sighed theatrically. "If you're not here in fifteen minutes, I'm leaving."

"We'll be there. Thank you." He ended the call and looked at Leung. "How do you want to handle this, Dennis?"

"I'll take the lead," Leung replied. "Have a look around the place while I'm talking to her."

"Sounds good." He knew what Leung was thinking. If Kevin spotted something in plain sight that might give them probable cause to file for a search warrant, it would help move things along.

As they worked their way back down Sussex Drive, Kevin couldn't help but compare the neighbourhood they had just visited to the street on which he lived in Sparrow Lake. Janie's modest ranch-style house would easily fit into the front entryway of Crichton Lodge. Its value would be about ten cents on the dollar compared to what John Scott's home would bring on the open market. But it wasn't the value of the properties so much as the differences in lifestyle that struck him. Things that were difficult for Janie and him to do would be easy for people like this. Things like good day care for the kids, university tuition when they graduated from high school, the best clothing and footwear and food that money could buy. Things that he and Janie struggled for and worried about, the basic fundamentals of a normal, healthy life, were things these people took for granted.

He watched the pedestrians on the street and thought about the faces of the men he'd seen lounging in front of the Ottawa Mission as he and Leung had driven downtown from the Queensway. Ottawa was a city of haves and have-nots, a city of bleak contrasts.

Then he thought about Jeremy Pool and Larry, his father. Caitlyn and Brendan were well-off compared to what Jeremy had experienced in his young life. Contrasts were everywhere you cared to look. Well-being existed on a sliding scale. Why be envious of people far above you on the scale when you were envied by people struggling below you on the same scale?

As they drove south on Sussex, Kevin admired the long sandstone and granite building that housed the National Research Council laboratories. Its neoclassical style of architecture reminded him of something one might see in Europe. Across the road he could see the Lester B. Pearson Building, headquarters of Canada's global affairs department. It had a more modern design with an ancient Egyptian inspiration. Despite his mood, he felt himself interested in the landmarks all around him. He'd never driven through this part of the capital city before. Perhaps Janie and the kids would enjoy coming up here sometime, during his day off, to see the sights.

Soon they were passing the Royal Mint, a granite castle with tourists crowded out front, and the National Gallery of Canada. Leung followed the split onto Mackenzie Avenue and turned left onto Murray Street just before the American embassy. The next block down they were surprised to find an empty parking spot not far from the corner. As they walked back up toward Sussex, they passed the mouth of the laneway that ran behind the buildings. Looking down, Kevin saw a large white cargo van parked about where the rear entrance to Battaglia's gallery would be. He touched Leung's arm and pointed.

"Let's take a look," Leung said.

They started down the laneway. The cargo van was a Mercedes Sprinter. Kevin remembered that according to their wheelbase measurements and tire tread evidence, the vehicle which had been at Spencer Farm was likely a Mercedes Sprinter. He felt a little jump of excitement and glanced at Leung, who raised his eyebrows. As they reached the front end of the van, a woman stepped out of the back door of the building. Taking a cigarette from her mouth, she frowned at them.

"Detective Constable Walker," Kevin said, holding up his badge. "We spoke on the phone. Could we step inside? It's a little hot out here."

"I don't have any time for this," Battaglia said, dropping the cigarette on the ground and crushing it with her foot. She was short and a little overweight, but her good looks were still evident despite the lines on her face and the puffiness under her eyes. Her long, dark hair was pinned up in a business-like arrangement at the back of her head. She wore jeans, sneakers, and a blue short-sleeved blouse.

"We won't take long." Leung stepped inside the door. "We just have a few questions."

"Nobody's allowed back here except staff," she said, following him inside.

Leung turned around and smiled. "I'm sorry. Maybe we could go up front into the gallery and talk there? It's through here, isn't it?"

As they disappeared into the front of the gallery, Kevin memorized the licence plate on the van and then did a slow tour of the back room. It was about twenty feet wide and twenty-five feet deep, with a high ceiling. He passed flat-file cabinets stacked against one wall, their long, skinny drawers likely filled with unframed artwork. There were hand-lettered labels on some of the drawers, suggesting that their contents were organized alphabetically. He resisted the impulse to take a look inside them.

He walked around work tables covered with prints in colourful mattes and paintings mounted on wood frames. Along the wall on his right were shelving units containing supplies and tools. He saw jars and boxes of cotton swabs, foam tip applicators, cheesecloth, sponges, anti-static wipes, and protective gloves. On another shelf he frowned at cans of aerosol spray varnish, adhesives, and several containers of acetone. Another shelf held tools, including large and small hammers, power drills, pry bars with rubber grips and larger crowbars, boxes of nails and screws, and other miscellaneous hand tools.

At the far corner of the room he turned and walked past a set of vertical bins made of two-by-twos. Inside the pigeon holes were framed oil paintings, many of them quite large. None of them appeared to have been painted by Darius Lane, at least not the ones he could see from where he stood.

Just before the door leading into the gallery he stopped, distracted by sound and movement back in the open doorway leading out into the alley. A bird had landed just outside the door. It cocked its head, pecked at something on the ground, and flew away. Kevin's eyes moved from the open door to a hand truck leaning against the wall behind the door. It was the kind that converted into a four-wheeled cart. It looked like the sort of thing that had been used to move whatever had been taken out of the house at Spencer Farm on the night of Lane's murder.

On his left he saw a small bathroom through an open door. He looked in at a toilet, a vanity and washbasin combination, a utility sink, and a tall waste can with a swinging removable lid. He resisted the impulse to peek inside it. A shelf on the wall held cleaning supplies, extra toilet paper and paper towels, hand soap, and other items commonly found in a bathroom. Behind the open door he saw a bucket and mop. He inhaled. Was there a lingering odour of vomit in the air, or was it just his imagination? He backed away, thinking it over.

"Like I told them before," Battaglia said, her voice coming from the gallery, "we had dinner and he left. I didn't see which way he went. I paid my bill and came back here. End of story."

"Why did you have dinner with him?" Leung asked. "I was under the impression you two didn't get along very well."

"That's an understatement, but I had a client who wanted to offer him a big commission for a piece in the main gallery of his office building in Victoria. We're talking a lot of money. I thought he'd jump at it."

"But he didn't, I take it?"

"He told me to fuck off. Typical Darius language. He was such an asshole."

As Kevin listened from the back room, his eyes ran up to the rafters in the high ceiling and down along the floorboards between the tables and the filing cabinets along the wall on the right. The floor was made of wide pine boards, probably original to the building. They'd been sanded and varnished at some point in an effort to preserve them, but foot traffic had worn the finish down again to the point that it was only visible close to the walls. The natural sunlight coming in through the open door made the floor look even paler than where it was lighted by the overhead fluorescents. Kevin frowned. The paler area was irregular, not uniform. He looked behind him and saw a light switch just inside the door. Using his elbow, he turned off the overhead lights. The irregular patch was a little more distinct. He walked down and stood above it. He could no longer see it. Gingerly, mindful of the burns on his chest, he eased down and felt the floor with his fingertips. Smooth, clean, free of grit. He looked under the table at dust bats and specks of sand, shreds of tissue paper, and other detritus. If the room had been vacuumed or swept recently it had been a rather careless effort, but this spot was particularly clean. Grunting, he lowered his face and sniffed. Bleach? Or was it just wishful thinking once again?

Still on his hands and knees, he looked at the hand truck behind the door. Its rubber tires were covered in dirt and grit.

He got back to his feet with an effort and went up front to join Leung.

"Yes, that's right," Battaglia was saying, "we're separated. I'm staying in the Westin. So what?"

"Your husband didn't seem to like Darius Lane very much," Kevin said.

"John has a very low opinion of all artists," she said, "even the ones who make him a lot of money."

"He seemed to get particularly angry when we asked him about Lane," Kevin said, stepping closer to her. "Does he have a temper?"

She raised her eyebrows. "Who, John? Of course he does."

"Does he ever get violent? Hit people?"

"What are you getting at?"

"You and he must have had some fights. Did he ever hit you?"

"Yeah, sure. I'm divorcing him, aren't I?"

"Did you fight back?"

"Of course I did. I'm nobody's punching bag. What's this got to do with anything? I'm not answering any more questions without my lawyer."

Kevin raised a hand. "I understand. I'm sorry to get into something this sensitive, but if John Scott is capable of violent behaviour, we need to know about it."

She narrowed her eyes. "You've got to be kidding me."

"Darius Lane was brutally murdered by someone capable of extreme violence, Ms. Battaglia. We wouldn't kid about a thing like that."

"We're aware of his background," Leung said, catching on to Kevin's play. "We're concerned that all the recent mob-related violence back in Hamilton might have spilled over into our jurisdiction."

"You really think he might have done it?"

"Do you think he could have?" Kevin asked. "Did you ever see him threaten Darius Lane? Or make any kind of physical move toward him in the past?"

"No. Well, not that I'm sure of. Maybe when I wasn't around." She seemed to consider the possibility, then frowned at them. "I don't understand. Why would they order something like that on Darius? It doesn't make sense." She bit her lip. "Unless he wanted the paintings. He's not doing well, and he borrowed money from his uncle to make some pretty important loan payments. Even if he got fifty cents on the dollar for them, it'd be a decent payday for him. That could be it, couldn't it?"

Kevin glanced at Leung. "What paintings are you talking about, Ms. Battaglia?"

"Uh, paintings by Darius. They're worth a lot, especially now he's dead."

"Are you referring to certain paintings in particular?"

She looked out the window at the traffic passing in the street. "No, just paintings in general. Maybe he knew where to get his hands on some and figured to cash them in as soon as their value went up."

Leung stepped forward. "What's your financial situation like right now? I imagine things must be difficult, being separated from your husband."

"I've got my own bank accounts, thanks very much. That's none of your business. Are we through now? I have things to do. I'd like you to leave."

Leung handed her a business card. "If you think of anything else, maybe about your husband and his connection to Darius Lane, please give us a call."

"Sure. Now let's go." She walked up to the front door and opened it. "This way," she called out to Kevin, who'd turned to go back through the back room.

Kevin obediently followed Leung out onto Sussex Drive. Battaglia slammed the door behind them and locked it.

They walked down to the corner and turned onto Murray Street. Leung looked at Kevin. “Well?”

Kevin smiled. “I’m pretty sure I can get us in there.”

Leung grinned back. “Let’s do it!”

chapter THIRTY-FOUR

Detective Constable Monica Sisson sat down at Ellie's desk to make some sort of adjustments to Ellie's laptop that would allow her better access to files on the detachment's local area network. A short, wiry blonde nearing fifty, she pounded on Ellie's keyboard for several minutes in total concentration before getting up from the desk with a grunt. "There you go. You're all set."

"Thanks, Mona." Ellie sat down. "Must be nice to know how all these programs work."

"Simple problem solving." Sisson leaned against the doorframe and glanced down the hall.

It was quiet at the moment. They were waiting for Scott Patterson to come back to the detachment from a call out near Frankville, where a house had been broken into and an old man had been beaten up during the robbery. When Patterson returned, Leung and Kevin would bring the team up to date on the progress they'd made in Ottawa. Then Ellie and Carty would decide on next steps for the investigation.

Ellie watched Sisson put her fist on her hip and purse her lips. She waited, and after a moment the question came.

"Can I ask you something?"

"Sure."

Sisson turned on the doorframe to look at her. "Do you

think there's a glass ceiling for people who go from civilian employee to sworn officer?"

Ellie shrugged. "Not really. It depends on the individual."

"I was thirty-five before the light went on for me," Sisson said. "I got a clerical job with Kingston and caught the fever. I've just been wondering lately whether to put in for the sergeant's competition when it comes up."

"Why not? What have you got to lose?"

The corners of Sisson's mouth turned down. "I don't get a lot of respect around here. I'm not sure if I want to waste my time on something I don't stand a chance at."

"If you think you'd be wasting your time, then don't do it."

"I—"

"All right all right," Patterson's voice boomed out from down the hall, "where the hell is everybody? In the meeting room, right now!"

Ellie turned in her seat to face the door.

"Maybe we can talk about it later," Sisson said, rolling her eyes.

"Sure." Ellie watched her push away from the doorframe and disappear toward the meeting room. She believed that Sisson had already reached her ceiling as a detective constable and wouldn't do well as a sergeant, but it wasn't her place to open her mouth on the subject. It was a matter that lay strictly between Sisson and Patterson, her immediate supervisor. As far as Ellie was concerned, Sisson might as well compete for the position along with everyone else. Who knew, she might actually succeed, and the promotion might bring out qualities in Sisson that had been hidden to this point. Either way, it was none of Ellie's business to offer Sisson encouragement she didn't deserve or criticism that might be unfounded.

She turned back to her laptop and checked her e-mail. Danny Merrick had sent her a polite note asking if things were going well and if possible could he bring down a case some time to replace the beer he'd guzzled during his visit Tuesday evening. She thought about it for a moment before typing, "I'll think about it." She sent the reply, shut down the laptop, grabbed her notebook, and went down to the meeting room.

Once Sisson had made the connection with Dave Martin via speakerphone in Smiths Falls, Ellie asked for an update on Detective Constable Wiltse's progress with the warrants that would get them into the Scott Gallery, Scott's residence, Rosa Battaglia's hotel room, and the Mercedes Sprinter van, which turned out to be registered to the gallery business. Carty reported that the detective was hopeful he'd have the paper in hand within an hour.

She then asked Leung to walk them through the interviews with John Scott and Rosa Battaglia. She'd already skimmed through the reports he and Kevin had filed with Sisson, but she now wanted to hear from them verbally, to get their gut reactions. She knew what they'd cited as their reasonable and probable grounds for the searches; now she wanted them to talk about the smaller things, the details not strong enough on their own to be included in the Information To Obtain but which, when taken as a whole, had led them to believe that the focus of the investigation should be narrowed to Rosa Battaglia and her estranged husband.

"Scott first," Carty said after Leung had delivered descriptions of the interviews that were very close to a verbatim report.

"Mr. Scott's very self-confident," Leung said. "Very poised. But I believed him when he said he didn't know anything about the portraits of Battaglia that Lane had painted back in Kingston. Right, Kevin?"

"Agreed." Kevin shifted in his chair, trying to find a comfortable position. "He was genuinely confused when you brought them up."

Leung nodded. "He didn't see the connection at all."

"You seem convinced," Carty said, "that these so-called 'lost portraits' are behind this whole thing."

"I'm reasonably confident," Leung replied carefully, "they're what were taken from the house at Spencer Farm. I believe they were the reason the killer tortured the victim and searched the studio and house."

"How much are we talking about?" Carty asked. "If someone stole them to sell through the back door to a private collector?"

"Hard to say for sure. From what Madeleine Menzies was telling us, his work was getting anywhere from eighty-five thousand to one twenty-five. Given the fact not only of his death but also its sensational nature, and the reality that these nudes, which experts seem to consider seminal pieces, probably represent the last of his work not yet on the market, I'd say they might go at auction for anywhere from one-fifty to two hundred thousand dollars."

Carty frowned at his notebook as he jotted down the information. "Times how many paintings?"

"Dr. Stewart claims he saw six, and thought there might be more."

"Let's say six." Carty did the arithmetic. "One point two million."

"In a public auction." Leung glanced at Ellie. "In a private black market sale, they'd bring a lot less because of the risk attached to the collector. Probably only ten per cent of their value."

"Are you kidding me?" Bishop sat up. "All that work to swipe the damned things, and that's all you get? Ten per cent?"

Carty tapped his pen. "So you're telling me that if someone killed Lane for these paintings, they'd only get about a hundred and twenty thousand for them?"

Leung shrugged. "I guess so, yes."

Carty looked at Ellie. "To a guy like John Scott, it

wouldn't be worth it. If what Battaglia said is true, that he borrowed money from his uncle and is having trouble paying it back, we're talking millions. The paintings wouldn't come close to touching that. I don't see them as a motive for Scott."

"I would agree," Ellie said.

"Unless the private collector is someone connected to the family," Kevin said. "Then it's not about cash value but someone wanting to own them."

"It's possible," Carty conceded. He looked down the table at Bill Merkley. "What about it? Is anyone down there known for black market artwork?"

Merkley shrugged. "I'll look into it. Generally in southern Ontario the Siderno group, which is the largest 'Ndrangheta association down there, are into narcotics, money laundering, cigarette smuggling, the usual stuff. And gambling, right, Dennis?"

Leung nodded. "There are a couple of families in the GTA who were a big problem for us at AGCO."

Ellie leaned forward to catch Merkley's eye. "See if you can find us anything about stolen art in either Scott's or Battaglia's family, or their associates." When he nodded, making a note of it on his tablet, she looked at Carty. "I think Tom and I are on the same page with this. I'd say the odds are less likely that it was an art theft than something personally motivated, given the violence of the torture and murder." She turned to Kevin. "Did you get a sense that Scott had that kind of emotion invested in Darius Lane?"

Kevin shook his head. "Not at all. Not anger or hatred. Just a strong sense of contempt, I'd say."

"You don't beat the shit out of a guy with a crowbar like that out of contempt," Bishop said.

Kevin nodded. "Exactly."

Ellie said to Kevin, "Okay, so talk about Rosa Battaglia."

"Evasive," he said, looking at Leung. "Surly."

Bishop laughed. "Sounds like Mona."

Fuck off, Sisson mouthed across the table at him.

"Kevin's right," Leung said. "She was unco-operative, hostile, and very uncomfortable with us being there."

"For good reason, apparently." Ellie looked again at Kevin. His eyes were dark-rimmed and sunken from fatigue, but he stared back at her with an intensity that she found encouraging. "Talk to us about that back room."

"Battaglia probably was with Lane outside on the sidewalk after he left the restaurant," Kevin said. "The gallery's only a block and a half away. She got him there one way or another, confined him in the back room, and started in on him with the wrecking bar."

"During which time he gave her reason to believe the paintings she wanted were at Spencer Farm," Carty said.

Kevin nodded. "She drove down there with him probably tied up in the back. Hauled him into the studio, thinking the paintings were most likely there. Tied him to the chair and picked up where she'd left off with the wrecking bar."

"He finally told her they were in the house," Carty said.

"She might have searched the house first," Kevin said, "to find them, before coming back and killing him with the blow to the head."

"Why bother?" Sisson asked. "If she had what she wanted, the paintings, why not just leave him there?"

"She wanted him dead," Kevin said. "In part because it would increase the value of the paintings, but mostly because she hated his guts."

Carty exhaled loudly. "It's a theory," he said to Ellie.

She nodded. "It's a probability."

"More so than the John Scott scenario," Carty agreed.

Ellie looked at Patterson. "We need to talk resources, right now. As soon as the warrants come through I want us to hit the gallery, the house, the hotel room, and the van at the same time. Let's get our ducks in a row right now."

As everyone stood up, Ellie looked at Kevin, who remained in his seat. His eyes were closed, but there was a faint smile at the corners of his mouth.

chapter THIRTY-FIVE

That evening they executed search warrants in Ottawa at the home of John Scott, the hotel room of Rosa Battaglia, and at the Scott Gallery. They were unable to follow through on the warrant to search the Mercedes Sprinter cargo van because they weren't able to find it. As a result, a Be On the Lookout alert for the vehicle went out through the OPP and the Ottawa Police Service.

The warrant for the house on Acacia Avenue in Rockcliffe Park authorized Dennis Leung and his team to search for any evidence connected to the victim, Darius Lane. Scott's Mercedes was included in the warrant, which made him distinctly unhappy about the whole thing. His attorney happened to live three blocks away and got there in a hurry. Leung immediately developed a headache that dogged him throughout the evening as they combed the house from top to bottom and turned the car inside out.

At the same time, Carty led a smaller team on a search of Rosa Battaglia's hotel suite. Although she wasn't there she hadn't yet checked out, and her things were still in the suite. Carty watched Detective Constable Mark Allore and Identification Constable Landry conduct the search and kept his fingers crossed.

Meanwhile, what was to Ellie's mind the most important search was underway at the Scott Gallery. Ottawa police assisted by sealing off the area for the duration. They blocked off both ends of the alley running behind the buildings and went door to door ensuring that each domicile with a back entrance facing out onto the alley was sealed up until the search was completed. They also went into the buildings on either side of the gallery, which pressed up against it with no space in between, to make sure there was no possible way someone could pass from one building to the other through an upper storey or the basement or via the roof. Ellie wanted to be completely certain there was no way Battaglia or anyone else might have been able to move evidence out of the gallery building surreptitiously from within the structure.

Identification Sergeant Dave Martin and his team began with the back alley, lifting tire tread marks and footprints he hoped would match what they'd found at Spencer Farm. Detectives searched the length of the alley for anything connected to the murder that might have been hidden or thrown away. Once Martin was satisfied that they'd gleaned whatever they could from the outside, he brought their van into the alley, and his team got to work on the back room.

Ellie and Kevin stood in the alley outside the open door, watching as Martin and one of his scenes of crime officers concentrated on the spot on the floor where Kevin believed a clean-up had taken place. Eventually Martin came over and pulled down his mask.

"You done good, kid. We've found blood. I'm reasonably sure we'll be able to recover enough DNA evidence from it to try for a match to the victim." He nodded at Ellie. "We're green-lighted. We'll be here for a while, now."

"How is that possible?" Kevin asked. "I didn't see you do a luminol test. And wouldn't the bleach destroy all the blood cells anyway?"

Martin rolled his eyes. "Luminol can give you a false positive in the presence of bleach. But as luck would have it, our offender used chlorine bleach, which is slightly less deadly to haemoglobin than oxygen bleach. Most importantly, though, we have the substrate working for us."

"Substrate?"

"The floor, Kev. The floor. Nice, porous wood grain worn by years of foot traffic into neat little channels and grooves invisible to the naked eye at a height of six feet, five inches, but plain as day to your friendly neighbourhood forensic specialist down on his hands and knees. The clean-up wasn't as thorough as she would have liked, and there's lots of blood down in those grooves for us to dig up and test." He winked. "Leave the science to us, and stick to what you do best, huh?"

Kevin grinned.

Ellie walked away and made a few calls to get updates on the other searches. She was just ending the call with Carty when a detective called out her name.

"Someone at the perimeter wants to see you," he said. "Says he's with the RCMP."

Ellie followed the detective down the alley to the sidewalk fronting on Clarence Street, where barriers had been set up as part of the outer perimeter. At the front of the small crowd of spectators, Danny Merrick gave her a friendly little wave.

"Sign him in," Ellie told the uniformed provincial constable in charge of the perimeter log.

When Merrick had been processed in, Ellie walked with him down the alley to a courtyard enclosed by a tall wrought iron fence. The courtyard was normally used by the restaurant facing out onto Clarence Street as an outdoor patio. The OPS had ordered the restaurant to close it down for the night, and the search team was using it as a command post. Many of the tables and chairs had been cleared away to give them ample room to work, but there was one in the near corner against the restaurant wall that was free. She led him over to it, and they sat down.

"I'm here as an interested observer," Merrick said, draping his suit jacket over the back of his chair. "Although we've ruled out a national security nexus in the case, I've been directed to monitor its progress, so that's why I'm here. To monitor your progress."

"Okay." Ellie studied him for a moment. His blue dress shirt was open at the neck and the sleeves were turned up on his forearms. His navy tie was stuffed into the breast pocket of his jacket like a pocket square. His hair, as usual, was untidy, his eyes were red-rimmed and tired, but his smile was genuine, and the look he returned to her was steady and focused. While she was experienced enough not to trust anyone from the RCMP any farther than she could throw them, her instincts told her that for whatever reason Merrick would not use any information she gave him to her disadvantage, or to the disadvantage of her case.

It occurred to her suddenly that he might be monitoring her progress on behalf of the prime minister, who would be waiting for an update later tonight.

"We've gotten very little from the Scott residence," she said, leaning forward and folding her hands on the table. "No murder weapon, no artwork by Darius Lane, no suggestion that the Mercedes Sprinter cargo van has been there recently. We've turned the place upside down, but I'm not hopeful. We'll process everything we got, of course, but my gut's telling me John Scott's not the guy."

"What about as an accomplice?"

Ellie shrugged. "Possibly. Maybe something will pop when we process all the physical evidence and go through all the electronic records, but our detectives aren't getting that vibe from him. We'll see."

"We looked at him, as you know, and didn't see anything either. If he was involved, we both missed it."

"Battaglia's looking good for it, though. As you suggested she would." Ellie glanced down the alley, where voices were being raised in the vicinity of the gallery back door. "We found a pair of sneakers in the hotel room that look like they might match the shoe prints at the scene. They've been wiped clean, but that doesn't mean much." The voices continued, along with a sudden whoop. Ellie stood up. "Excuse me for a minute."

Merrick got to his feet. "Sounds like something's going on."

Ellie left him at the table in the courtyard and hurried down the alley. Kevin met her halfway, a grin on his face.

"She forgot to empty the garbage can in the bathroom," he crowed. "Paper towels and a hand towel with blood and vomit. We've got her!"

"We don't have her yet," Ellie cautioned. "We've got more of the story. Now we'll be able to prove he was held here and beaten before being transported to Spencer Farm. But we still have to find the damned murder weapon and put it in her hand. Any luck with the tools in there?"

He shook his head, the grin disappearing. "The one she used isn't here. If you ask me, it's still in the van."

"You may be right." Ellie patted him on the arm. "You've been right so far. This was excellent work, Kevin. You should feel proud of yourself."

"Thanks," he smiled, a little self-consciously. "I appreciate it."

She glanced around him at Dave Martin, who was capering around the end of the Ident van with one of his scenes of crime officers as they loaded up on more equipment to continue their assault on the crime scene. The SOCO pumped a fist in the air. Martin, his mask down, grinned.

She looked up into Kevin's eyes. "They've got this under control, and it'll take a while. Why don't you come with me and sit down for a bit? Take a load off."

"I'm okay," Kevin replied, unconvincingly.

"We'll get you a Coke. I don't want you collapsing on me."

"All right."

"Besides," she said, "there's someone I think you should meet."

"Oh?"

"I think you'll like him. I know he'll like you." *And besides*, she thought, leading the way back to the courtyard where Danny Merrick was waiting for her, *it's about time your star had a chance to shine a little, my young friend.*

chapter THIRTY-SIX

Ellie spent Saturday morning in her office at the cottage, alternating between the cellphone and her laptop as information related to Thursday night's searches began to stream in. Sipping coffee, she made notes in her notebook as Dave Martin called to bring her up to date on lab results coming back from the CFS. The Ontario Centre of Forensic Sciences in Toronto had assigned an analyst to move Martin's evidence to the front of the line for around-the-clock processing.

Carty called to brief her on the search for Rosa Battaglia. A Canada-wide warrant had been issued for her arrest. Normally an arrest warrant was valid only in the province in which it was signed, but in serious cases such as this one, a Canada-wide warrant allowed for the suspect to be arrested anywhere in the country and transported back to the jurisdiction in which the crime occurred. Carty assured her that everyone on the team was working the phones to make sure their contacts were on high alert for the Mercedes van, the stolen artwork, and Rosa Battaglia.

As soon as Ellie ended the call with Carty, Dave Martin called back with another update, and she scribbled down more notes. Then Carty called to tell her that updated reports had been filed in the case management system, routed through Mona Sisson, and she spent some time looking through them, making still more notes.

After her third cup of coffee, the phone went quiet. She made a quick trip to the washroom, then stood in front of the whiteboard and condensed her pages of notes into a bulleted list of highlights. That done, she went out onto the back deck, smoked half a cigarette and dropped the rest of it into a mason jar she kept on the railing for that purpose, poured another cup of coffee, took it into the office, sat down, and picked up her cellphone.

When Commissioner Moodie answered, Ellie could hear the voices of children in the background against the distant sound of traffic.

"I'm at the park with my grandchildren," he said. "A Saturday ritual."

"I'm sorry to interrupt. I should call back later."

"No, Ellie. It's fine. My daughter's watching the kids; I'm basically just watching her watch them. What have we got?"

"CFS confirms the DNA recovered from the art gallery matches the victim," Ellie said, her eyes on the top bullet on her whiteboard.

"That's from samples of the blood and vomit found in the bathroom trash can, correct?"

"Yes, sir. Also from trace amounts recovered from the floorboard. We can definitely place Darius Lane in that back room and confirm that he was beaten before being transported down to Rideau Lakes."

"What about the stolen artwork?"

"Still unaccounted for," Ellie replied. "We found records at the gallery for an off-site storage facility. Their security system shows that Battaglia was there last evening. She's changed the licence plates on the van. Early this morning we learned that she'd stolen the plates from a car in long-term parking at the airport. So we've updated the BOLO."

"You believe she has the artwork in the van?"

"It's a reasonable assumption at this point."

"Sounds like she might be getting ready to make a run

for it."

"Yes, sir. We're covering all the bases."

"What's our position on the husband, John Scott?"

"There's no evidence supporting the idea he was involved. We're reasonably certain the story Rosa Battaglia told us, that Scott borrowed heavily from family in Hamilton and was scrambling to make good on it, is bogus and intended to throw us off track. Plus, there's no intelligence suggesting the families in Hamilton have any particular involvement in moving stolen art. We're now concentrating on Battaglia as our only suspect."

There was a scuffling sound in the background. "Wait one." The phone went silent as Moodie put her on hold. A few moments later he was back. "Sorry, someone sat down on the next bench, so I moved. I was going to ask you about the weapon."

"Still looking for it. We found a disposable dish cloth with blood, hair, and other matter on it in the storage unit. We think she used it to wipe off the murder weapon."

"She's leaving a trail a mile long, Ellie."

"Yes, sir. She profiles out as a disorganized amateur who's basically making it up as she goes along. Stealing a licence plate and then driving into a secure compound with video surveillance, along with the burning of Lane's body to throw us off the track and the clumsy way she did it, are examples of her lack of planning and foresight. It wouldn't surprise me to find the wrecking bar in her van along with the paintings and everything else we need to ring her up for this."

"It has to happen ASAP. I trust that's clear."

"Yes, sir." Ellie ran her eyes down the bulleted list on the whiteboard. She'd covered everything that the commissioner needed to know at the moment.

"By the way," Moodie said, "I heard the young detective constable, Walker, did a great job for us on this."

Ellie frowned, surprised. "Oh?"

"Apparently the feds are considering poaching him away from us. What's your take on him?"

"Walker? He's raw, but he's got a lot of potential." Ellie bit her lip. After introducing Kevin to Merrick Thursday night, she'd left them alone in the courtyard while she talked to Martin and his team. Merrick must have asked Kevin about his current situation and career plans.

The snake.

"Kevin's very intelligent," she added, "shows a high level of sensitivity and responsiveness in how he deals with the public, and has all the physical attributes. This is the second case he's worked under me, as you know, and as far as I'm concerned he's just the kind of person we need more of."

"Noted. Anything else I need to know right now?"

"No, sir. That pretty much covers it."

"Make this arrest, Ellie. The pressure's ramping up."

"Yes, sir." Ellie ended the call and stared at the cellphone in her hand. Almost immediately it began to vibrate, startling her.

She hoped it was good news.

chapter THIRTY-SEVEN

Kevin finally got his day off.

Janie left early for the hair salon in the village, where she was completely booked for the day, and Kevin had a second chance to look after Caitlyn and Brendan. They enjoyed a leisurely breakfast, watched some cartoons on television, and then got dressed. After a prolonged search for Kevin's magic book, which was eventually discovered nestled, for some inexplicable reason, in Brendan's sock drawer, they piled into the car and headed off for the library.

Brendan was not in a particularly good mood, having slept poorly the night before because of an upset stomach. He felt better physically this morning but he was tired and grouchy. He fussed all the way to Springville. Caitlyn, as she often did, tried to compensate by being extra nice to Kevin. As he waited at the end of County Road 46 to turn onto Highway 29, she caught his eye in the rear-view mirror. "You're a very careful driver."

"Thank you," Kevin replied, making his turn and accelerating into the southbound lane.

"May I ask you a question?"

"Of course you may." He smiled at her reflection in the mirror. "You don't need to be so formal, Cait. Although it proves you have excellent grammar as well as good manners."

"Caitlyn doesn't have any glamour!" Brendan chirped.

"Not glamour," Caitlyn corrected. "Grammar. Be quiet, Brendan."

"I *won't* be quiet! *You* be quiet!"

"Brendan," Kevin said, "Caitlyn and I are talking. Please wait your turn."

After a moment's silence, Kevin glanced again in the mirror. Brendan sat in his booster seat with his arms folded, frowning out the window. "What's your question, Cait?"

"How come your magic didn't work when that man burned you?"

"My magic?"

"From your book. Why didn't you use a magic trick to keep him from burning you?"

Kevin took a moment to think about it, checking his speed and setting the cruise control. "It wasn't the right situation for magic tricks," he finally said.

"Why not?"

"He was too upset and he wouldn't have liked it."

"Why not?"

"He wanted people to be honest with him and not to play games." Kevin frowned out the windshield, dissatisfied with his answer. "Anyway, it happened too fast."

"Why did he burn you, Kevin?"

He bit his lip, hearing the emotion in her voice. "He burned himself, Cait. I got burned when I covered him up to put out the flames."

"Is he all right now?"

"He's still in hospital. They have to do a lot of stuff to heal his burns. They were a lot worse than mine."

They drove in silence for a while until she said, "Do you still like it?"

"Like what, Cait?"

"Being a policeman?"

"You bet I do." He grinned at her in the mirror. "I

wouldn't want to be anything else."

The Elizabethtown-Kitley Township Public Library was an L-shaped frame building located about ten kilometres northwest of Brockville. It sat next to the OPP detachment office in the middle of its own large paved rectangle. The former Spring Valley Community Hall, the building had been converted into a library with the help of federal funding several years ago. As Kevin turned into the entrance off the highway, he was surprised to see that there were quite a few cars parked in the lot. Then he remembered it was Saturday.

It was a bit of an ordeal to get Brendan out of the back seat and into the building. At first he wouldn't talk or move or acknowledge Kevin's existence. Then he wanted to stay in the car by himself. Then he wanted to see what the kids were doing behind the library. When told they were big kids playing with a Frisbee, he wanted to join them. When Caitlyn objected, saying she wanted to go inside, Brendan told her off.

Kevin got down on one knee and held Brendan lightly by the elbows so that he could make eye contact. "We can see what the kids are doing after we go inside, Brendan. Caity needs to get her books first."

"I want to see *now*!" He squirmed impatiently.

"Do you have to go to the bathroom?"

Brendan pooched his lips in and out, then nodded.

"Well, thank goodness, so do I. Let's take care of that first while Caitlyn gets her books, then we can see what the big kids are doing. Okay?"

"Ohhh-kay."

Kevin grabbed his book and locked the car. As they went inside, he dropped the book into the return slot and led Brendan over to the washrooms. Caitlyn skipped lightly ahead of them on her way to the back corner, which was set up as the children's area. Thankfully, the men's washroom was unoccupied. Kevin got Brendan set up in the stall and then used the urinal. As he was washing his hands, he heard the toilet paper roll making its distinctive sound, over and over. He hastily dried his hands and went into the stall. Brendan had unravelled half a roll of toilet paper onto the floor.

"Are you all done?"

Brendan nodded.

"Did you wipe?"

No answer.

Kevin gently moved him forward on the toilet and peeked down. No solids, just liquid. He moved Brendan the rest of the way off the toilet. "You didn't have to poo?"

Brendan shook his head.

"You feel okay now?"

Brendan nodded, pulling up his drawers.

They washed their hands and went back out. Down at the children's end they discovered that someone was giving a reading. A woman with short grey hair and glasses sat cross-legged on the floor with a picture book, surrounded by young children and their mothers. As soon as Brendan saw the book from which she was reading, he tugged on Kevin's hand. "Dragons!"

"You want to listen?"

Spotting Caitlyn on the far side of the circle, Brendan shed Kevin's hand and hopped over to his sister's side. They sat down together at the edge of the circle. Brendan put his elbows on his knees, cupped his face in his hands, and began to listen with an intensity that was almost shocking to Kevin, given the boy's erratic behaviour up to now.

Caitlyn looked over and Kevin pointed meaningfully at her brother. When she nodded, acknowledging that she would keep an eye on Brendan, Kevin retraced his steps up to the front desk.

A sandy-haired woman with glasses smiled up at him. "How are you doing, Kevin?"

"Not bad, Megan, thanks. I didn't realize there was a

reading today. Who is she?"

She touched the ring on her right index finger self-consciously. "Carolyn Wells. She's a local artist." Megan turned in her seat and pointed at the wall behind her. "That's one of her paintings."

Kevin looked at it, a large still life dominated by red poppies and blue glassware. He'd noticed it before but hadn't paid it much attention. It seemed as though paintings and painters were cropping up all over the place these days. He remembered reading somewhere that 40 per cent of Canadian artists lived in Ontario, and that 13 per cent of artists in the province lived in eastern Ontario, some seven thousand altogether. On the downside, people who reported earning income as artists in Ontario declared around $26,000 a year, a quarter less than the average earnings of the workforce overall. He remembered now that he'd read these figures in a local newspaper article basing its commentary on a report by the Ontario Arts Council. The report had also said the average earnings by artists in Leeds and Grenville amounted to slightly more than $11,000 a year. A long way from Darius Lane territory, obviously.

"Were you looking for something in particular today, Kevin?"

He broke off this train of thought and nodded, removing his wallet. "Can we do another inter-library loan thing?"

"Sure." Megan beamed at him. By now she was used to his diverse interests and got a kick out of them.

He pulled a folded slip of paper from his wallet and handed it to her. As she unfolded it, he returned his wallet to his pocket. "It's a book about mirror-touch synesthesia. I heard about it on CBC Radio the other day."

"Okay, I give up. What's mirror-touch synesthesia?"

"Well, synesthesia is when the senses get crossed, right? When people smell colours or feel certain sounds as a touching on various parts of their body."

"That sounds interesting," Megan said.

"One of the best dramatizations of it," Kevin ploughed on, "is in Alfred Bester's *The Stars My Destination*. Remember? At the end?"

She nodded, having read the well-known science fiction novel at Kevin's suggestion last winter.

"Well, mirror-touch is a form of synesthesia where people feel the same sensations other people feel. If they see someone burn their hand, they feel the pain as well, sympathetically. A rare form of empathy."

Megan smoothed out the piece of paper on the desk in front of her. "It really exists?"

Kevin nodded. "That's why I want to read this book, to learn more about it. Fascinating, huh?"

"You never cease to amaze me, Kevin. I never know what you're going to discover next."

Kevin felt a tap on his shoulder and turned around to look at John Bishop.

"Hey, Kev. Got a sec?" Bishop motioned with his head toward the front doors.

"What is it?"

"Outside? For a sec?"

"Okay." Kevin checked on the reading circle and saw that Brendan and Caitlyn hadn't moved. He followed Bishop outside.

"What is it? What's going on?"

Bishop stopped at the corner of the building and leaned against the wall. "I know it's your day off, Kev. I saw the car over here and thought I'd come over and tell you in person, instead of calling."

"Tell me what?"

"The kid. Pool. He killed himself."

Kevin closed his eyes. The burns on his chest tingled with pain, and he found it difficult to breathe. "What happened?"

"They were getting ready to transport him for his psych

eval. They found him dead. He hanged himself with a sheet. I'm sorry, Kev. I know you gave a shit about the kid."

"Damn." Kevin felt overwhelming disappointment and regret. There must have been more he could have done. Ways in which he could have helped the young man find himself. But then he shook his head. No. There was no way Jeremy Pool would ever have trusted him. Or trusted anyone. He'd been struggling all alone at the bottom of a very deep well, and now he was dead. Beyond anyone's help.

He opened his eyes. "Thanks, JB. I appreciate you telling me."

"No problem." Bishop dropped a hand on his shoulder. "It's okay. Every now and then one of them gets us where we live. It's okay, Kev." He clapped Kevin's shoulder and pushed away from the wall. "Are you okay?"

"I'm okay."

"All right. See you tomorrow."

Kevin watched Bishop cut across the parking lot on his way back to the detachment building next door. Then his vision blurred and he had to wipe his eyes before going back inside. Instead of browsing the stacks, he decided he'd rather sit cross-legged on the floor with the kids and listen to the painter lady read the story about the little girl and the dragon.

It was one of those days when he wished he could be only eight years old again.

chapter THIRTY-EIGHT

"When I called," Scott Patterson said, leaning back in his chair to allow the server to remove the remains of his lunch, "you sounded distracted. Everything all right?"

Ellie nodded. When the server disappeared she glanced at her cellphone on the table and said, "I was briefing the commissioner. He was at the park with his grandkids."

"How'd that go?"

"Fine. He wants Battaglia arrested, ASAP."

"We'll find her. She's basically a bonehead. She'll screw up something and we'll drop down on her like a ton of bricks."

"It better be soon." Ellie stared out the window at the water without seeing it. After receiving Patterson's invitation to lunch, she'd taken a call from Todd Fisher, who was reacting to the pressure trickling down from the top. She'd reminded him that the primary job of her team—*his* team—right now was to make certain they assembled an airtight case against Rosa Battaglia so that once she was in custody, the Crown could prosecute and convict without encountering any procedural difficulties that could allow her to slip free. It wasn't as though they could all jump in their cars and trawl the highways and back roads hoping to catch sight of their fugitive in her white Mercedes Sprinter. The Canada-wide warrant on Battaglia and the BOLO on the van would have to do the job for them.

Just the same, she understood Fisher's stress. She felt it just as much as he did, in the tightness of her stomach muscles, the headache pounding at her temples, and the shortness of breath she kept trying to relieve by sighing and inhaling deeply. No matter how much experience you carried into the job, situations like this were difficult to weather.

She hadn't been in the mood to take a lunch break with Patterson, but she'd realized he had something on his mind, something he needed to talk about. Both of them ended up calling the other to set the time back, until they finally met a few minutes before 1:30. So here they were, a late lunch heavy in their stomachs, staring out the window at the St. Lawrence River, waiting for their bill. The restaurant was on the top floor of a waterfront building in downtown Brockville that gave them a view of the river and Morristown, New York, on the far shore. The weather was good and, because it was Saturday, there was a lot of activity on the water. Boats trolled back and forth, kayaks roamed the shoreline, and in the distance a cargo ship inched closer.

"There's a shipwreck right out there," Patterson said, pointing.

"Out where?" Ellie frowned at the water.

"See where the buoy is with the flashing yellow light?"

"Mmm hmm."

"It was a three-masted ship, the *Robert Gaskin*. It sank in the 1880s or 1890s right out there."

"And it's still there?"

"Sure. Where else is it going to go, Ellie?" He grinned at her.

"You sound like Kevin. Always ready with some esoteric piece of information."

Patterson's grin faded. "He's a project, that's for sure."

Ellie opened her mouth and then closed it again. She wanted to talk to Patterson about Kevin and his future, but she suddenly remembered Mona Sisson asking her advice on whether or not to write the sergeants' exam. In Sisson's case Ellie had remained overtly neutral, not wanting to get involved on the assumption that it was better for her to have that conversation with Patterson, her supervisor. It had been a way to avoid saying something negative. Now she felt slightly hypocritical.

Screw it.

"Mona Sisson asked me whether she should compete for sergeant when it comes up," she said. "She wondered whether there was a glass ceiling for officers who start out as civilian employees."

"What did you say?"

"I ducked it," Ellie admitted. "I said that there wasn't necessarily a glass ceiling and that it depended on the individual, but I didn't really encourage or discourage her."

"She's talked to me about it several times. I've told her she has a lot of work to do before she's ready to take that step. I gave her the list of competencies for the position and told her to check off each one she felt she was ready to match. Then to come back to me and we'd talk some more."

It sounded to Ellie as though Patterson was handling it well. "So why the hell did she ask me about it? Because she wanted a woman's opinion?"

"Probably." Patterson shrugged. "Nobody cares if she started out as a dispatcher as long as she's a good cop. But right now I don't see supervisory abilities there, and that's what'll hold her back." He nodded as the server placed the bill in front of him and went away again. "Everybody thinks they're going to be the next commissioner."

When Ellie reached out for the bill, Patterson shook his head. "On me." He took out his wallet and tossed down a credit card. "Speaking of which..." He made no move to get up.

"Yes?"

"I'm moving to Smiths Falls. I got the word yesterday."

Ellie cocked her head. "Oh?"

Patterson nodded, embarrassed. "I got the ops manager acting assignment."

"Congratulations," Ellie said, genuinely pleased for him. The incumbent operations manager for East Region, Rick Tobin, had recently been promoted to a position at General Headquarters, creating an opening on Fisher's staff. It was an acting assignment at the staff sergeant level, which would bump up his pay more than 10 per cent. Plus, it was a given that any acting assignment helped to prepare for future promotional opportunities. "You must be excited."

"I should have my head examined. Stuck all day in an office next door to The Fish?"

"You'll do fine. Todd could use your no-nonsense approach." Ellie could have said more, but left it at that. Rick Tobin was intelligent and competent, but he was overly conscious, in Ellie's opinion, of the political ramifications of any particular decision he might make. She thought he'd probably do well at GHQ. Patterson, on the other hand, would always be a little rough around the edges. Which was why she liked him.

"Fisher asked who should backfill for me. I told him Carty, hands down."

"I see."

"I know what you're thinking, that he's a soulless hard-ass who doesn't get along with anyone." Patterson shrugged. "Big deal. No change from me, right? Same shit, different day."

"I see your point," Ellie replied, acknowledging the joke. "Do they know you're leaving?"

Patterson shook his head. "Not yet."

Ellie held eye contact with him, knowing he wanted

her to give her blessing on his choice of Carty as his replacement. They'd been friends long enough that her opinion mattered to him, particularly since she would have to work with Carty as the crime unit commander if another major case brought her back to the detachment.

"He's the best internal choice," she said, "but what about going outside to other detachments? I can think of several good possibilities Fisher might consider."

"He mentioned a couple of names. I said the staff would probably prefer the devil they know to one they don't."

Ellie knew Patterson didn't want her to sugar-coat it, so she said, "Carty has a pretty low opinion of the others in the unit, Scott, and he doesn't make a secret of it."

"I know, I know."

"Some of them may end up transferring out. I think it's a good group right now, but anyway, it's none of my business."

Patterson stared at her. "You're thinking of Kevin."

"I am."

"He's got to grow a thicker skin, Ellie. If he can't be tough-minded enough, maybe he *should* look for something else."

"It's not about being tough-minded. Well, yeah, it is, but I'm thinking about finding and keeping a balance between being a tough guy and being able to bring out the best in others. Kevin has that ability, and so do you, but I haven't seen any sign of it in Carty."

Patterson nodded. "He's fair-minded, though."

"Perhaps."

"We all learn how it has to work, Ellie, the first time we step into a supervisory role. God knows I had to. Carty's smart. He'll figure it out."

"And you, my friend," Ellie tapped the table in front of him, "will have to learn how to swim with the sharks at RHQ. Think you're up for it?"

Patterson stood up, grabbing the bill and his credit

card, which hadn't yet been retrieved by the server. "Sure, Ellie. They won't have a fucking clue what hit them."

At that moment, his cellphone began to buzz. He pulled it out, frowning.

As Ellie got up and started to reach for her cellphone on the table, it too began to vibrate.

Something was happening.

chapter THIRTY-NINE

When the reading was finished and Caitlyn had chosen her books for the week, Kevin took them into Brockville, where Janie's mother would keep them for the afternoon while Kevin went grocery shopping.

Brendan had enjoyed the reading and had peppered the woman, Carolyn Wells, with dragon-related questions afterward. It was as though she'd flipped a switch on his back that transformed him from demon seed to sparky angel. He babbled joyously all the way to Barb's house. Kevin and Caitlyn exchanged glances in the mirror.

Let's just keep our heads down and go with the flow.

Kevin stayed for lunch, gave Barb a peck on the cheek, and went out to his car. He checked his text messages and read several updates from Bishop that had been sent late in the morning. He learned that a Canada-wide warrant had been issued for Rosa Battaglia. The lab results coming back on the gallery search were all thumbs-up. A rumour was circulating that Patterson was moving up to RHQ and that Carty would replace him.

Run and hide, kid, Bishop texted after passing that one along. *Run and hide.*

Kevin put the cellphone into sleep mode and drove to the big grocery store on Parkedale Avenue. Because it was Saturday the place was very busy. He spent just over an hour finding everything on his list and adding a few extras, like a couple of loaves of reduced-to-clear bread he'd never tried before and a big chunk of salmon on sale that he thought he'd try grilling for supper. Caitlyn liked fish and Janie loved salmon, so it was a reasonable gamble. Brendan, as always, would be the wild card.

He loaded his purchases into the trunk of the car and walked back up to the pharmacy next door. He stocked up on bandages, ointment, and a few other things for Janie, but decided to pass on the analgesics. The pain from his burns was manageable today, and he didn't like taking too many painkillers.

He tossed the bag containing his pharmacy purchases into the back seat of the car and started the engine. Immediately a light flashed on the dashboard and a chime sounded. He was low on fuel.

He drove across the wide parking lot to the gas bar down at the edge of the street. Again, because it was Saturday, the line-ups at each of the eight self-serve lanes were long. He idled in front of the far outside lane, the fuel tank being on the passenger side, and checked his texts again while he waited. There was nothing new from Bishop, but Janie had texted him that she'd just been given a twenty-dollar tip. He responded back with his congratulations and told her about the salmon he planned to grill for supper. She responded immediately that she'd rather have hamburgers.

No problem, Kevin replied, glad he'd also just bought a box of frozen Angus burgers and a package of buns.

Someone tapped a car horn and Kevin looked up. The line-up had moved forward. He put down the cellphone and lifted his foot from the brake pedal, easing up to the pump. He got out and filled the tank, watching the heavy traffic in the street in front of him. When the tank was full he returned the nozzle, checked the pump number on the pillar, and started off for the hut at the other end to pay for his gas.

As he passed the next set of pumps, he pulled his wallet

out and removed his gas card, which he always kept in the front slot for easy retrieval. He glanced up in time to avoid bumping into the back fender of a blue Impala with a bumper sticker advertising the Red Pony Continual Soirée Bar & Grill, and found his way blocked on the other side of the pillar by a large white vehicle. He paused, frowned at the chrome word *Sprinter* on the back door of the vehicle, and looked up.

The driver's side door was open, which was necessary on a Mercedes Sprinter van in order to open the little hatch next to it to get at the fuel filler pipe. Rosa Battaglia stood in the doorway, the diesel fuel pump in her hand, cigarette between her lips, about to begin fuelling the van. She wore a tight black t-shirt, black jeans, and white sneakers.

"Jesus fucking Christ," she muttered, staring at him.

"Rosa Battaglia," Kevin said, shoving his wallet and card into his back pocket, "you're under arrest for the murder of Darius Lane. You have—"

"Fuck you, asshole!" Face twisted in anger, Battaglia jabbed the gas pump nozzle at him as he stepped forward to put his hand on her arm.

The nozzle struck him on the chest, in the middle of his burns. He grunted, stepping back involuntarily, and continued, "You have the right to retain and instruct—"

"You son of a bitch!" She jabbed the nozzle at him again, but this time squeezed the trigger and splashed fuel at him.

It jetted out in a stream that soaked his pant legs. Battaglia dropped the hose, grabbed the cigarette from her mouth and threw it at him, then swung up into the driver's seat of the van.

The cigarette bounced off Kevin's knee and fell into the pooling fuel as Kevin lunged forward and grabbed her, hauling her out from behind the wheel. She came out bottom first, landed on the ground, and promptly aimed an upward kick at his crotch.

Kevin saw it coming and twisted enough so that it glanced off his thigh. Her heel struck with enough force, given the weight behind it and the fury with which she kicked, to cause him considerable pain. He grunted, bending over, but managed to grab her ankle as she drew back her leg for another kick. She pumped the leg ineffectually, pulling Kevin forward and off balance, then kicked out with her other foot.

Falling forward, Kevin avoided this kick. Her foot went up over his shoulder and he fell down on top of her. Her hands immediately began clawing at his face. He jerked back in time to avoid her teeth, which almost bit off the end of his nose.

He looked up and saw several people watching from the back end of the van. "Police!" he managed, as Battaglia's fist bounced off his ear, "OPP! Call 911! Call 911!"

Her fist drew back again and punched him in the mouth.

Enough was enough. He surged upward, grabbed one of Battaglia's arms, and forced her over onto her back. It took several tries, as they were confined in the narrow space between the cement foundation of the gas pump island and the van's rocker panel, but he finally managed to roll her over and pin her arm in a half-nelson, straddling her on the backs of her legs, just below her buttocks. Her back was wet with oily diesel fuel, and the stink of it caught at Kevin's throat.

"You bastard!" she screamed, her cheek pressed against the pavement, "I'll kill you! You fucking son of a bitch!"

After several attempts while sitting on her buttocks, he managed to corral her other arm and bring it up behind her back. "You're under arrest," he began again, "for the murder of Darius Lane. You have the right to—"

Her heels began pounding into his back, one after the other, as she continued to struggle.

"—retain and instruct counsel without delay. You also

have the right—"

A lucky shot caught him in the kidney, and he twisted in pain.

"Bastard! You should have burned! Why didn't you burn like him, you fucking bastard?"

Trying to catch his breath as pain throbbed in his back, Kevin looked up and saw several people holding up cellphones, recording the incident. "911?" he managed.

"Are you really a cop or her boyfriend?" a young woman asked, staring at her cellphone screen.

"Does anyone—"

"Let me go, you fucking bastard!"

"—have plastic locking strips in their vehicle? Big ones?"

"I do," said a man standing behind the young woman, "in the toolbox in the back of my truck."

"OPP. Making an arrest. I'd appreciate it," Kevin grunted as another heel landed in the middle of his back, "if you'd get them for me."

"Okay."

As Kevin twisted, trying to avoid more blows on his back, he saw the man put his hands on the young woman's shoulders and lean down, peering at her phone.

"You're getting all this?" the man asked.

"Oh yeah," the young woman replied.

The man patted her shoulder and said to Kevin, "I'll be right back."

chapter FORTY

While being placed in the back of a police cruiser, Rosa Battaglia injured a provincial constable by kicking him in the shin hard enough to fracture the bone. As she struggled with officers attempting to get her under control, she was told that if she continued to resist arrest she would be Tasered. After this warning was repeated several times, it penetrated the haze of her anger and she stopped struggling. Once inside the cruiser, hands restrained behind her back, she settled down and remained quiet for the duration of the trip to jail.

By this time Patterson and Ellie had arrived at the gas bar. Witnesses were interviewed, and the young woman who had video-recorded Kevin's struggle with Battaglia was persuaded to turn over her phone as evidence. In the meanwhile, she'd managed to upload the clip to the Internet, and it had already started to receive multiple views. Other witnesses also gave up their recordings, but the young woman's vantage point had been the best. The only problem, as far as Kevin was concerned, was that she had begun recording only after the scuffle had already started. However, he knew that the security camera right above them in the canopy of the gas bar would have captured the entire incident and would help clear him of any charge of excessive use of force that might result from the incident.

Paramedics called to the scene offered to treat Kevin's chest, which had started to bleed after the poke from the gas nozzle, but he shook his head. His lip had already stopped bleeding. He'd been punched harder than that in more than one hockey fight, he joked. The woman examined his right side, noted that a bruise was already beginning to show over his kidney, and warned him to go to the hospital right away if he developed a fever or saw blood in his urine.

When Battaglia was examined, she was found to have only sustained a few scratches on the cheek from grit on the pavement when Kevin had wrestled her into a face-down position. Suspects subjected to the use of force to one degree or another during arrest often complained of various injuries in order to pave the way for future lawsuits against the arresting officer, but Battaglia declared herself unharmed by the altercation. She swore bitterly that Kevin was lucky to have remained alive, and that since burning him had failed, all she wanted was another chance to knock out his teeth.

A few hours after her arrest and her subsequent telephone call with her lawyer, Carty began the interview process. While the others watched the video feed, he tried with minimal success to coax her to answer basic questions that would establish a pattern of relative truthfulness. She had lapsed into a sullen mood in which she answered him in monosyllables or shrugs, but after more than forty minutes of sparring, she abruptly lost her temper.

"I want to talk to that other guy, the young fucker!" She pounded on the table with her fist.

Carty was on his feet, ready to end the interview before her aggression escalated again into violence. "Who are you talking about?"

Outside, Patterson had started for the door of the interview room, but he stopped abruptly when Battaglia barked, "That big son of a bitch! The one who caught me!"

"Walker? You're talking about Detective Constable

Walker?"

"Bring him in here! I won't talk to anybody else."

Patterson looked at Kevin, who was sitting in a chair directly in front of the video monitor. "Well?"

Kevin slowly hauled himself to his feet.

"I want—" Ellie started.

"Bishop, go with him," Patterson finished.

Carty was reluctant to yield the room but Patterson, outside in the corridor, insisted. As Kevin sat down in Carty's chair, Battaglia eyed Bishop. "Who's he? Your bodyguard?"

"If you want to talk to me," Kevin said calmly, "you need to settle down."

Battaglia leaned forward. "I can take you. I can take him, too. There isn't a man born I can't beat in a fight."

"I'm sure that's true," Kevin replied, "and I have the bruises to prove it. But if you want me to sit here and listen, you have to dial it down. Way down. Do you understand?"

"Not with Magilla Gorilla standing there. He goes, and you and I can talk. One on one."

"Not a chance," Bishop rumbled.

"It's okay," Kevin said.

Bishop glanced up at the camera in the corner of the ceiling, unwilling to move.

Kevin moved his chair a little closer to his end of the table. "As Detective Constable Carty told you, this interview is being audio- and video-recorded. Detective Constable Bishop will be watching on the monitor. He'll come back in at the first sign of a problem from you, and we'll have to take this in a different direction. Is that understood?"

"Sure. Whatever."

Bishop glared at her. Kevin nodded. Bishop nodded back and left the room.

Battaglia sat back in her chair and stared at him. Kevin maintained eye contact, waiting.

"Explain something to me," she finally said. "Why

didn't you burn, you son of a bitch?"

"It was diesel fuel. It's not flammable the same way regular gasoline is. The cigarette went out as soon as it hit the puddle."

"Christ. Can you believe that? Just my fucking luck."

"A lot different than the acetone you used to set Darius Lane's body on fire, wasn't it?"

Battaglia said nothing, staring at him.

"Why did you set fire to Lane's body after you killed him?"

Battaglia shrugged. "Look, that other guy seemed to know everything already, so what's the point? I don't feel like talking about it."

Kevin opened the file folder Carty had handed him and flipped through a few pages. Following a well-established interrogation technique, Carty had moved from his preliminary questions into a more assertive presentation of the evidence gathered in the case in order to convince Battaglia that she should admit her guilt. The photographs and reports in the file folder represented a healthy portion of what the CFS and Dave Martin had assembled in their case against Battaglia, but when Carty trotted them out for her one by one, she'd refused to co-operate, responding with non-sequiturs and shrugs.

"I know Detective Constable Carty went through all this with you," Kevin said. "The crates in the van contained paintings signed by Darius Lane. All of them nudes, featuring a model who looks remarkably like you." He held up a photograph of one of the paintings. "This is you, isn't it? You modelled for these?"

"Like what you see?"

"They're beautiful," Kevin said without hesitation. "Absolutely stunning. Romantic modernism at its best."

After a moment, she raised an eyebrow at him. "They are, aren't they? Beautiful?"

"Stunning. I can understand why you wanted them."

She sighed, shaking her head as he appeared to miss her point. "*I* made them what they are. *I* made them beautiful. Lane's job was just to get it down on canvas. To get my beauty down on canvas for the world to see."

"You wanted him to tell you where they were, didn't you? You wanted them for yourself."

"We both knew they were masterpieces, as soon as he finished the first one. He couldn't stop. He did them one after the other, different poses, different sets, we couldn't stop. It was like we were both stoned for an entire week. And the sex was incredible. He was a different man. Like a god. It was unbelievable."

Kevin paused, wanting to pursue the actions leading up to the murder, but understanding that at this moment her head was in the past, in Kingston. He realized he might be able to get her to say something that could contribute to motive and state of mind, so he asked, "Why didn't it last, Rosa? Why did your relationship with Lane end?"

"I thought I loved him and I thought he loved me back, but I was wrong on both counts." She sat quietly for a moment, her eyes unfocused, her thoughts inward, and she seemed to be trying to decide whether or not she wanted to talk about it.

Kevin stayed quiet.

Finally she said, "He was in love with his work. He actually quit drinking and stayed up all night painting and slept all day. He didn't use me as a model any more after he finished these pictures, the bastard, and I was working on my MFA and had to sleep at night, for Christ's sake. We hardly saw each other. Then when I realized that John was interested in me, I thought, what the hell. Let's see where this goes."

"John Scott? He was doing his MBA at that time, wasn't he?"

"He swept me off my feet, but that's ancient history." She widened her eyes at him. "He's a little too old for me now. I like younger men. More stamina."

"You were working on your Master of Fine Arts, weren't you?"

"I've always been attracted to a man who fights back."

Kevin felt his face go warm. He hoped the others watching the video feed couldn't see him blushing as he said, "Did you ask Lane, back then, for the paintings?"

She shook her head.

"But you wanted them, didn't you?"

"It would have been nice to have had just one. But he put them away and wouldn't talk about them. I thought at first he'd destroyed them. He did that a lot, back then. I asked a couple of times. But after a while, once John and I were going out together, I hardly saw Darius any more and the chance to get them slipped away."

"But you never forgot about them, did you? You still wanted them."

"Obviously."

"Later, when you took over the Gibson Gallery in Ottawa, did you ask Lane about them again?"

"Once."

"Was that the time when you put all his paintings out on the sidewalk?"

She laughed, an abrupt bark. "Yes! That felt so good. And the look on his face! The bastard. I stood in front of the door and wouldn't let him outside until they were all gone. That was sweet."

"You did that because he wouldn't give you the nudes?"

"Because he wouldn't even admit they still existed, the son of a bitch. He was a stubborn sack of shit and he deserved everything he got."

"Everything you did to him?"

"Yes! It was sweet."

Kevin pulled a photograph out of the folder and held it up. "Is this what you used on him, to get him to tell you where they were?"

She looked, then shrugged disdainfully. "I have a bunch of those."

"We know. This is a photograph of the wrecking bar we found in your van. As Detective Constable Carty told you, our lab will prove that this one in particular has Lane's DNA on it along with your fingerprints. Did you use this to beat Lane until he told you where the paintings were?"

"I don't think I want to answer that question right now."

"Okay." Kevin put the photograph down. "Let's talk about your meeting with Lane last Sunday at the restaurant. Whose idea was it, yours or his?"

"I already talked to the Mounties about all that."

"Talk to me about it, Rosa. Was there really a commission in the works for Lane?"

She shook her head. "I stopped trying to sell his stuff a long, long time ago. Menzies is the only one he'd co-operate with."

"But you told him you had a potential client lined up, didn't you?"

"Sure."

"Why did you tell him that?"

"To get him to meet with me, obviously. He wouldn't give me the time of day otherwise."

"But there wasn't a client?"

She rolled her eyes. "Don't pretend to be thick. Obviously there wasn't. And we were only halfway through the appetisers when he figured that out."

"But you wouldn't let him leave, is that it?"

"He was hungry. The food was good. And he thought I was paying for it, so he stayed."

Kevin tapped the photograph of the painting. "Did you ask him then where they were?"

"I asked him, once again, if they were still around. I reminded him how wonderful they were, how great that week had been, tried all that sucky bullshit, but he wouldn't bite. I could tell by his expression, though, that he knew where they were, so I asked him if he'd sold them. He said no. That's all he'd say. So I knew then that he still had them."

"How did the rest of the meeting go? What else did you talk about?"

She shook her head. "Typical Darius. He got surly and shut up. We ate."

"It doesn't sound like it ended well."

"It ended," she replied with acid, "the way everything ended with him, in a fucking pout. Pissy, grouchy old bastard."

"After you left the restaurant, he went with you to the gallery though, didn't he? How did you get him to go with you, if the meal had ended on such a sour note?"

"What's your name again?"

"Walker. Detective Constable Walker."

"No, no. Your first name."

"Kevin."

She leaned forward. "Well look, Kevin. He wasn't a nice, muscular young man like you, was he? Once I had hold of his elbow he didn't have much choice in the matter."

"You forced him to come with you to the gallery?"

"He wasn't going to come on his own."

"You took him into the back room, did you?"

"Sure, why not? I took him down the alley and in through the back door."

"And that's where you questioned him? In the back room?"

"That's where we had our little chat, Kevin. You guessed it, didn't you?"

"Did you try to reason with him first before you hit him?"

Her face grew cold. "You couldn't reason with that son of a bitch."

"Where did you hit him?"

"If he'd co-operated," she growled, "none of this would have happened. But he was so stubborn. Even when I waved that fucking thing under his nose," she motioned with her chin at the photograph of the wrecking bar, "he still wouldn't budge. So I let him have it on the elbow."

"Which elbow? Left or right?"

"Well, he was right-handed, so I hit him on the left arm. Christ, Kevin, I was trying to give him a break and not cripple his painting arm, wasn't I?"

"What did he do when you hit him?"

"Wet his pants and passed out, the fucking geezer."

"What did you do when he lost consciousness?"

"Well, I was pissed for starters, wasn't I? He wasn't going to do me any good out cold."

"You tried to revive him?"

"I put him in a chair and poured water over his head to wake him up."

Kevin frowned again. "I don't remember seeing a chair in the back room, Rosa. What chair did you use?"

She rolled her eyes at him. "It's in the basement, genius. One of the folding chairs we drag out for special events."

"What happened when he came to?"

"A lot of crying and blubbering. All I could get out of him was how much it hurt."

"What did you do then?"

"I hit him again, of course. Look, when somebody makes me mad, I can't help it. You saw it for yourself, didn't you?"

"Where did you hit him, the second time?"

"On the other elbow. I was done fooling around. He was either going to talk or I was going to cripple him for life."

"What happened when you hit him then?"

She made a face. "He fucking threw up, that's what happened. Then he passed out again."

"What did you do then?"

"It took me, like, almost an hour to clean up the mess."

"It must have given you time to cool off. Maybe reconsider what you were doing?"

"Are you kidding? Obviously I wasn't seeing red any more, no, but having to clean up all that barf and blood and piss? Oh, he was going to tell me where they were if I had to break every bone in his fucking body. No doubt about it."

Kevin paused, looking through the other material in the file. He'd asked the last question hoping to obviate any "heat of the moment" defence claims after the fact, and he felt the gamble had paid off. Such a claim would be a no-brainer on the face of it, given Battaglia's obvious hair-trigger temper and deep-seated anger management issues, but Kevin felt he'd just gotten her to undercut this potential defence by saying that she intended to keep hitting him until he told her what she wanted to know.

"So what happened when he woke up the second time?"

"More of the same, Kevin. More of the same."

"Did he tell you the paintings were down on Spencer Farm?"

"I figured it out. I had to hit him on the knee first, but once I did that, I knew where they were. It was a mistake, though."

"Why do you say that?"

"Well Christ, Kevin. He couldn't walk after that, could he? I had to carry him into the van. Stupid old bastard."

"Then what happened?"

She sat back suddenly, closing her eyes and sighing loudly. "I don't want to talk about this any more."

"That's when you drove him down to Spencer Farm, isn't it?"

"I'm tired. I'm tired of talking."

"Do you want to go back to the cell, Rosa?"

She didn't reply.

He waited. Up until now he felt he'd maintained a good pace and had coaxed several important admissions from her. If she withdrew completely now, though, they still wouldn't have a statement from her on the killing blow, the shot to the head that had caved in Lane's skull. They would have to bring her back out and wade through all the preliminary questions with her once again before getting into the rest of what had happened, and there was no guarantee she'd be as co-operative as she was right now.

Weighing his options, Kevin thought the best thing to do was to sit tight and wait out the silence. If she asked to be taken back to the cell, then so be it. If she said anything else, though, he'd get right back to work. He decided to gamble that her impatience, her restlessness, and her cockiness would prevail.

Eventually she opened her eyes again and looked at him. "Did you see the paintings? I mean in person, not in a picture?"

He nodded.

"What did you think of them? Honestly?"

"Incredible," Kevin replied, again without hesitation. "Beautiful."

She smiled, faintly, as though through a severe headache. "When I saw them again, when I found them, I couldn't believe it. They were even more stunning than I remembered."

"Lane finally told you where they were?"

She nodded, staring at the wall.

"Where did he tell you to look?"

"Upstairs. In a spare bedroom. All six of them, hanging on the walls. What a sight. I nearly fainted."

"You boxed them up and brought them out?"

"Oh, yeah."

"Do you always keep packing supplies and crates in the van?"

She shook her head. "I loaded up before I went down. I knew I was going to find them down there. My blood pressure was through the roof, I was so excited."

"So you crated them up and brought them down into the van. You used the hand truck I saw in the back room of the gallery, didn't you?"

"It's the one I always use."

"You used it this time to bring Lane's paintings out of the farmhouse and put them into the van?"

"Yes. That's what I just said, didn't I?"

"What was happening with Lane while you were doing this?"

"He was out cold, I guess. I don't know."

"You left him tied in a chair in the studio, didn't you?"

She said nothing, looking down at her hands.

"Did you use rope to tie him in the chair?"

She shook her head. "Duct tape. There's always some in the van."

"When you finished loading the paintings, what did you do then?"

"Went back."

"To the studio? To see Lane?"

She nodded.

"Was he conscious?"

She looked away, her face twisting. "I hate that old bastard. I've always hated him. I never loved him. I mean, who the fuck could? Great sex for a week, back when he was still young enough to get it up, and then a lifetime of fucking migraines and stomach acid afterward from the son of a bitch. All I wanted from him was those fucking paintings. That's all I ever fucking wanted from him."

"But he was conscious when you went back, is that what you're saying?"

"Yes, he was conscious," she snarled.

"What happened then?"

"He fucking—" she broke off, baring her teeth, her eyes

boring into Kevin's, "the fucking bastard called me an ugly old cow. Can you believe that?"

"Why did he say that?"

"Because I said the paintings were mine, like they should have been all the time, and he said they had nothing to do with me. I said, 'What the fuck are you talking about? They're beautiful works of art because of me. Because of me!' And he had the fucking nerve, the stupidity, to say they were beautiful because *he* made them beautiful, that the *model* had nothing to do with it. Then he called me an ugly old cow, and I showed him what he had coming to him, the old fucker."

"You hit him on the head with the wrecking bar?"

"I should have used both hands. I probably could have knocked his fucking head right off."

Kevin paused. There was only one more thing he wanted to get out of her right now. He took a moment to decide how to approach it, then asked, "Why did you burn his body after that? Why not leave him there, where he was, and just drive away?"

She shrugged. "Viking funeral, I guess."

"Did you know about the other barn fires in the area?"

She stared at him for a moment, then stirred. "Yeah."

"How did you know about them?"

"From the news. How else?"

"Is that why you decided to burn his body after you killed him? So that we'd think it was another fire by the same arsonist?"

She shrugged. "It seemed like a good idea at the time." She fell silent for a moment, then said, "Could have worked. Don't you think?"

Kevin put the photographs back into the file folder. "Is there anything else you'd like to tell me at this time?"

She thought about it and then shrugged. "Like I said before, I like a guy who fights back."

Outside in the hallway, after Battaglia had been

returned to her cell, Bishop came up to him and ruffled his hair. "I like a guy who fights back too, Kevvy."

Kevin gave him a tired smile. "Who's Magilla Gorilla?"

"Fuck you, dickwad." Bishop slapped him on the back and pushed him down the hall to where the others were waiting for him.

chapter FORTY-ONE

Sunday morning found Ellie driving west on Highway 401. She was on her way to General Headquarters in Orillia where she was expected to attend a press conference being held by the commissioner at 11:00 AM. It was a four-hour drive from the cottage to Orillia, and when she'd left, the sun had just begun to lighten the sky in the east.

She was now passing The Big Apple, a bakery and gift shop on the south side of the highway near Colborne that featured an observatory in the shape of a gigantic red apple with a big happy face on it. It always served Ellie as a landmark indicating the halfway point in her trip. She glanced at the dashboard clock and saw that it was only a few minutes after eight, meaning she would have about an hour after arriving at GHQ to find a washroom to freshen up and change into her Class A uniform before the commissioner got things rolling.

Moodie and John Goss, the corporate communications director, were anxious to put an official face on the arrest of Rosa Battaglia. News broadcasts last night and this morning had featured clips of Kevin Walker's take-down at the gas bar, which the media had obtained from the Internet. Moodie's objective was to replace these images with toned-down, factual statements from a panel of senior departmental officials including Deputy Commissioner Ron Belanger, provincial commander of Field Operations,

Chief Superintendent Leanne Blair, and Ellie. The tone of public commentary so far was mixed, with many people wondering aloud if the arrest was perhaps another example of police brutality and improper use of force. As a result, while Moodie's statement would focus on the successful conclusion of the investigation, he was prepared to answer questions about Kevin by stating the official position that the arrest of Rosa Battaglia was carried out by the detective constable involved in a manner that was completely within departmental procedures and guidelines.

Ellie was glad that Ted Moodie and the other senior executives at GHQ had chosen to back Kevin. They had already watched the video obtained from the overhead security camera at the gas bar, as she had, and everyone was confident Kevin had acted properly. Battaglia had resisted arrest, attempted to flee, and had assaulted a public officer engaged in the execution of his duty, all of which would be added to the list of charges being brought against her. Counter-charges of excessive use of force would be a publicity stunt at best, and the Crown attorney had already told them Battaglia's counsel had hinted to her that they weren't interested in pursuing them.

As she approached the off-ramp to Grafton, her cellphone rang through the hands-free device. She immediately reduced speed and eased onto the ramp, pulling over onto the shoulder as she answered the call. "March."

"Ellie, it's Danny Merrick. Did I catch you on the road?"

"It's okay," she said, shifting into Park. "I just pulled over. Too bad I don't have a driver, like you."

"You should. Listen, I don't want to keep you because I know you need to get there on time, but I just wanted to say break a leg this morning. I hope it goes well."

The sound of passing tractor trailers rose and fell behind her. "I thought you'd be there too."

Merrick laughed lightly. “That’s not my sort of thing. Janitors stay in the wings, right? Bob Jones will be there, and so will Eric Melanson.”

“You know me, Danny. I can’t tell the players without a program.”

“Pardon me. RCMP Deputy Commissioner of Operations Robert Jones and Assistant Commissioner Melanson, Criminal Intelligence Directorate. They’ll make official statements on behalf of the commissioner. By the way, the prime minister reminded me to tell you he expects you in very soon for that visit to his office in Langevin Block. He took the whole thing rather personally, and he’s grateful you’ve brought Darius Lane’s killer to justice.”

“I think he’s getting a little carried away. And so are you.”

“Speaking of which, you said you’d think about it. Have you?”

A battered pick-up truck passed her on the ramp. She stared at its brake lights as it rounded the curve and came to a stop before turning left. “Things have been pretty busy,” she lied.

“I understand. That’s okay. Maybe a rain check. I’ll just drink this case and buy you another one later.”

“I’m staying with some friends in Orillia and coming back tomorrow,” she said. “There’s a ton of work to do with Ident and the Crown attorney to get everything ready for court, but I’ll probably have some free time next weekend.”

“Just a minute, let me check my calendar ... mmm, yes, I believe I’m available then.”

“Hey,” Ellie said, “I’ve got an idea. My next-door neighbour—”

“Ridge Ballantyne.”

“Yes. Oh, right. You did a background on me. Anyway, he and his friends are playing at a thing in Merrickville on Saturday night. Why don’t you come down for that?”

"I'm more of a black-metal kind of guy, I'm afraid." He made a sound resembling a satanic chant coming from the bottom of a half-clogged sewer drain. "Sorry, my attempt at 'In Defiance of Existence'."

"Don't know them."

"That's the name of the song. Old Man's Child is the name of the performer. Galder. He's Norwegian."

"Never heard of him."

"That's okay. Just as well, I suppose. Black metal is an acquired taste, at best. Although, you know, I'm actually a fan of The Happy Teazel as well. I have one of their CDs."

"Now you're just patronizing me. I have to go, Danny."

"No really, I do. Shall I bring the case of beer?"

"There's an after-party thing, or whatever they call it, at Ridge's. We could go to that and have a beer. Or not."

"I'll leave it entirely up to you, but I'll bring a case of beer anyway. I always pay my debts."

"See you Saturday." Ellie ended the call and threw the Crown Vic back into gear. She drove up the ramp and stopped. She looked both ways and drove down the on-ramp back onto the 401.

She made a conscious effort not to do the arithmetic on how long it had been since she'd gone out with someone on what could be considered a date. It didn't matter. She wasn't a hermit, and she needed to socialize. She wanted to socialize. Danny Merrick was amusing. And it would give her an opportunity to tell him to his face to keep his hands off Kevin Walker.

Oh, what the hell. And yes, it was true. She *did* actually like the guy.

chapter FORTY-TWO

Janie's house had three small bedrooms upstairs and another room in the basement that she'd offered to Kevin as an office and den when he moved in, four years ago. At the time, Kevin had been renting an apartment above the hardware store in Sparrow Lake. He didn't have much in the way of furniture that was worth bringing with him, so he left most of it behind. Janie hadn't been using the basement much for anything other than laundry, so she had no problem with him setting up his few possessions down there. His weights, exercise machine, and treadmill were arranged in a separate area in the basement near the furnace. His desk, a nice old oak specimen he'd found in Mrs. Shipman's second-hand store, went into the spare room that had become his office and private space. In a burst of enthusiasm, he'd covered the walls with shelves, but he'd only unpacked a few of his books. The rest were still in boxes piled in the corner. His personal computer was set up on the desk, but he seldom came downstairs to use it. Everything seemed to happen upstairs on the main floor, and as time passed he found fewer and fewer opportunities to wander down here to spend a little free time on his own.

Sunday afternoon, however, he was on a mission. Janie was at her mother's with the kids, and he had the rest of the day off. He was downstairs in his office, searching through the cardboard boxes for his copy of *Kirk's Fire Investigations*. The text book by DeHaan and Icove was regarded as one of the primary references on the subject, and his recent exposure to the barn fire cases had emphasized how little he knew about arson and fire investigation in general. Ordinarily it would make great bathroom reading, allowing him to catch up on the subject a chapter at a time over the course of a week or two, but it wasn't the sort of thing he could leave lying around for the kids to see. The photographs of dead bodies and burned homes were not appropriate viewing for young ones.

He had decided to spend the rest of the afternoon today getting started on it, and then take it to work with him, where he could use it for bathroom reading at the detachment office without upsetting anyone. First, however, he had to find it.

He searched through box after box. His progress was often slowed by the discovery of other books he'd forgotten he owned. He browsed through Dylan Thomas's *Collected Poems*, read the first chapter of Frank Herbert's *Dune* for the fourteenth time, and leafed through a glossy text on herbs and spices. He was admiring the photographs in a book about stone houses along the Rideau Waterway when he heard footsteps upstairs.

Dropping the book back into the box, he listened. There was only one set of steps, crossing the dining room above his head and stopping at the doorway into the living room. It was Janie, and she seemed to be looking for him.

He went upstairs and found her coming back up the hallway from the bedroom.

"There you are," she said. "Where were you?"

"Downstairs, looking for a book. Everything okay?"

She stopped, her chin an inch from his sternum, and looked up at him. "We need to talk."

"Okay," Kevin replied without enthusiasm.

She put a hand on his forearm and gently moved him

out of her way. He trailed her into the kitchen, where she handed him a can of Coke from the refrigerator and took a can of root beer for herself. “Let’s go out back,” she said. “It’s shady.”

He followed her outside and around to the back of the house. Kevin had built a small deck out here two years ago, and Janie had decorated it with a patio set and a barbecue. She opened the big umbrella above the table and they sat down, their eyes automatically moving around the yard. There was a swing set and slide for the kids, a sand pit littered with toy vehicles, the little metal shed at the back housing the lawn mower and a snow blower that didn’t work, and Janie’s flower garden, dominated now by her sunflowers and dahlias.

She quietly belched gas from the root beer and said, “I’m sorry I’ve been so bitchy.”

“That’s okay. It’s been hard lately.”

“I’ve had a lot on my mind.”

“I know,” Kevin said. “I could tell.” When she didn’t say anything else, he said, “The kids are still at Barb’s?”

“She wants us to have supper there. I said I’d come and pick you up.”

“Okay.” Kevin didn’t mind; Barb was an excellent cook.

“I don’t want you driving until you feel better.”

“I’m okay, Janie. Really, I’m fine.”

“Mom said I should talk to you now. Get it over with.”

“About what?”

“Everything, Kevin. Frigging everything.”

“Should I be worried?” Kevin asked, starting to feel distinctly worried.

“Well Jesus Christ, Kevin, how do you think I feel? I’m worried sick. What am I supposed to do?”

Kevin took a drink of Coke, unsure of what to say. He was sitting in the middle of a minefield with no idea which direction he should take. His chances of surviving this conversation with his hide intact were slim to none. No matter where he stepped, he was going to blow himself to kingdom come. So much for his quiet afternoon tooling up on the chemistry of combustion and sources of ignition. He was about to become a living case study.

"What are you worried about, Janie? What is it?"

She slammed her root beer down and glared at him. "I'm pregnant. I'm going to have another kid. What are you going to do about it?"

Kevin stared at her, mouth open. Sandbagged. Pregnant. Having a baby. His? Of course it was; she was fiercely loyal to him. His. A child. His. A baby. His. "A baby?"

"Now's your chance, Kevin," she said, bitterly. "Now you can make up your mind. Stay or go. It's up to you. I don't care any more." She began to cry.

He knew there were important things he needed to process from what she'd just said, but his mind was stuck in first gear. "A baby? We're going to have a baby?"

"That's what I said! This is what we have to talk about, Kevin. What the hell are you laughing about?"

He hadn't realized he'd been grinning like a fool. He got to his feet and went around to her, dropping to his knees and grabbing her hands. "We're having a baby? How long?"

"Six weeks. You're not acting pissed."

He squeezed her hands. "Pissed? Why would I be pissed? I'm thrilled! Excited! I can't believe it!" He released her hands, stood up, took two blind steps and spun around. "You're sure? There's no mistake?"

Her shoulders dropped. "Of course I'm sure, Kevin. Jesus. Do you think I'd be wrong about something like this? I went to the doctor, remember? The tests were positive." She began to cry. "I need to know what you're going to do."

"I don't understand." He blinked at her, confused. "What do you mean, what I'm going to do?"

"Look," she fumed, "all you've been talking about lately is how shitty work is, how they give you all the crap stuff to do, how people transfer around all the time, and then you tell me this morning about this job offer you got in Ottawa and now I have no idea what's going to happen. I don't want to move. I told you that before. Now, with a baby coming, I need to know whether it's going to have a father who's around all the time or if I'm going to be stuck raising it all by myself again, like I was with Brendan. I need to *know*, Kevin."

He stared at her. It was true that he'd received a call this morning from RCMP Assistant Commissioner Merrick, who'd given him the name and number of a contact who was very interested in meeting with him in Ottawa to discuss a transfer from the OPP. He'd told Janie about it mostly because he was flattered by the attention, and of course he wanted to take a few days to savour the moment before turning them down. But he realized he hadn't explained that last part to Janie. Stupidly, he'd thought it was obvious. When he looked at it from her point of view, though, and put it alongside all the grumbling and hard feelings he'd had over the last six months about the crime unit and his place in it, and his absent-minded comments about transferring to another detachment where he could make a fresh start, he understood where she was coming from.

He crouched down in front of her. "I'm not going anywhere, Janie. This is incredible news. Incredible!"

"But the job in Ottawa. You were so excited when you got off the phone."

"I was excited to be asked," he said, "but that's all. I'm not interested in working in Ottawa."

"What if you have to transfer to another detachment?"

He shook his head. "I don't think I'll have to, right now. Maybe in a few years, if they decide they want to move me, but we'll cross that bridge when we get to it. I can always jump to Brockville Police. I know the guys there. I could get a job, no problem, and we could stay put, right where we are."

"But you want to move somewhere else, don't you?"

"No! I don't. I'm perfectly happy right here with you."

"Then why haven't you asked me?"

He bit his lip, confused again. "Asked you what, Janie? If you wanted to move? You already told me you didn't."

"That's not what I'm talking about."

He looked at her, waiting.

"Why didn't you ask me if I wanted to get married?"

He stared at her once again, mouth open. Sandbagged. Get married. On his mind all the time, but never a good time to bring it up. "Um. Do you want to?"

"Of course, you big frigging dope. Why didn't you ask me?"

"Because—I thought—you didn't." He stopped. There was no good answer. He started to laugh.

"I don't think it's *funny*, Kevin."

"It's not," he said, still laughing, "I'm just, it's okay. I'm happy. Shall we get married, Janie?"

"Oh, why the hell not," she replied, sarcastically. Then she suddenly grinned back at him through her tears.

"When? Next month?"

"We can't afford a honeymoon."

"Your mom could keep the kids for a weekend. We could go, oh, I don't know. Ottawa?"

"The hell with that. I want to go to Buffalo and shop my ass off."

"I thought you said we couldn't afford it."

"I'll borrow the money from Mom. It's only for a weekend."

"The hell you will. We won't borrow a penny from your mom."

"We'll figure it out," she said, grabbing his hand and giving it a squeeze.

"Yeah. We will, won't we?"

She nodded, her face wet with tears.

I'm going to be a father, Kevin thought.

His world was filled with sunlight.

Acknowledgments

This novel is a work of fiction. Names, characters, institutions, places and events are either the product of the author's imagination or are used fictitiously.

The author wishes once again to thank OPP Detective Inspector (Retired) Randy Millar for his invaluable advice and guidance. Any inaccuracies or errors are entirely the responsibility of the author.

The author was also guided by John E. Douglas, Ann W. Burgess, Allen G. Burgess and Robert K. Ressler, *Crime Classification Manual* (San Francisco: Jossey-Bass, Inc., 1992) and John D. DeHaan, *Kirk's Fire Investigation, Fourth Edition* (Upper Saddle River, NJ: Prentice-Hall, Inc., 1977).

Finally, thanks once again to my wife, Lynn L. Clark, for her superb editing, her endless support, her encouragement as we deal with life's challenges, and for remaining my best friend throughout it all.

About the Author

Michael J. McCann lives and writes in Oxford Station, Ontario. A graduate of Trent University in Peterborough, ON, and Queen's University in Kingston, ON, he worked for Carswell Legal Publications (Western) as production editor of *Criminal Reports (Third Series)* before spending fifteen years with the Canada Border Services Agency as a training specialist, project officer, and program manager at national headquarters in Ottawa. He is married and has one son.

He is the author of *Sorrow Lake*, a finalist for the 2015 Hammett Prize for excellence in crime fiction in North America. He's also the author of the Donaghue and Stainer Crime Novel series, including *Blood Passage*, *Marcie's Murder*, *The Fregoli Delusion*, and *The Rainy Day Killer*, as well as the supernatural thriller, *The Ghost Man*.

If you enjoyed

Michael J. McCann's **BURN COUNTRY**
you won't want to miss the exciting
debut of Ellie March and Kevin Walker in

Ask your local independent bookstore
to order it today!

Sorrow Lake
Michael J. McCann
ISBN: 978-1-927884-02-7

Lightning Source UK Ltd.
Milton Keynes UK
UKHW010846260719
346860UK00001B/10/P